Pop Star

Also by Meredith Michelle

Star Struck: A Pick Your Own Plot Bedventure

Pop Star

A Pick Your Own Plot Bedventure

Meredith Michelle

LYRICAL SHINE
Kensington Publishing Corp.
www.kensingtonbooks.com

LYRICAL SHINE BOOKS are published by

Kensington Publishing Corp.
119 West 40th Street
New York, NY 10018

All Kensington titles, imprints, and distributed lines are available at special quantity discounts for bulk purchases for sales promotion, premiums, fundraising, educational, or institutional use.

Special book excerpts or customized printings can also be created to fit specific needs. For details, write or phone the office of the Kensington Sales Manager: Kensington Publishing Corp., 119 West 40th Street, New York, NY 10018. Attn. Sales Department. Phone: 1-800-221-2647.

Lyrical Shine and Lyrical Shine logo Reg. U.S. Pat. & TM Off.

First Electronic Edition: May 2017
eISBN-13: 978-1-60183-745-5
eISBN-10: 1-60183-745-3

First Print Edition: May 2017
ISBN-13: 978-1-60183-746-2
ISBN-10: 1-60183-746-1

Printed in the United States of America

Dedicated to my wonderful agent, Amy Tannenbaum, who took a chance on a new concept, who provided invaluable support and feedback, and with whom I have enjoyed sharing the adventure!

You are Honey Noble. Your perfect pout, poised over the lustrous sphere of a ruby red Blow Pop, wrapper partially peeled and dangling from its white cardboard stick, gleams in close-up from the cover of *Rock 'N' Roll* magazine. THE BUZZ ABOUT HONEY! screams the headline. You have made it.

Hugging the magazine to your chest, you do a little happy dance in the privacy of your tour bus. You fall back onto the supple leather bench and allow your eyes to gaze unfocused at the polished wood ceiling as you savor this moment.

"What? Are you sleeping?" The door abruptly squeals open then slams shut as Sasha Fortier, your constant companion and the stabilizing force in the dizzying trajectory your life has taken, sashays across the little entryway. He pauses at your side, towering above you from his lanky height of six-two, then tilts his head to the side and slides a hand onto his hip. "Oh. My. God." In one quick motion he slips the glossy magazine from beneath your folded arms. "Oh my god! Girrrrl. . . ." He draws the word out in a throaty growl, "This is beyond! Look at those lips! And I thought your first platinum was exciting! Do you know what this means?"

You sit up and Sasha plops down beside you. "I know," you tell him, "I seriously feel like I'm dreaming."

Sasha doesn't miss a beat, instantly reaching around to deliver a quick pinch to your behind.

"Ouch!" you squeal in surprise.

"Well, you ain't dreaming! I just wanted you to know for sure."

"Thanks" you laugh, "I think."

Sasha flips through the magazine until he finds the article. NOBILITY, is the title.

"*I* haven't even read it yet." You give the precious magazine a little tug.

"Well then, let me oblige," Sasha clears his throat, pushes an imaginary pair of glasses up the bridge of his nose, and begins to read.

Honey Noble is all legs, long jet-black hair, and huge green eyes as she strolls into the room. Taller in person than I expect, her supermodel stature dazzles even without the elevated stage and backdrop of eye-numbing pyrotechnics that are the hallmark of her live performances.

Honey pauses to look over her shoulder and raises a finely arched eyebrow as she leads the way through the black-and-white tiled atrium of her newly completed home, set in a stunning and very private location in the Hollywood Hills. Her glam squad meets us in her enormous living room, a nod to old Hollywood glamour, decked out in a sophisticated mix of burnished antiques and low contemporary pieces in muted hues. An elegant baby grand piano gleams from the corner of the room, its cover open and sheet music perched at the ready.

Professional lighting and photography gear also litter the room, which served as the location for today's photo shoot. Fresh from being photographed, Honey is dressed in a red-carpet-ready gown with a glittering beaded bustier and body-con silhouette highlighting her tiny waist and her ample curves.

She pauses momentarily to thank her costume designer and "best friend," Sasha Fortier.

"Awww, thanks," Sasha looks up to bat his long eyelashes before he continues reading.

"I've had a little guidance from my decorator," says Honey, in response to my admiration of her to-die-for digs. She gently pushes her long, glossy black hair, set in retro-style waves that reach almost to her waist, behind one shoulder. "But I do a lot of the shopping myself. I love finding just the right piece. It's one of my passions."

Often called one of the hardest-working performers in the industry, Honey is quickly amassing a mini empire built upon her many passions—her music tops an extensive list which en-

compasses fashion (she's currently working on her Hive label, which includes shoes, jewelry, and a ready-to-wear lingerie line inspired by her tour costumes); romance (her on-again, off-again relationship with former Brit boy-bander and current white-hot solo artist, Crispin Hershey, is the constant fodder for tabloid headlines); and her fans, who affectionately call themselves The Honey Bees and swarm en masse outside of every Honey Noble concert, hoping for an audience with their queen.

Honey is happy to oblige, and routinely takes time for backstage meet-and-greets, often pulling a handful of thrilled black-and-gold clad Bees from the audience at random. They leave with a hug from Honey, an autograph, and a story they'll be buzzing about for years.

"I wouldn't be where I am today without my fans. They are the reason I perform. They mean everything to me," Honey says as she glides through a pair of towering French doors to the shaded patio at the back of the house. The stone-and-wood structure overlooks a sparkling swimming pool surrounded by lush gardens and bordered by high walls overgrown with thick bougainvillea, a deceptively beautiful security feature. Atop the walls, not quite hidden by the foliage, perch a series of cameras that pan constantly, slowly scanning the property.

Honey declines to comment on the status of her romance with recent Grammy winner, Crispin Hershey, telling me instead, "Right now I'm focused on my music."

Honey offers me the silver tray of blueberry scones, and gingerly selects one for herself, "I'm starving," she says before taking a dainty bite of the pastry. "Dry," she pronounces, and returns the scone to the tray, trailing bits of the pastry down her front as she does. She is disarmingly unabashed as she dips her manicured fingers into her décolletage to retrieve an errant scone crumb. "Oops," she laughs, popping her finger into her mouth and drawing it slowly between her lips. She dries it on the linen napkin in front of her and looks up, huge, emerald eyes full of mischief. "Where were we?" she asks.

This reporter has to clear his throat and take a sip of cold water before he can continue."

"You did not," howls Sasha as he flips the magazine closed. "I bet that poor Clark Kent had to harness his Superman!"

Sasha's spot-on one-liner has you doubled over with laughter. "Those scones were crumbly," you explain. "It was innocent. But he was kind of cute."

Sasha smirks and flips the magazine closed. "Something is not right with you." He laughs.

"A lot of things," you agree, playfully straightening Sasha's shirt collar.

"Don't think everyone who reads that article won't notice your artful dodge, though." Sasha is suddenly serious and looks you in the eye. "How long has it been since you've heard from Crispin anyway?"

"No comment," you respond, dropping your eyes back to the magazine.

Sasha takes his hand and brushes away the thick veil of hair that has fallen over your face. "Seriously, is this fake? This hair does not look real. How can it possibly be so perfectly straight? You are not letting them stick extensions in there, are you? Those things will ruin your hair."

You're grateful Sasha has taken the hint and changed the subject, despite his uncanny ability to read between the lines. But part of you does want to talk about Crispin, and Sasha is the perfect sounding board. Although he's been by your side since long before you and Crispin met, Sasha was careful to keep a distance when you and Crispin were first together, giving you all the space you needed to cement your blossoming romance. And he has gracefully moved back in to keep you company now that Crispin's comeback has him traveling nonstop.

You disentangle his fingers from your hair and take his warm hand in yours. "Hands off the hair," you tease.

Sasha looks you in the eye and reads you like a book. "Stop trying to be evasive," Sasha says. "Answer my question. How long?"

"A couple of weeks."

"Weeks? So, since the Grammys."

"It's not a big deal. He's been doing a ton of press since he won. And he's still recording. He knows the tour schedule. I'm sure he'll visit as soon as he gets a break."

"If it's not a big deal, why do you seem so worried?"

You hesitate to answer, but you know Sasha won't let it go until you do. "It has to do with Trixie," you mutter, halfway hoping he won't hear you.

But Sasha's hearing is perfect, and he slams his hand hard onto the table, making the magazine—and you—jump. "What did that boy do? I swear I will kill him!"

"Jeez, Sasha, chill. This is exactly why I didn't say anything to you before. It's not that bad."

"I am breathing, I am breathing," Sasha inhales dramatically, pulling in a huge breath and then pushing it out in a long gust. "I am fine." He sits up straight and smiles, the picture of perfect composure. "Go on."

You pause, not sure whether to continue. "I actually don't think I should tell you the rest."

"Don't wrinkle your nose like you smell something nasty. I have a right to protect the person I love most in this whole wide world." Sasha lays his long fingers gently over yours. "I am calm, and I do not own a gun. Tell me. Now."

"Fine, but you have to promise to just listen." You pause to see whether Sasha will say any more, but he remains silent, so you continue. "You know the last time Crispin and I broke up? How it was kind of part PR stunt and part trial to see what would happen if we did . . . you know . . . decide we should take some real time apart?"

Sasha nods, his eyes focused on yours.

"And we both did some, um, exploring I guess you would call it. You remember Han?"

"How could I possibly forget?" Sasha asks.

Discovered on Korea's reality TV singing show, *K-Pop,* Han Lee was imported by legendary music producer, Colton Powers, and made over into an American media-ready heartthrob. Han was already a sensation in his native Korea and Powers put his massive PR machine into action to thrust Han to the U.S. media forefront. Often compared to a young (and Asian) Elvis Presley, Han's provocative dance moves have made him almost as famous as have his brilliant rap lyrics. Even before you met, Han had dated a string of actresses and pop stars, but you were by far the most well-known.

Not long after you started dating, Han's shows began to sell out, and they have ever since. Sasha contends that having you on Han's arm is what catapulted him into the stratosphere, bringing Han platinum-album success and making him the subject of tabloid stories week after week. He stops short of saying Han used you to get to the top, although you suspect that's what he really thinks. You know the truth—Han's incredible talent, undeniable sex appeal, and unwavering hard work made him a success. You also know it's not worth arguing over, especially since Han is solidly in your past.

You decide to let Sasha's comment pass. "And you know Crispin was really in rehab—even though everyone thought he had vocal nodules."

"Mmmm hmmmm . . ." Sasha replies patiently.

"Well, Trixie was at The Pines too. You know, recovering from 'exhaustion.'"

"Exhaustion. Riiiiiight. I heard about that."

The once-adorable star of the hit kids' series, *Showstoppers*, Trixie veered wildly away from her squeaky-clean TV image to become an edgy adult pop star. More known for her onstage antics and racy selfies than her music, Trixie manages to stay in the public eye by using the "all PR is good PR" theory. Her most recent tabloid coverage revolved around her use of a bucket to relieve herself between sets and her penchant for growing premium-grade cannabis plants under lights in her tour bus. She's always in the headlines for something scandalous and she's always linked to someone more famous than she is.

"Anyway, Crispin and Trixie kind of bonded. Apparently they were dealing with similar underlying issues."

Sasha purses his lips, "I can only imagine."

"It was just a fling."

"I knew it!" cries Sasha. "That bastard!"

"We were on a break. They hooked up one time. And then it was over."

"According to Crispin," Sasha says.

"I believe him. He didn't have to tell me."

"Your trust is admirable."

"Thank you. Even if you are being sarcastic. But here's the real issue. They see each other from time to time at some kind of post-rehab support group. Supposedly they were assigned as each other's *recovery advocates*. And I guess Trixie's getting 'exhausted' again. She texted him the day after the Grammys. I know Crispin is probably just trying to help her, but I worry he could be getting sucked in."

"I bet he's getting sucked one way or another."

"Sasha!"

"I'm sorry, but what could he possibly see in her? There's a reason the tabloids call her *Trashy*. As if the name Trixie isn't already bad enough."

"Crispin is probably the most empathetic person I know. If someone needs him, he's going to be there, no matter who it is."

Sasha purses his lips and stares straight ahead.

"Thanks for trying to make me feel better about it," you say.

"I'm not doing you any favors by hiding the truth. Crispin is a player. Always has been, always will be. Just because he's hot as hell doesn't mean he gets carte blanche to flit in and out of your life as he pleases. And now that he's got that Grammy, I guarantee his ego is going to be even bigger, if that's possible."

"Did you just say Crispin is hot as hell?"

Sasha halts for a moment, caught, then continues. "I'm just saying he has a very high opinion of himself. As does Trixie, obviously. You can't tell me Crispin doesn't eat that up."

"You are being so judgmental."

"Am I? Maybe you should listen to your own instincts if you aren't going to listen to me. Maybe you're finally realizing you deserve more, as I've told you a thousand times. Is it possible you're just seeing things clearly in Crispin's absence?"

"No, that isn't it." You stop to think for a minute, trying to work out what exactly is making you feel so uneasy. "It's not Crispin I don't trust, it's Trixie. There's something about her. She has this innocence, this kind of adorable vulnerability."

"She has something all right." Sasha agrees. "Probably herpes."

"Sasha!" you can't help but laugh. "Seriously, though. I'm going to trust Crispin until he gives me a reason not to. I'm focusing on the positive"—you pick up the thick *Rock 'N' Roll* magazine—"and I'm going to enjoy my time in the spotlight."

"As well you should"—Sasha smiles—"as well you should. And I'm going to enjoy it right along with you. But I am telling you I will kill that figgy-pudding-eating Brit with my bare hands if he breaks your heart." He takes a dramatic breath. "At which time we shall revert to the pact." Sasha nods reverently, referring to the promise you and he have made to each other to live together in a platonic partnership if you haven't found the loves of your lives by the time you turn thirty-five.

"Thanks, Sash." You laugh and give his hands a squeeze. "You are the best."

"You think I don't know that? Now come on, I think we better go figure out that peacock."

Besides being your best friend, Sasha has taken on the role of your personal stylist and costumier for the tour, something he was born to do. Not only does he help you choose every costume for your performances, he's begun to design some of his own pieces and consults with you on your apparel line, providing invaluable advice.

You flip the magazine open to the first page of your article one more time, let out a squeal, and then head for the door.

Parked just a few steps from the tour bus, your wardrobe trailer is filled with endless racks of costume pieces and counters stacked with an eye-popping array of candy-colored wigs and extensions. Your carefully choreographed costume changes happen backstage, with Sasha there to help you slip quickly in and out of your clothing in the seconds you have between songs. It's almost like a magic act, and it has to be seamless.

One of your costumes, the show-stopping peacock piece, has an elaborate and incredibly heavy, feathered and sequined train that has to be hooked onto the bustle at the back of the costume's corset. The full ensemble also requires a change of your stockings, your shoes, and your headpiece. Even with the help of two stagehands, the costume change is taking too long. Sasha is determined to get the timing right—and your manager, Freddie, is insistent that he does.

You wrap your hair quickly into a messy bun. "Do you think we should start in the waterfall?" you ask Sasha, referring to the costume you wear right before your change into the peacock.

"No," answers Sasha. "That's easy."

The waterfall is a relatively simple, one-piece costume with a flowy skirt and a simple closure. One zip and it's off.

"I think part of the problem is that we keep getting in each other's way attaching the train at the same time the headpiece goes on. There's no room to work around it once that peacock is attached," Sasha says. "It would work better to have someone doing the headpiece at the same time the waterfall is coming off."

"Okay, let's try that." You quickly strip off your leggings and baggy black tee, tossing them on the stool behind you. Then you peel off your panties and reach around to undo your bra. The costume has all the support you need built right into it, so there's no need for extra undergarments.

The door to the trailer flies open as you stand there in your naked glory. "Hey!" you shout, pulling the closest garment you can find, a sheer, sparkly skirt, across your bare torso.

"My, my, my, what have I stumbled into?"

You quickly let your guard—and the skirt—down as the door closes behind the gorgeous, chiseled body, and equally perfect face of your MIA boyfriend, Crispin Hershey. Instant, enormous relief surges through you. Somehow you are still surprised by just how beautiful he is. In a form-fitting white T-shirt, distressed jeans, and black boots, he looks more like a movie star than a rock god. The sight of him makes you melt, and that accent . . . every time you hear it your stomach feels like you've just veered over the highest drop of the best roller coaster in the world.

Crispin takes in the scene. "I'm not interrupting anything, am I?" He cuts his eyes dramatically at Sasha.

"Actually," you explain, taking a playful step in Crispin's direction, "we were just working on timing. It can be a little tricky backstage."

"Yes," Sasha agrees, his voice dripping with sarcasm. "Timing. Something you seem to have a small problem with."

"The only problem I have," answers Crispin, playing along, "is that I never seem to have enough time. But when I find a spare moment"—Crispin steps toward you, leaving only the smallest distance between your naked body and his—"how"—he takes another step, pulling you to him, wrapping his strong forearm around your bare waist—"can I possibly"—now his face is inches from yours, and you can smell the heady scent of his cologne and feel the rough scrape of the fly of his jeans against your bare stomach as he presses you to him—"resist this?" Crispin kisses you, pushing you back into the rack of costumes and making your head swim. You laugh around the swirl of Crispin's tongue as you feel the scratch of the tulle and sequins against your bare back and buttocks.

"Don't mind me," Sasha calls from as far away as he can get in the cramped trailer, bringing you back to your senses.

You open your eyes, bite your lip, and look into Crispin's hypnotizing, amber eyes. "I'd better . . ."

Crispin silences you with another kiss then looks over his shoulder at Sasha. "You're welcome to join us," he teases.

"Puh-lease," Sasha crosses his arms and rolls his eyes. "You, Mr. Hershey, are most definitely not my type."

"All right, boys, that's enough." You disentangle yourself from the jumble of costumes and give Crispin another long kiss. "I am so happy you're here! But that's going to have to tide you over until after the show. I have a ton of prep work to do."

"Oh, I see how it is," Crispin says. "I fly all the way from LA and now you don't have time for me." He plunges a mock dagger into his heart and falls dramatically into the rack of costumes.

"Stop wrecking my wardrobe!" You giggle, pulling Crispin out of a frothy skirt.

"That's nothing compared to what I plan to do to you later," Crispin growls into your neck. His eyes twinkle with mischief.

"You're welcome to stay," you tell him. "Maybe you can help. We could use a third set of hands."

Crispin wraps his arms around you tighter, pulling you close. "I think one set of hands is more than enough." He gives your backside a squeeze.

"You really do have a one-track mind," Sasha tells him. "But if you can refocus long enough to help us figure out this costume conundrum, I agree you are welcome to stay."

"No, no, not my forte," Crispin answers, giving you another kiss before pulling away. "I'll leave you to it." He walks toward the door, adjusting his waistband slightly. "Catch you after the show, baby." He looks at you hungrily and slips out.

"Oh my god, I feel so much better!" you exhale. The weight of worry you've been carrying is entirely lifted. You feel as if you've just drunk a glass of champagne, bubbly and light.

"I'm so glad," says Sasha, dryly, "but now I have a mess to clean up and we're running late. We still have got to figure out this costume change."

Sasha bends to lift the clipped edge of the peacock's feathered train and as he does he lets out a gasp. "Well, what have we here?" He spins to display the cell phone he's retrieved from under the rack of costumes.

You extend your hand to take it. "I can give it to him later."

"Not so fast!" Sasha swipes a finger across the dark screen and arches an eyebrow. "Aren't you even a little curious?"

"Sasha, that's private." You reach for the phone but he pulls it away. "Besides, I'm sure it's fingerprint protected."

Sasha glances at the screen. "Not even password protected. He really is as dumb as he looks."

"Sasha, be nice."

"I'm sorry, you know I cannot help myself. Come on, let's just take a quick peek at what Mr. Crispin has been up to during his absence. Then your mind will be fully at ease."

You pause to think about it, but not for long. "No, I wouldn't want him—or anyone—snooping around in my phone. A relationship has to be built on trust. And I trust Crispin. You saw how he was just now. He's here, just like he said he would be. Everything is fine."

"Seems like Mr. Hershey came in here with a little too much pent-up energy, if you ask me."

Now that you think about it, he did seem a little frantic. Still, you haven't seen each other in weeks, so his extra enthusiasm only makes sense. You do trust him, but a niggling worry eats at the corners of your mind. You realize it's not him you don't trust, it's that manipulative Trixie.

Sasha is like a dog with a bone. "Would it really hurt to look? Once you see there are no suspicious texts or photos, it will just confirm what you already know."

There is some truth to that, but at the same time, you know you'll feel guilty once you spy, and it's a slippery slope. Next will you feel the need to start checking his pockets for questionable receipts?

Sasha waggles the phone in front of you, his finger poised over the message icon. "You know you want to look."

What should you do?

To say no to Sasha, turn to page 75.
**To give in to Sasha and look through Crispin's phone,
keep reading.**

"I guess it wouldn't hurt to take a quick, innocent peek." you say.

"That's my girl!" Sasha swipes his finger across the screen.

You slip your shirt back on and pull it over your knees as you both hunker down, cross-legged on the floor. "Hold on," you tell him, popping up for a second to lock the trailer door. Feeling a little criminal, you sit back down and lean in, your forehead almost touching Sasha's as you hover over the illuminated screen.

Sasha presses the green message icon and quickly scrolls through the lengthy list of texts. He hits the second text in the series, apparently an exchange between you and Crispin. "What is he doing calling you *Henry*?" Sasha asks.

"He thought it was cute," you shrug.

"I thought that was just our thing." Sasha drops his eyes to his lap, clearly stung by Crispin's use of your childhood nickname. Crispin is the only person you've trusted with the truth of your given name, "Henrietta," and your related nickname, "Henry," since you became a successful pop star. Your agent, your manager, and your PR team have done everything in their power to hide the offensive moniker from the media. Even Sasha has taken to calling you "Henry" only in private, and then only in moments of affection or frustration—though he's barely known you by any other name since the time you were children.

"Sasha, are you seriously going to pout about this?" you ask.

Sasha scrolls freely through texts between you and Crispin, most of which are single words from you trying to elicit a response from Crispin during his absence. Finally Sasha sighs and looks up.

"How can I stay mad at someone so pathetic," he turns the screen to show you the recurrent green bubbles containing the single word *Hello?* from you to Crispin. "I'm sorry, but that is just rude."

"He gets busy," you explain.

"I bet he was gettin' busy," Sasha smirks, gazing intently into the phone. "This is interesting," he announces, scrolling slowly through a new set of texts. "Very interesting indeed . . ."

"What?" you reach for the phone but Sasha pulls it back.

"Not so fast. I need to be sure these are fit for public consumption—oh my!"

"Sasha, give me that," you lunge for the phone again, not sure whether he's just teasing you or truly reading something horrendous.

"Just . . . give me a second . . ." Sasha rises slowly to his feet as he reads, holding the phone inches from his face. "No you did not!"

"Sasha!" You leap and make a grab for the phone, but instead of releasing it Sasha pulls it away and simultaneously loses his grip, flinging the phone backward as he does. For a slow-motion moment you watch the phone fly through the air and then, impossibly, plunge with a sickening plunk in the huge, cylindrical vase in the corner. It is slowly swallowed by filthy water left by the vase's deceased contents, disposed of just this morning.

Sasha watches the phone bubble and gurgle as it submerges to the bottom of the vase. "I could not have done that if I'd tried," he observes wryly.

You run to the vase to retrieve the sodden phone. "Oh no! No, no, no, no!" Water immediately runs from every crevice, much more water than you would ever have imagined the thin device could possibly hold.

"Sasha, get me something!"

"Oh, all right," Sasha answers, nonchalantly walking to the tiny powder room and retrieving a hand towel.

"Hurry up!"

"It's not the end of the world, Henrietta." Sasha holds out a hand for the phone. "Let me see it."

You hand over the phone, which is still leaking an alarming volume of water, and watch as Sasha shakes it hard then uses the corner of the little towel to dab at its screen.

"Sasha, what are you doing? You're going to make it worse! Use the whole towel—you have to get it completely dry!"

"I know what I am doing, Henry, there's an art to this."

Watching Sasha, you have a sneaking suspicion there's at least an artifice, if not an art, to what he is trying to accomplish.

He gives the phone a few more ineffectual pats and then tries to power it on. "Hmmmm," is all he says.

"What?" you ask.

"Be patient." He pushes and holds two buttons on the phone, then counts slowly to twenty. "Hmmmm."

"It's not working is it?"

"Not yet, but these things can take time," he shakes the phone up and down vigorously, causing more droplets of water to fly into the air.

"Rice!" you announce, remembering something you read about how to dry out a phone that had been dropped in water. "We need rice!"

"I can call for takeout, but I don't really think this is the time—"

"Sasha, this isn't funny! We have to get his phone fixed! How are we possibly going to explain this?"

"We just tell the truth—we found his phone on the floor, reached down to get it, and it somehow leapt out of our hands and into that dunk tank over there. We'll just leave out the part about looking through his texts and you viciously attacking me."

You roll your eyes. "He is never going to believe that."

"I don't know why he wouldn't. It's the truth. Pretty much."

"I'm going to get some rice. I'll dry it out and give the phone back to him when I see him after the show tonight. He'll never know the difference."

There's a sharp knock on the trailer door and you both freeze in place.

"Who is it?" Sasha sings out innocently.

"It's me, Freddie." The unamused voice of your manager comes from the other side of the door.

"Uh, just a second," you answer.

"I don't have all day," you hear Freddie grumble.

"Shit, shit, shit!" Sasha looks feverishly around for a place to stash the phone.

"Just stick it in your pocket!"

"What? But it's all wet, and these are Balmain leggings."

"Stick it in your pocket!" Sasha grimaces as he slides the phone into his back pocket, smoothing his thin, silk shirt back down over his pants.

You reach for the door handle but turn back to Sasha before you open it. "And go get some rice. Uncooked rice," you instruct him.

Freddie ducks to enter the trailer. "Just checking in on you."

You've adored Freddie since the moment you met him. A full twenty-two years older than you are, Freddie feels almost fatherly. He's been around the business long enough to understand the ins and outs of fame and he genuinely seems concerned about your well-being, even committing to travel with you to ensure everything is just right on your first national tour.

Freddie has dated a string of supermodels since his infamous divorce from fiery Telenovela legend, Angelique Angel, but describes himself as a sworn born-again bachelor. "She scarred me for life! The temper on that woman—like you've never seen!" he says with a mock-shiver whenever the subject of Angelique arises.

Dressed impeccably in a suit tailored to fit his broad chest and shoulders, his head of thick, black hair, just beginning to grey at the temples, brushed back from his handsome face, he glances around the trailer, lifts his sunglasses off the bridge of his nose, and points toward the peacock costume. "Still haven't figured that out yet?"

"That's actually what we were working on when you came in," Sasha tells him nervously.

"So let's see it." Freddie's intimidating stature, his direct delivery, and the Bronx accent he's never managed to shed despite his decades on the West Coast make him seem tougher than the teddy bear you know he really is.

"We didn't quite get it one hundred percent perfect yet," Sasha explains, obsessively zipping and unzipping the costumes as he speaks, "but we're close."

"So, close meaning . . . ?" Freddie prods impatiently, "Rocket science it ain't."

"The problem is the timing of the train and the headpiece—we have that part figured out. But we really need to try it with another person. There are always at least two of us on it backstage."

"Well, what are we waiting for?" Freddie gamely shoves his sunglasses on top of his head. "Let's give it a shot."

Sasha cuts his eyes at you.

"I actually need Sasha to run out for a second," you jump in. "I need some, uh, feminine hygiene products." You pull the hem of your long t-shirt down and hide behind the costume rack, hoping Freddie won't notice your lack of undergarments.

Freddie wrinkles his nose.

You widen your eyes at Sasha and he takes the hint.

"Uh, okay, Honey," Sasha says, trying to sound natural but failing miserably. "I will run right out and be back as soon as I find you your—um—you know the supplies you need. Unless you want to get them for her, Freddie?"

Freddie looks aghast. "No, that is most definitely not my department."

"Well, then, I guess it's mine! Ta-ta!" Sasha fumbles awkwardly behind him for the door handle and stumbles out the door. You can hear the scratchy staccato of his steps as he runs across the gravel lot.

"He is a funny one," observes Freddie, holding the peacock costume out in front him. "Sure you don't want to give this a try? We really need to work out these glitches."

"No, that's okay," you answer. "We really do have it figured out. We'll run it a couple of times before the show tonight."

"Terrific." Freddie slides his sunglasses back over his eyes then peers at you over the rims. "Are you hiding back there?"

You feel a blush rise to your face as you answer. "I'm not exactly fully dressed."

Freddie jumps back a step. "Oh! Why didn't you say something?" He scrambles for the door handle, adorably flustered.

"It's fine, Freddie," you assure him. "I'm mostly dressed."

"Right. Okay. Just stay back there, I'll let myself out." He holds his hand in front of his eyes as he backs toward the door. "I'll see you backstage."

"See you." You laugh as Freddie exits the trailer.

As you lift the heavy peacock train and do your best to hang it back on the rack, you realize Sasha left without telling you what he read on Crispin's phone. Maybe he really was reacting to something, though he could have simply been acting like his normal, overly-dramatic self. It was probably nothing. But now you won't have a chance to ask him about it, not until after the show. Once you're in hair and makeup you won't have any privacy. You pull out your phone and shoot Sasha a quick text.

So, what's the intel?

You see the familiar oblong bubble encircling a series of dots appear as Sasha writes a reply.

Intel?

You know what I mean—what were you reading?

The series of dots appears again, then after a pause quickly disappears.

Hello?

After another pause, he answers.

I am currently occupied trying to find uncooked rice. Who knew it would be so elusive? And then I have to go ISO your oversized panty liners.

Ha ha

OK found white rice. Be back shortly.

Sasha?

Yes.

Are you going to answer my question?

Getting in the bus. No text is important enough to die for. See you when I get back.

Well, that got you nowhere. You pull on your clothes, switch off the light, open the door, and head back across the lot toward the arena.

The sun is beginning to dip lower in the sky and you feel a familiar pulse of energy as you walk through the talent entrance. This prelude to your performance, the long walk down tile and cinderblock halls lined with offices and dressing rooms, leads to the one place you feel truly at home.

The low thrum of the pre-pre show music intensifies as you approach the arena. You feel your senses heighten, your heart beat quicken. You pull the rubber band from your hair and let it flow freely around your shoulders.

At an intersection in the long hallway, a haggard-looking twenty-something trying way too hard to look rock 'n' roll suddenly intercepts you. Behind her, a thin rope clipped across the corridor barely keeps a throng of screaming fans at bay.

"Oh thank goodness," says the twenty-something. "I thought I was about to be trampled!" The ID card hooked to the lanyard around her neck is emblazoned with the title, EVENT MANAGER.

But it's too late. One of the fans at the front of the line has caught a glimpse of you and now the whole crowd is screaming. The rope is far too flimsy to hold and before you know it your fans are upon you. The first in line holds up her backstage pass inches from your face.

"Oh my god!" she screams, apparently oblivious to the fact that you are in fact a human being and that at this distance her volume could cause hearing loss. "Is it really you?"

You decide to answer her hysteria with a calm smile, which you find does the trick most of the time. "What's your name?" you ask, gamely taking the Sharpie and T-shirt she's thrusting in your direction.

"You are even more beautiful in person!" she gushes. "Oh! I'm Kristin!"

"Thank you!" You smile and sign the T-shirt. "Just one second."

You turn to the event manager, who is in fact not managing the event very well. "I thought the meet-and-greet was supposed to be after hair and makeup."

Her eyes are pools of pure fear. "I am so sorry! I thought you were already finished. They've been lined up here for hours." She gulps then looks at you apologetically, "This is my first week."

"It's okay," you tell her. You can handle this. You calmly address the rabid crowd, using your concert voice. "Everybody!"

The single word elicits a new round of screams. The group is a mix of your baseline demographic: teenaged girls, a few adolescent boys, a handful of post-pubescents, and a smattering of middle-aged moms and overly calm and cool-seeming dads trying too hard to appear uninterested. You look down and realize in your hurry to dress following the cell phone fiasco you forgot to throw on your bra. Oh well. You pull your long hair forward over your shoulders to cover what you can, fully aware that some of the men—and likely some of the women—in this crowd are followers of @honeyshives, a renegade Twitter account set up by fans in homage to your much-admired assets.

"This way!" you call, then lean toward the event manager, yelling in order to be heard. "Help me get them to the meet-and-greet room— I'll take them in one at a time—but we have to make it quick."

"Got it," she replies, and together you corral the crowd down the hall to the holding area outside of the little room bedecked in glittery, oversized hives and adorable cartoon bees.

One by one, you bring each group of fans into the room, take a photo, scribble a hasty autograph, and then send the group off with a Honey Swag Bag containing a honey-bee shaped lip gloss, honey-flavored lollipops, Bit-O-Honey candies, and a glittery tiara complete with glowing bee antennae to be worn during the show (also sold for $14.99 at the many Nobility Tour kiosks sprinkled throughout the venue). The fans are universally wowed and gushingly grateful, and you know they'll be posting their selfies on social media for weeks.

The last of the pre-show guests is preempted by a frenetic Freddie berating the flustered event manager as she tries in vain to explain the meet-and-greet mix-up.

"All right people, move it along!" Freddie yells as he barges into the room. The final group looks crestfallen at the prospect of a foreshortened visit.

"No, you don't have to leave," you tell them. And to Freddie, "We have plenty of time."

"We do not have plenty of time!" Freddie insists. "You are almost an hour late for hair and makeup."

You hop down from the photo platform in the center of the room.

"Freddie," you say as quietly as possible. "These people have been waiting in line for hours. It's the last group. And now we actually have more time since the meet-and-greet is already done."

Freddie breathes in a deep breath. "You got ten minutes."

"Thank you," you tell him, half-seriously. "I'll meet you in the dressing room in ten."

But Freddie plants himself by the door like a sentry, folding his arms across his chest. "I'll wait."

You can't help but smile at his protectiveness as you finish up with your last guests and send them on their way back to the arena.

Your glam squad, Marco (your hair stylist) and Margot (your makeup artist)—M & M, as you affectionately refer to the duo—wait in the dressing room and immediately go to work. Sasha saunters into the room, noticeably calmer than when you last saw him.

"The supplies you requested are in the corner," he tells you, then leans to whisper in your ear, "under the rainbow wig."

Marco waves Sasha away in irritation, but luckily appears not to have heard him.

"Okay . . ." You look toward the corner but see nothing but the rainbow wig, styled and ready, resting on its usual wig stand.

An hour and a half later, you step out of the makeup chair and take a careful sip of your Red Bull through a straw. You blink your eyes as you look in the makeup mirror, after all this time still slightly surprised at the transformation the layers of makeup, the fake eyelashes, and the sleek up-do accomplish.

For the first song, your own hair will be exposed, pulled up high with the ends of your ponytail just touching the middle of your back. During the first costume change, the pony gets wrapped into the tight bun that will be hidden under the wigs you wear for the rest of the show until the finale.

Sasha holds your first costume in front of you, ready for you to step into. It's a heavily sequined minidress, and weighs at least ten pounds. The intricate beadwork creates a prism effect under the lights onstage, and draws gasps from the crowd as you make your entrance, lowered down from above onto the platform projecting out into the center of the arena.

Sasha zips the back of the dress and helps you into your four-inch silver heels. The rest of your Act One costumes hang backstage, ready for the many split-second changes you'll make during the show.

Your dancers and backstage crew trickle into the dressing room as you listen to your opening act play their second-to-last song. The nervous energy in the room is palpable, the adrenaline increasing by the second. The dancers joke, laugh, and stretch as they form the little pre-show circle you've grown to love.

"All right, everybody," you bring the circle to attention "Let's make this the best show yet. I am so excited to be here in"—you realize you actually have no idea where you are—"what city are we in?"

The group laughs, probably not sure whether you are joking. "Albuquerque!" one of them tells you.

"I knew that." You wink. "Let's give this Albuquerque audience the best night of their lives!"

The group cheers and you initiate the energy pulse, a quick hand squeeze that travels around the circle. When it's come back to you three times you are ready. "On three: one, two, three . . ."

"Nobility!" they cheer in unison before scattering to take their places.

Backstage, Sasha gives you a little squeeze as he passes you in the dimly lit wings, "Kill it, Henry!"

Two of your dancers accompany you up the winding staircase to the catwalk, where you'll wait to make your entrance. They walk directly behind you, at Freddie's insistence, in case you should stumble backward and fall, which thankfully hasn't happened yet. You can hear their playful banter as they follow one step behind.

"You better not be talking about my ass," you tease.

One of the dancers, a ripped eastern European transplant who goes only by his first name, Serge, laughs, "We cannot even see your ass. We are blinded by so many sparkles."

You giggle and ascend to the top of the stairway, where you're met by two burly crew members who affix a sturdy harness to the back of your costume before they assist you over the six-inch gap leading to the catwalk. You dare to look down, and the sheer height brings on a swooping sense of vertigo.

Flanked by a dancer on each side and with the two crew members behind you, you carefully navigate to the platform that will carry you down to the stage.

As the stage lights darken, the buzz in the arena erupts into applause and cheers of anticipation. "She's secure," one of the crew announces into his walkie as he gives the harness a tug. "We're a go." The dancers are clipped into their harnesses, set to drop onto the stage as soon as you land, and choreographed to gracefully unclip you as the show begins.

You take in a long breath, slowly exhale, and shake out your nerves. Every sense is immensely exaggerated in the moments before a show, but the nerves you feel now will become pure energy the minute you step on stage.

Serge reaches over and squeezes your hand. "Break a leg!"

You smile at him in the dark. "Thanks," you whisper.

He leans in and brushes his rough cheek against your smooth skin. "Your ass," he tells you, "is dazzling."

You laugh as you hear, "Go, go, go!" and the crew pushes the button that initiates your descent. *What was that?* You wonder, but not for long.

Surrounded by two huge spheres of shining silver, the platform appears to levitate as it slowly floats to stage level. Pyrotechnics in rainbow hues explode behind you as you make your descent. The sea of audience members that encircles the stage, as far as you can see, sparkles with neon tiaras and illuminated signs, and cheers at a deafening volume. You lift your face to the sunlight of their adoration, bring the microphone to your lips, and give them what they came for.

Three hours and two encores later, you are bundled into a soft terry robe as you walk back to your dressing room, thanking the crew as you pass them in the hall. "Great show!" they yell back and high-five one another. Sasha meets you at the door, ready to remove the headpiece still attached to your aching scalp.

"That blasted peacock!" he says as you ease into a low chair and prop your feet up on an ottoman.

Along with bottled spring water, a footbath warmed to precisely one hundred degrees (though you never check), a mint-infused neck pillow, loose-leaf brewed passionflower tea, and peanut M&M's (a nod to your glam squad), your concert contract rider calls for a comfy chair with an ottoman. You're not a diva with an extensive list of demands, but you do have a few basic requirements that help you unwind after a grueling stage performance.

"It wasn't that bad." You drop your feet slowly into the footbath, the heavenly warmth of the water beginning to relax your aching muscles. "It seemed faster tonight to me."

"Well, it wasn't," Sasha says. "I'm sure the sound booth was dying a slow death waiting for us to get you out there."

There's a quick knock at the door as Crispin enters the room, grabbing a fistful of M&M's and bending to kiss you on the cheek.

"Brilliant show, darling," he tells you. "That bit with the tightrope always gets me. Plus I got to have a glimpse straight up your knickers."

"You and the rest of the world," Sasha comments as he gathers an armful of costumes and begins hanging them piece by piece on the rolling rack.

"Not like there's anything to see. I'm in full granny panties during that song." You reach down gingerly to touch a fresh blister that's appeared on your big toe. "Ouch. Looks like I still haven't broken in those shoes."

"Aww, let me take a look," Crispin sits on his haunches in front of the little bath and lifts your foot from the water. He rests your heel in the palm of his hand, and takes your big toe between his fingers. "This little piggy goes to market . . ." He glances up and lets his gaze run the length of your leg, a look of mischief on his face as he lowers his voice, "No granny panties in sight now, if I'm not mistaken." He drops your foot and runs his thumb along your bare thigh. He follows his thumbstroke with a little bite and growls. "This little piggy is ready to go all the way home."

"I do not need to be a witness to your freaky X-rated nursery rhymes," Sasha rolls his eyes as he breezes past, pushing the heavy rack of costumes toward the door. "I will catch you in the morning."

Before he can exit the room, a high voice you can't place emanates from the other side of the rack of clothes. "Crispin? Are you in there?"

Crispin jerks around, clearly startled. "Just here," he calls out. He straightens his shirt and smooths the front of his pants before turning back to you. "You don't mind, do you?" he asks.

You shake your head and shrug, unsure what he is asking.

"Oh boy," Sasha mutters as puts his weight into the rack and rolls it swiftly out the door.

"There you are!" trills the voice you finally place a moment before Trixie enters the room. "I thought you'd run off!"

"No, I'd never . . ." Crispin looks oddly abashed in her presence, and for a moment you feel like you're a fly on the wall of a private moment you are not meant to witness. The moment passes quickly, though, as Trixie finally notices you.

"Honey!" she drawls, racing over in a series of stilted baby steps on her towering platforms. Her breasts and her extensions bounce merrily as she approaches to give you a bubble-gum scented squeeze. "Your show is just magical—truly one of the best! Technically it's just—to die! Thank you so much for the pass!"

You can't help but laugh at her sheer enthusiasm. "You're welcome," you tell her, although you had no idea you had given her a pass. You can only imagine that Crispin must have given her one of his comps.

She does an abrupt about-face and begins to circle the room, alternately cracking her gum and making an aggressive display of bubble-blowing, like a howler monkey inflating its throat. She stops to pick up a bottle of water and then considers and rejects the colorful bowl of M&M's.

"It's amazing," she continues, "how you make all of those songs sound so authentic. I know all the little tricks, but it is truly like you're really singing up there. And we all know how much of our music is auto-tuned," she says with a conspiratorial wink.

She pops a huge bubble then twists the masticated wad of gum disgustingly around one finger, pulling it into a long string before popping it back into her mouth. She holds the same finger, glistening with saliva, up to her lips, "Shhh!" she assures you, "I won't tell a soul."

You know you should take nothing about this girl seriously, but still you feel your blood pressure rising. "Um, I actually do perform my music live. That's really me singing up there on stage, Trixie."

Trixie laughs as though you've just told the funniest joke she's ever heard. "Oh my goodness, you are too precious!" she cries.

You glance over at Crispin to see whether he thinks her behavior is as bizarre as you do. He looks completely uncomfortable, his back hunched as though in pain.

You straighten up in your seat and pull your robe more closely around you, tightening the sash. As you do, you see Trixie headed toward the counter, inches from the rainbow wig and the phone you remember is stashed there. She moves from one wig to the next, gently stroking a tendril on each.

"Trixie," you've got to get her away from those wigs. "I don't mean to sound rude but if you could just not touch those wigs that would be great. My stylist just reset them after the show, and he's pretty protective of them."

Trixie seems to consider this for a moment then slowly withdraws her hand just inches from the rainbow wig.

"Hmmm," she says, "they don't look very styled. No offense."

"Yeah, well, that's what we do . . . kind of . . . unstructured," you trail off, immensely relieved she's moved away from the wig.

"Yeah . . ." Trixie suddenly turns to you and makes full eye contact, as if measuring you up.

Crispin seems to sense the tension and breaks in. "Hey, I've just remembered—I seem to have misplaced my mobile. Have either of you lovely ladies seen it lying around?"

It doesn't escape you that Crispin appears to think it's just as possible that Trixie might know where his phone is as it is that you do.

Trixie seems to sense your unease and jumps at it. "My hotel room is such a disaster. I guess it could be there. I don't think I would have even noticed." She appears to ponder for a moment. "Or could it maybe be in my car?"

Your head is spinning. *Crispin's been in Trixie's room? And in her car?*

"We should probably go look." She stands just inches in front of Crispin. You watch, horrified, as she uses two fingers to walk baby steps up his chest. "You know, retrace our steps." The loud crack of her gum is the straw that breaks the camel's back.

Suddenly every jealous, competitive nerve in your body is on fire, and you know you need to do everything you can to keep Crispin from leaving with Trixie. "Actually, Crispin"—you keep your voice as even as possible—"there's something I need to talk to you about. I was hoping we could have a few minutes"—you look pointedly at Trixie—"alone."

Trixie pivots slowly to face you. She wraps her gum around her finger again and stands on her heels, looking like a five-year-old being punished with a timeout. She pops the gum back into her mouth and draws her lips into a thin line. "I can take a hint. I know when I'm not welcome."

She backs slowly toward the door and dips a quick curtsy, holding out the hem of an imaginary skirt, "M'lady, I'm ever so grateful to have been allowed into your presence," she says in an awful English accent, then laughs raucously, mouth open wide. "Naw, I'm just playing." The wad of gum is fully visible, stuck to her molars. "I really just wanted to thank you for the ticket. The concert was dope."

Dope?

She pauses at the door and waggles her fingers at Crispin. "We'll talk later, right? After you two lovebirds have your alone time?"

"Right," says Crispin. "I'll ring you. Oh right. I suppose I can't do that after all, can I?" He turns both palms toward the ceiling and shrugs. "No mobile."

"Oh . . . darn." Trixie looks crestfallen. "We can't even text. What will I do if I need you?"

Once again, Crispin looks intensely uncomfortable. He clears his throat and glances at you before he answers. "I think you'll be fine for one evening. As soon as I locate my mobile I'll check in. I promise."

"Well, okay then, I guess. You two have a good night." At last she is out the door.

An awkward silence descends, the dynamic completely changed after Trixie's visit. You have a feeling whatever you say next will come out wrong so you let the silence linger. Luckily, Sasha breezes back into the room to fill it.

"Sorry, I forgot this." He bends to retrieve a shoe from the corner. "What happened?" he asks, noticing Trixie's absence. "Did the trailer park call?"

"Sasha," you reprimand him, "be nice."

"You know I can't help myself." He smirks.

You know Sasha has some ulterior motive for returning to the dressing room, and that the errant shoe is not it.

Crispin seems to sense this, too. He stands with arms folded. "May we help you?" he asks.

Sasha looks him up and down before answering, "No thank you. I think I can help myself. I won't be a minute." He appears to think for a few moments then makes a decision. He slinks over to the corner of the makeup counter. "Marco didn't get a chance to style one of the wigs—he, uh, asked me to bring it to him. Let me just grab this then I will be out of your hair. Ha! No pun intended."

"Actually," Crispin announces suddenly, stepping toward the door. "I really can't stay. I just wanted to come tell you brilliant show. I've got to find my mobile. I think retracing my steps is just the ticket."

"Crispin." You jump up from your seat and subtly loosen your robe. "There really is something I need to discuss with you."

You use your best bedroom voice, a little embarrassing in front of Sasha but desperate times call for desperate measures. You take two long strides toward Crispin. "It really is very important."

Crispin remains oblivious. "Unless it's about my mobile I'm afraid it will have to wait, won't it?" He kisses you softly on the lips and walks toward the door. "Until tomorrow?"

"Uh, Crispin?" you begin, flying by the seat of your pants, "there's a chance I might have some information about the whereabouts of your cell phone."

Now you're trapped. You either need to spill the beans about the location of Crispin's phone and give up the chance to see for yourself what is going on between him and Trixie—not to mention try to explain to Crispin how it ended up here—or keep your secret and risk Crispin running back to Trixie in a futile attempt to find his phone. Should you tell him you have his phone or keep your secret? You have to make a choice.

To tell Crispin you have his phone, turn to page 101.
To keep your secret and hide the phone from Crispin,
keep reading.

"You might?" asks Crispin, drawing his eyebrows together.

"I might," you say uncertainly, "I was thinking we should check with lost and found. Maybe it fell out during the concert."

You cut your eyes to Sasha, who lifts the wig along with the heavy vase of rice, trying to make it appear as lightweight as possible. You shake your head subtly and silently implore Sasha to read your mind, but he doesn't get the message.

"Sasha!" you shout a little too loudly, "Actually, I need that wig—uh—Marco just texted me before you guys came in and asked me to keep it . . . he's coming back . . . early, tomorrow . . . to style it himself."

Sasha holds the wig in front of him uncertainly, shielding the vase of rice with his arms. "Okay . . ." he says slowly, narrowing his eyes at you and then slowly turning back to the countertop from which he took the wig. "I guess I will just leave it then," he asks, setting the vase and wig down gently and turning back around. "Right?"

"Yes," you tell him, immensely relieved, "Just leave it there. I'll tell Marco."

"Okay, that's great then. I think." Sasha walks slowly toward the door then turns back quickly. "Well, nighty-night!" he shouts in a high falsetto as he runs out the door.

"Not sure what that was all about," says Crispin, puzzled. "He can be very odd, that one, can't he?"

"Yes, well." You smile and bat your lashes. "Finally, I have you all to myself."

You walk past Crispin and shut the door to the dressing room, turning the bolt to lock it. You gaze up into the famous, whiskey-colored eyes you know so well and in one swift move tug the sash to let your robe fall open. Your body is tanned and glittered, and you put on hand on your hip, well aware that the pose thrusts your breasts out beyond the robe's opening. You take three long strides toward Crispin and place one hand on his chest.

He grins and a decisively red flush creeps up to his face. "Uh," he begins, "I thought you had some kind of important business to discuss."

"I do," you tell him, lowering your voice, "very, very important." You reach up to put your arms around his neck as you stand on tiptoe to kiss him. He returns the kiss in full, thrusting his minty tongue into your mouth, and reaches his hands around the back of your robe to pull you tightly to him. You feel the his urgency beneath the waistline of his jeans and reach your manicured hand gently down to touch the hot tip of him, then pull back dramatically.

"Oh my, Mr. Hershey," you tease, "I wasn't expecting *that*!"

Crispin laughs and plays right along, "Well, Ms. Noble, I wasn't expecting this," he says. "But, I most certainly appreciate it."

You shrug to let the robe fall from your shoulders but Crispin stops you. "No, he says, his breathing becoming shorter as he kisses you, "I kind of like this." He slips one hand beneath your robe and strokes his thumb up and down your lower back, skims along the top of your buttocks and then gently between them, while he brings his mouth to just below your jawline and kisses your neck, sending chills up your spine. "You smell so good," he tells you in a throaty whisper.

"It's my signature fragrance, eau de post-show glow, stage makeup, and body glitter," you laugh.

"It's absolutely intoxicating," he says, still kissing your neck. He brings his other hand up to your bare breasts, lightly running his palm over your nipple before he lifts your heavy breast and, groaning, gives it a squeeze.

He brings his other hand around to run his thumb down your firm stomach, trails it lower, then gently dips his fingers slightly into your most sensitive area. "Mmmm," he moans, as he feels how ready you are for him. He lifts one breast to his mouth and suckles, swirling his tongue in circles around your nipple.

You are ready, and sooner than you would expect. You push his hand away and begin to lead him to the soft pile of pillows at the corner of the room, but again Crispin stops you.

"Uh-uh, over here," he instructs. You stop to pull a condom from your LV clutch—you always use protection—before Crispin leads you to the makeup counter. He brushes aside the scattered mess of makeup and hair accessories and lifts you onto the counter's edge. Using his knee to separate your legs, he steps between them and, fully clothed, thrusts against you. The roughness of his jeans over the hard bulge of his desire is delicious. You reach your hand down again to feel his ready cock. You hurriedly push his jeans down his muscular thighs then run your palm up the inside of his leg. Reaching even lower, you give him a gentle squeeze but he stills your hand, looks you in the eye, pulls you to him, moves his mouth back to your neck, and thrusts into you. Something about the plush softness of the robe around you combined with the cold, sharp edge of the counter gently biting into your thighs and the heat of Crispin's body against yours makes you come almost instantly. You pull him into you and lock your legs around him as waves of pleasure wash over you.

It takes Crispin a little longer, but soon his breathing takes on the rough quality you've come to recognize and he buries his head into your neck and moans. As he does he thrusts into you, hard, and all at once you hear a crack a moment before the counter gives way beneath your combined weight.

You are jolted painfully to the floor, Crispin crushing you to the ground as the broken countertop jabs painfully into your legs and backside.

"Are you okay?" Crispin asks.

"I think so," you tell him.

Crispin's hands are pinned under you and your robe is providing a little extra padding, which has probably prevented a much worse outcome. You're more shocked than anything, and although you may feel it tomorrow, right now you're immensely grateful you aren't seriously hurt. Then all at once you remember the cell phone.

You twist around to try to assess the damage. The adjacent section of countertop is still attached to the piece that has fallen, and it remains upright—though it's tilted at an alarming angle. The rainbow wig-topped vase begins to slide ever so slowly from the back edge of the counter. You scramble to get out from under Crispin but you are hopelessly stuck.

"Honey, hold on, you are going to injure yourself. Just let me get up first," Crispin says as you wriggle and twist to free yourself.

Crispin pulls his hands out from under you, "Ouch," he wiggles his fingers, balling his hands into fists. "I may not be playing guitar anytime soon."

"Crispin, I need to get up!" you yell, as you watch the vase slide across the middle of the counter. You jerk the robe and finally free yourself, making a lunge for the countertop. The vase reaches the edge as if in slow-motion, but you're an instant too late to stop it. It teeters for a split second before plunging to the tile floor and smashing with a terrific crash followed by the slow flow of what must be thousands of grains of rice, pooling around the jagged shards of glass to reveal the top edge of Crispin's cell phone.

"No!" you shout as you make a grab for the phone. Instead, you connect with a jagged piece of glass which you don't feel until it is too late.

The pain having not yet registered, you are confused for a moment watching red droplets fall into the hill of rice, creating a stark crimson contrast against the white grains. Crispin, however, reacts immediately.

"What have you done?" he asks as he grabs your injured hand. Too late, you see the phone, still partially buried in the pile of rice, but peeking accusingly out from under the fringe of the rainbow wig. Crispin sees it, too. "Honey?" he asks, as he gingerly removes the phone, "what's this?"

"I can explain," you say quickly.

Crispin looks crestfallen. His mouth pinches into a thin, straight line.

"I was just trying to dry it out . . ." you offer lamely.

He eases up off of the floor and brusquely turns away from you to pulls up his jeans. You reach out to grab his arm.

"Crispin." He jerks away as if burned. Suddenly, the pain from your other hand registers, searing through your arm. "Ouch!"

"Come on," he tells you, his eyes cool and his voice slightly strained. "You're going the have to get this seen to."

"It's fine." You squeeze your fingers and a wave of nausea hits you as you glimpse the thin sheen of what looks like muscle through the gaping, bloody gash in your skin. You cup your other hand under the steady flow of blood, trying in vain to contain it, and the strength drains from your legs.

Crispin catches you around your waist just before your legs give out and he carries you back to your chair. "Sit," he tells you, "and stay."

You don't have the energy to argue. Crispin presses a thick wad of paper towels into your hand and jogs out of the room. What feels like seconds later, he returns with a wheelchair.

"Where did you get that?" you ask. "I can walk."

But as you attempt to get to your feet and feel your head swim, you realize the wheelchair is actually a good idea and allow Crispin to help you into the seat. He tucks your robe around you—you didn't even realize it was still open—and ties the sash snugly.

The ride to the hospital is a blur. A side entrance, hidden by a bank of ambulances, takes you discreetly to the triage area. A nurse wearing purple scrubs festooned with cartoon characters walks briskly into the room. The embodiment of efficiency, she doesn't bother to look up from the chart resting on the blood pressure cart she wheels in front of her. "Henrietta," she announces, "laceration to the left hand? Let's take a look."

You stretch your hand toward her gingerly and she peels away the paper towels. "I'm going to give that a quick rinse and then wrap it nice and tight until we can get the doc in to take a look. I'm going to ask you to keep it elevated. Okay?"

She turns away to grab supplies from the locked cabinet on the wall, then looks back over her shoulder when you don't respond. She turns away again for a moment then does a double-take. Recognition, doubt, then dismissal wash in quick succession across her face. She turns back to her work. "You okay, honey?"

Unsure whether she is using an anonymous term of endearment or your name, you answer hesitantly, "I'm fine."

She bustles over with a plastic bottle, a large container, and a roll of gauze. She makes small talk as she rinses your hand, the runoff from the water bottle turning the water in the container pink. "You know you look a lot like that singer the kids like? What is her name? Honey something?" She laughs off the remark as she pats your hand dry and begins to wrap it. "I bet you get that all the time."

You flinch a little as she wraps the sterile gauze tightly around your hand. "You have no idea," you tell her.

A dose of pain medication, twelve quick stitches, and an hour later, the doctor peels off his gloves and scrubs his hands in the sink at the side of the room. "That was a close one," he tells you, "one centimeter to the left and it would have been an artery. Next time, let someone else pick up the broken glass."

"Good advice," you agree.

"The nurse will be in to discharge you shortly," the doctor says as he heads toward the door. "Change the bandages daily. I used absorbable stitches, so they'll dissolve on their own. The wound should heal cleanly as long as you keep it dry and bandaged. You should be good as new in about two weeks. But you'll need to check back in with me if you notice any redness or the pain gets worse."

You don't bother to tell him that in a few days you'll be long gone, in another city doing another show.

"Can my friend come in to see me now?" you ask the doctor before he leaves.

"Your friend?"

"Yes, my friend, uh, Crispin, drove me here. Maybe he's in the waiting area?"

"I'll check in with the nurses' station. Someone will track him down."

Every time you hear footsteps approaching the little curtained room, you're sure it's Crispin returning to take you home. You doze off and on as you wait. Eventually you're sure the hospital staff has entirely forgotten about you and your request to locate Crispin.

At last, the footsteps stop at your room and the curtain pulls back to reveal Sasha, one hand on his hip, shaking his head. "What have you done to yourself?" He circles around to appraise your bandaged hand. "This," he says, surveying the hospital-blue sling elevating your injured appendage, "is not a good look."

"Where's Crispin?" you ask.

Sasha purses his lips and steps back, "Well, isn't that a fine how-do-you-do?"

"Sasha." You know he's trying to lighten the mood, but you are exhausted and now you're worried. "You know I'm glad you're here. It's just that Crispin was with me when this happened. He drove me here and I haven't seen him since. I have no idea where he is."

"Well, I for one could not care less where he is," Sasha tells you. "I just know he isn't here, and that he woke me from a very deep sleep to tell me to come retrieve you. At least he didn't leave you stranded. I guess I should give him that."

"Wait, he called you?"

"How do you think I knew to come and get you?"

"But his phone . . ."

Sasha pauses and looks at you with immense impatience. "Henry, he didn't call me from *his* phone." He gives you a moment to process. "Believe me, you do not want to know. Let's get you out of here."

Sasha makes a quick trip to the nurses' station. "Some kind of paperwork is apparently needed to set you free. Think they would have done that while you were waiting, but who am I to assume the health care system would run efficiently?" Sasha glances around the room as if looking for something. "Where's all your stuff?"

"You're looking at it," you answer.

"Oh lord," he sighs, shaking his head. "I am not even going to ask. Where is Crispin's phone anyway?" A look of understanding washes across his face as he awaits your answer. "Oh boy. You better tell me everything."

So you do—well, most of it.

The better part of the second and final day of your Albuquerque tour stop is spent in a fitful sleep. You awake in a sweat from a nightmare in which your hand has swollen to the size of a balloon and throbs painfully as it floats above your head. Opening your eyes, you realize the pain in your hand is quite real. At least the grotesque swelling was just a figment of your dream. You reach for your cell phone to check your messages and see a lengthy stream of texts from Sasha:

How's the hand?

You up yet?

Hello?

Okay you must still be sleeping but text me when you wake up.

I don't want to disturb you if you are still sleeping but pls let me know you are OK.

It's noon. Text me back.

You type a one-handed message.

I'm up. Where are you?

Costumes

OK be there in a few.

You can't believe Crispin hasn't checked in once. But then again, his phone probably isn't working. After a Red Bull and a quick shower with a baggie over your injured hand, you feel a thousand percent better. You pull on stretchy pants and a loose shirt then make your way across the parking lot to the costume trailer. On your way, you try Crispin. Your call goes straight to voicemail.

Sasha sits perched on a little stool, hunched over his sewing machine. "Well, good morning, Sleeping Beauty," he says without turning around, biting off a piece of thread as he greets you.

"What are you working on?"

"One second . . ." Sasha slides his hands skillfully across the machine and spins around to display the finished product. "Et viola!"

A long, glittered glove hangs in front of you, reflecting the fluorescent lights of the trailer like a disco ball.

"I don't think—" you begin.

"You are right," Sasha cuts you off. "You don't think, and that is why we have found ourselves in this unfortunate situation. You should have let me take that ridiculous phone when I could have, then this whole crisis would have been averted. And once again I am left to find a solution. So here you go." Sasha holds up the glove again. "Now let's see if it fits over that unsightly bandaged paw."

Sasha's clearly irritated and likely a little overtired himself—and you do appreciate his coming to your rescue. You hold out your hand obediently and wince as you feel the pain begin to throb anew.

Sasha notices immediately. "You okay, Henrietta?"

"It's ridiculous that a tiny cut could hurt this much."

"Well, we all know you have a very low pain threshold," Sasha says sardonically. "I will be careful."

He slides the glove slowly over your hand, intently monitoring your expression to be sure he isn't causing too much pain.

You move to the mirror to observe the effect. "It works, I guess." You twist your hand gingerly left and right. "But I'm thinking it may be a little too Michael Jackson."

"I'm going to make another one, obviously," Sasha rolls his eyes. "Michael Jackson. Puh-lease." Sasha spins back around to show you the makings of the other glove, the pattern already cut and ready to be sewn.

The ripple effects of your little post-show calamity become increasingly evident as you enter the backstage area. Your dressing room has been relocated to a small crevice the size of a closet on the other side of the hall and rolling racks of your costumes now line the hallway. Your previous dressing area is taped off like a crime scene. You ease into the makeup chair, now squeezed into a cramped corner, as Freddie pops his head into the crowded space. "Sorry," you apologize.

"You don't have to apologize to me," he tells you. "But I gotta tell you I don't think Albuquerque is going to be sorry to see us go."

"I know. I feel awful."

"Eh. It was an accident. How's the hand?"

"It's okay. It kind of throbs off and on."

"Well I'm glad it wasn't worse. I talked to the doctor. He says you'll be good as new in a couple of weeks. But don't push yourself too hard tonight. And you let me know if you need anything, you got it? You need extra rest? You leave it to me. Did they give you medicine at the hospital?"

"Just some extra-strength Tylenol," you tell him. "Didn't make a dent."

"I have something I can give you for tonight if you have trouble sleeping, but it's strong stuff. You shouldn't take it unless you absolutely need it." He fishes inside his pocket and extracts a chalky, round pill.

"Thanks," you close your fist around the little pill. "Thanks, Freddie," you smile at him in the mirror, "You're the best."

"Yes," he agrees with a satisfied smile. "I am the best. Don't you forget it." Then he disappears into the hallway.

Getting into your first costume is a nightmare. Thank god for Sasha's silky glove, which helps the tight sleeves slide over your throbbing hand. Your stomach clenches when you reach the next obstacle, the long stairway leading to the catwalk. You place your foot onto the first step and suddenly the climb seems much steeper than it did last night.

Your dancers wait behind you.

You take another step onto the stairway and vertigo overwhelms you. You begin to fall back, and are gracefully caught in a pair of muscular arms.

"Oh!" you exclaim as Serge literally sweeps you off of your feet.

"I got you," he says, his bulging biceps pressing into your back. In one swift motion, he carries you like a baby up the stairs, depositing you gently down at the top.

"That must be exactly what Lois Lane felt like in Superman's arms," you say, your head still swimming a bit.

"I am honored to come to your rescue," Serge says with a huge smile, then leans in close and whispers into your ear. "I would tell you to break a leg, but I think your hand is already enough." Then he's gone with a wink and you are harnessed into the platform and ready descend to the stage. Once you're there, the pain melts magically away and you are one with your music and your audience.

Sasha keeps you company after the show as you wait in vain for a visit from Crispin. Sasha's incessant yawns and the thought of a long travel day tomorrow finally convince you to give up and return to the bus. Sasha air-kisses you goodnight as you close the door and burrow beneath the covers.

You lie awake in the dark, then pick up your phone to try Crispin again. This time, it rings once and then goes to voicemail. You can't believe he hasn't even checked on you all day. You know he's probably angry about the phone, but still you'd think he would have been worried enough about you to get over it. You decide not to leave a message but text him instead.

U there?

The text hangs on the screen, unanswered.

You slip out from under the covers to pace around the little bus, the adrenaline from your performance still not completely out of your system. You check your text every few minutes even though you know a message would have popped up on the dark screen if Crispin had responded.

Finally, you give up and decide to return to bed. As soon as you lay down the pain in your hand returns with a vengeance. You can't seem to find a comfortable position. Even propping your hand on two pillows doesn't help. You roll over to grab the bottle of Tylenol the hospital prescribed when you remember the little pill Freddie handed you before the show. You pop back up to find the pill, and you examine it as you try to determine what exactly you are taking. You can't find any kind of identifying mark.

You fill a glass with water and hesitate for a moment. You don't have any allergies you know of and you know Freddie would never give you anything dangerous, but still something in you is giving you pause. The Tylenol would be the safer bet, but you know it is useless and the last thing you need is to be up all night and miserable all day tomorrow, with nothing to distract you from the pain on the long ride to your next stop in Vegas. Should you listen to your gut and deal with the pain? Or should you take Freddie's pill and hope for a solid sleep?

To take the Tylenol, turn to page 82.
To take Freddie's pill, keep reading.

You pop the little pill into your mouth and wash it down with a quick swallow of water.

What feels like minutes later, pounding at your door jolts you awake. "Just a second!" you yell. Your breath comes out in little puffs in the frigid air as you race to the door. You feel insanely refreshed and incredibly awake. Even your hand is miraculously painless.

"The circus has pulled up stakes," Sasha announces the minute you open the door. "You ready to roll?" He rubs his hands back and forth, "Did you forget to turn on the heat or something? "

The desert nights are truly freezing and you realize you did in fact forget to switch the heat on, and now the bus is frigid. "I was so exhausted after everything last night I completely passed out."

"Hmm," Sasha comments. You were so tired you didn't even change your clothes?" Sasha purses his full lips. "What's up, Henrietta?"

"What do you mean?" you ask innocently, "I was just really tired."

"Are you seriously going to lie to me right now?"

"Okay," you give in, realizing there's no point in trying to hide anything from Sasha. "Freddie gave me a sleeping pill or something last night and it totally knocked me out."

"I'm sorry, come again?" Sasha shakes his head in disbelief. "Freddie gave you what exactly?"

"I don't know. Some kind of little round pill. It was totally harmless, obviously. And I slept like a baby."

"I bet you did," says Sasha. "Let me see the pills."

"He only gave me one."

"Hmm," Sasha folds his arms across his chest. "Best you keep it that way." He walks to the front of the bus, settles into the driver's seat, and puts on his sunglasses. "Why don't you come up and keep me company, since you're so bright-eyed and bushy-tailed."

"I'd be glad to," you tell him, and take your seat beside him.

Eight hours, fourteen games of twenty questions, and three unproductive attempts to call Crispin later, you pull into downtown Las Vegas. The city is lit up magically, the setting sun barely visible behind the rows of high-rise hotels and casinos. The sky is a blood-orange backdrop for silhouetted palms and twinkling neon lights. Sasha pulls the bus expertly into the wide circle in front of the Maxamillion Resort and Arena, or "The Max," as the famous Vegas landmark is known.

"You ready to sleep in a real bed?" Sasha asks. "I know I am."

"So ready," you tell him, heading to the back of the bus to grab your hotel bags, pre-packed with comfy PJs, cosmetics, and two fun outfits—one for an obligatory appearance at the resort's Max nightclub, and one just in case.

The hotel lobby bustles with energy, color, and light. Men in tuxedos and women in floor-length gowns and glittering jewels glide in and out of elevators and casino entrances. The *clang* and *chime* of slot machines, the *click* of spinning roulette wheels, and smell of money waft past as you make your way unnoticed to the service elevator. A uniformed elevator operator turns a key, opens a locked panel, and pushes a button that whisks you to the penthouse suite. The doors glide open onto an expanse of sleek marble ending at a wall of windows overlooking a breathtaking view of the Strip. "Wow!" you exclaim, as you step into the dimly lit suite.

Sasha rolls your bags into the living room and opens the little bar refrigerator. "I love it when they get Freddie's memos," he says, cracking open a Mountain Dew and taking a deep draught. "Ahhhh," he sighs, "that hits the spot."

He tosses you a frosty can of Red Bull, which you manage to catch. "Thanks," you say, and begin to explore the suite.

You round the corner and almost run smack into Freddie's chest. Red Bull shoots straight up and out your nose as you laugh in surprise. "Owwww! That stings!" you howl, tears streaming from your eyes.

"My god," Sasha tosses you a towel from the bar. "I cannot take you anywhere."

"That really is not very ladylike," agrees Freddie, hoisting his bags on a chair in the far corner of the room.

"Sorry," you mop your face and then the floor.

"Nice, right?" Freddie asks, looking around the suite. "What took you so long to get here?"

"You know Sasha," you answer. "Drives like an old lady."

"You're welcome to drive anytime, miss thing," Sasha snaps.

"I'm good." You smile and take another swig of Red Bull. "Sasha," you yell, "can you grab me a straw?"

Sasha rifles around under the bar and saunters over twirling the straw then sliding it into the Red Bull can. "I am only here to serve you," he says before dipping a curtsey and leaving the room.

"That stuff is toxic," Freddie says as he watches you drink. "A straw does not make it any better."

"I know, but at least it won't ruin my lipstick." You're glad Sasha and Freddie are here to distract you from thoughts of Crispin. You can't believe he still hasn't called you back.

"Is your hand bothering you?" Freddie asks as he carries his bag into the smallest of the suite's bedrooms.

"Not too much. It's actually a little better."

"Oh, you had kind of a funny look on your face."

Is Freddie really able to read you so easily? For a fleeting moment, you consider confiding in him, but you immediately think better of it. Crispin isn't Freddie's problem.

"I had an amazing sleep, which helped. That pill you gave me worked wonders."

"Oh, so you took it?"

"Yup, and I slept like a baby."

"That's great." He gives your shoulder a little squeeze and heads off in the direction of the bathroom.

An hour later, Marco and Margot put the final touches on your hair and makeup. Your makeup is a dramatic smoky eye with a glossy, natural lip, and your hair is swept up high and slick, a thin braid wrapped around to conceal the hairband. "Thank you," you tell them as they pack up their bags and cases. "It's perfect." You rise from the hair-and-makeup chair and hear the strains of "Starry Eyes," Crispin's first solo platinum single. You grab your cell phone from your pocket and answer it as quickly as you can.

"Crispin?"

"Henrietta!" Crispin's unmistakable British clip sizzles from the other end of the line. "How in the world are you?" He draws out the word *are*, not actually pronouncing the "r", so that it sounds like a low *ahhhhh*.

Something definitely isn't right. "Where are you?" you ask him.

"The question is," he answers brightly, "where . . . are . . . you?"

"Crispin, what's going on?" You don't like the tone of his voice, the slight slushiness of his words.

Then you hear a chiming laugh in the background followed by a familiar drawl. "Crispin! Come on! Hang up the phone," Trixie cries. "Just hang it up!" The exaggerated slur of her words is evident, even in the background.

"Is that Trixie?" you ask, even though you know the answer.

"In the flesh, love," Crispin answers. "In the flesh!"

"What are you two doing?" you ask carefully. You know you should just hang up the phone, that Crispin is clearly in an altered state, but you are afraid to let him go. "Do you need help?"

"Help?" he asks, "I do believe I have all the help I could possibly need."

Trixie laughs again in the background and begins to sing in a low, slow, drawl, a famous Beatles song about getting help from friends. Then she breaks into another hysterical peal, "I get high! Oh my god, I don't need any help with that!"

"No," laughs Crispin, "you most certainly do not!"

You are suddenly out of sympathy and out of patience, "Let me talk to Trixie."

Crispin is silent for a moment. "I'm sorry, what, love?"

"Please put Trixie on the phone," you repeat with all of the patience you can muster.

Crispin clears his throat. "Let me just see if she is available."

Crispin whispers loudly, then snorts a short laugh, "Ms. Taylor, are you available to come on the blower for a moment?"

"Ha!" Trixie barks. "You mean to tell me that Honey Noble, the world famous pop star, wants to talk to little old me?"

"I do believe she does, doesn't she?"

"Honey?" Trixie picks up the phone. "Honey Noble? Is it really you?"

"Cut the shit, Trixie." You are in no mood for her games. "I don't know what you have Crispin on, but clean yourselves up and get him back to rehab."

You feel tears spring to your eyes as you realize that Crispin's months of hard work and sobriety have come to this. He's an addict, and he needs more help than you can give him.

"Honey, I truly have no idea what you could be talking about." Trixie drawls sweetly. "We're just having a little party. Isn't that right, Crisp? There is nothing untoward going on here, nothing at all. I'm an official Rehab Advocate. RAs don't let RAs relapse. Or something like that. What was it Crispy?"

"Yeah, that was it, well done," Crispin says in the background. "Very well done, indeed!"

"Wooo!" yells Trixie loudly, and you pull the phone away from your ear.

"Put Crispin back on," you tell her.

"Yes ma'am!" she obliges.

"Crispin," you tell him. "I feel sorry for you, I really do. You worked hard to get clean and now in one night you've ruined it all. I wish I could help you, but I can't do this for you. You have to want it. And clearly you don't want it badly enough." You pause for a moment then let out a long sigh. "I'm just so disappointed."

Crispin gasps as though wounded. "Well, I certainly don't want to be a disa . . . disapp . . ." he snorts with laughter, unable to get the word out. "I don't want to let you down, baby, do I?"

"Crispin," Trixie whines in the background, "get off the phone!

Don't let that stick-in-the-mud ruin your good time. We were having fun!"

The phone goes quiet for a moment and you think he's hung up. Then you hear Crispin's low laughter, which quickly turns hysterical. "We were! Right you are! We were having fun!"

An immense sadness wells up in your chest. You've been through so much with Crispin, and you really hoped this time would be different.

"I'm sorry, love." Crispin is back on the line. "What were you saying, something very serious, wasn't it?"

You don't bother to respond, but instead lower the phone from your ear and look at the display, the words "Crispin Hershey" lit up in white against the dark screen. You have an overwhelming feeling this will be the last time you see his name there. In the black glass background, you catch your own reflection.

"Hello?" Crispin's voice is far away now, remarkably tiny at this distance. "Honey?" He says something else too muffled to make out then, "I think she hung up."

You pause for a long moment before you hit End and turn off the phone. The air suddenly seems very close, very still. You turn the slim cellphone facedown and set it on the counter in front of you and stare at it, your eyes unfocused.

"Honey?" Freddie emerges from his room as if on cue. "Are you all right?"

"Yeah." You suck in a huge rush of air and stand up straight, smiling as convincingly as you can manage. "I'm fine." But as you say it, an embarrassing sob escapes your throat and before you know it you are gasping for air, tears streaming down your face.

"Honey!" Freddie immediately wraps you into a strong embrace. "Honey! What happened?"

"It's just"—you can't even speak; your body is wracked with sobs. You lean into Freddie's solid chest and take in his comforting scent even as you soak his shirt with your tears.

"It's okay," he tells you, crooning soothingly as you cry. "I am here, whatever it is, I am here and it is going to be just fine."

Freddie strokes your back, running his strong hand in circles across your shoulders. Finally, your sobs begin to subside. "That's better," he tells you, "that's better."

He places one finger under your chin and tips your head up to look into your eyes. You know your makeup must be horribly smeared, mascara running down your blotchy cheeks. Freddie uses one thumb to gently brush a tear from below your eye. "You know you are beautiful when you are crying?" he asks.

You drop your eyes and sniffle. "Thanks." You smile.

Thank God for this man, who has the ability to be such an instant comfort. You reach for a tissue and dab at your face. "Sorry," you tell him, as the tissue comes away stained with makeup. "What a mess."

You look up at him, into his beautiful dark brown eyes, handsomely ringed by crinkles only years of smiles can produce. He holds your gaze for a long moment and for a single dizzying second you are certain he is going to kiss you.

Instead, he gently reaches for an errant eyelash and removes it from your cheek. "Just an eyelash," he says quietly.

"Oh good." You let out the breath you only now realize you have been holding. "That's good." You turn from him quickly to hide the blush that has risen to your cheeks. "I'm just going to run to the bathroom."

You use your uninjured hand to splash cold water over your face and shake your head to clear it. What on earth are you thinking?

An hour and a half of Margot's magic and a glass of champagne later, you're ready for the club—or as ready as you can be despite a pounding headache and fatigue that has hit you like a ton of bricks. Thank goodness the appearance is only a one-hour gig. All you can think about is the sweet oblivion of the downy hotel bed when you finish.

Sasha helps you into your five-inch Louboutins, which you could never have managed with just one hand. He's blissfully oblivious to the latest Crispin fiasco and you plan to keep it that way until you have time to mentally process it yourself.

"You look killer," Sasha says, rising after he finishes fastening the second shoe.

You turn to glance at your reflection and your mood begins to lift. Your leather pants are topped by a structured, midriff-baring corset. Your high ponytail swings so that the end just touches the top of your cleavage. Margot has managed to repair your smoky eyes, disguising some of the damage with extra-thick lashes, making your huge eyes look even larger. Your glossy lip pops with a subtle hint of color, making your still slightly reddened face look a bit paler in contrast.

"Hey Freddie," you ask before you walk out the door. "Would you mind leaving me one more of those pills? Just in case I can't sleep?"

Sasha is quick to respond for him. "Not on your life, Henrietta." He juts his chin accusingly in Freddie's direction. "What was it that you gave her anyway? Some kind of black market Ambien knock-off?"

Freddie turns slowly to face Sasha. "I would never give Honey some kind of *knock-off*. What are you insinuating?"

"Simmer down, you two," you tell them. "I'm sorry I even asked. Just forget it." You decide to drop it, not interested in causing any more friction. "Okay, I'm ready to roll."

"Good night Freddie," says Sasha, cutting his eyes menacingly in Freddie's direction. To his credit, Freddie laughs it off, which elicits a grin from Sasha, too.

You feel instantly happier, glad these two friends you hold so dear are over their little scuffle.

"I may see you down there," Freddie says as you walk out the door. "It has been too long since I had a night at a club and a little fun at a casino. Plus I hear DJ Jett puts on the best show in town."

"Really?" You smile, "I'll look for you. That is, if I don't run out of there right at the hour mark. You know how these appearances can be."

Sasha sighs in mock-empathy. "Yes, yes, the life of a pop super-star. It really is too taxing."

You laugh and walk out the door on Sasha's arm.

"One hour and I'm out, for sure" Sasha says. "You've seen one DJ, you've seen them all. I want to catch Carlie's show."

"You mean Carlton?" Sasha's told you all about his high-school classmate turned Vegas dancer.

"She's Carlie here, Honey," Sasha tells you.

The club is dark and smoky, pulsing with dancing bodies, blaring music, and strobing lasers cutting through the smoky darkness. A pair of promoters leads you to the DJ booth, where you plan to say a quick hello to the crowd, help the DJ play a few tracks, sign autographs, and then make your exit.

The DJ is a star in his own right. Now known as DJ Jett, Jett Johnston is former tween heartthrob who played a starring role on one of your favorite shows, a family sitcom called *The Silversmiths*. Though sunglasses hide the eyes you remember as being a remarkable shade of the lightest blue, his hair is spiked in the same style you remember, and his gorgeous, chiseled features are unmistakable. "Hi, Jett, I'm Honey," you reach out to shake his hand. Your hand trembles slightly and you realize you are seriously and surprisingly starstruck.

Luckily, Jett doesn't seem to notice. He lowers his sunglasses to the bridge of his nose, and fixes you with a piercing gaze. "Alright, alright!" he enthuses, leaning in close so he can be heard over the music. He smells like a mix of cologne, cigarettes, and alcohol. One deep breath and you know you'll be instantly intoxicated. "My sidekick for the night!" He runs his eyes from your face to your feet then back up again. "Honey Noble," he purrs in a very sexy Australian accent. "Welcome to the Max."

Jett authoritatively guides your good hand to one of the turntables in front of you. He slides a lever to lower the music and raises his hands in the air. "Ladies and gents of Las Vegas!" he announces, eliciting a cheer from the crowd. "May I present your very special guest DJ," he pauses dramatically and you can almost hear the silent drumroll. "She floats like a butterfly, but she stings like a bee! The one, the only, the incredibly sexy goddess of pop, Honey Noble!"

The crowd goes wild, almost drowning out your words, "I'm so glad to be here in Vegas with you tonight! Let's have some fun!"

"They love you!" Jett enthuses as he dials the music back up to full volume. He lowers his sunglasses to give you a wink. "But who wouldn't?"

You have to smile. Sometimes the events you dread the most turn out to be the most fun. Your headache has miraculously disappeared and you feel the beat of the music saturating your body. Before you know it you're dancing along with the crowd to Jett's tracks. Club guests who no doubt paid a hefty fee for a VIP visit to the DJ booth are brought up one by one to get a CD or photograph signed. The hour passes in what feels like minutes.

Sasha climbs up to the booth the minute your hour is up, looking sweaty and anxious to leave. "You ready?" he asks.

"Has it been an hour already?" Jett yells over the music, then leans in so that only you can hear him. "I'd love for you to keep me company, if you want to stay, that is."

"Actually, this has been really fun. I wouldn't mind hanging out a little longer." A second wind has filled you with new energy, and your time in the DJ booth has proved the perfect distraction.

Sasha falls backs into a swoon against the booth's metal rails. "Honey, you agreed to an hour," he reminds you. "And I promised Carlie I would be there tonight. I've got to freshen up and catch a cab." He surveys the crowd, jumping in unison to Jett's beat. "And now I have a pounding headache. I cannot imagine why."

"You go ahead," you offer. "I'll be fine. Freddie's here somewhere I think."

Sasha crosses his long arms, "Do you really think I am going to leave you in the middle of a Las Vegas nightclub by yourself? You must think I've lost my mind."

Jett glances over casually, one hand still on the turntable. "She wouldn't be all by herself."

"I'm sorry?" asks Sasha, affronted. "I don't think we've been formally introduced?"

"Sasha, this is Jett. You remember him—from *The Silversmiths.* We used to watch it all the time when we were kids."

Sasha cuts his eyes at Jett suspiciously, but a glint of recognition grows in his eyes. "DJ Jett is actually Jett Johnston?" he asks slowly.

"In the flesh," Jett lowers his sunglasses to give Sasha a better look.

"Well, you have certainly grown up," says Sasha, looking Jett up and down and instantly warming to his effortless charm.

Jett laughs, "Yeah, well, it happens."

Sasha leans on the booth's metal railing. "I loved that show—*The Silversmiths*—that episode where your dad remarries? Totally broke my heart."

"Yeah, the good old days. One sec." Jett holds up a finger and returns to his turntable, sets a new disc spinning, and returns his attention to Sasha, who continues to eat it up. "Anyway, I really don't mind walking Honey to her room after I'm finished here. I'm only on for another hour then I'll bring her straight back."

Sasha looks at you for approval. "It's fine, Sash," you assure him. "I'm a big girl."

"I mean, I'm not a bodyguard like you," Jett tells Sasha. It's impossible to tell whether Jett is serious or teasing, but it works, and Sasha doesn't bother to correct him. "But I can keep her safe in these mean hallways and elevator shafts. I know my way around the Max. And"—Jett flexes one impressive bicep—"I've been working out."

"Well," Sasha swoons, "who am I to argue with that? If it's okay with Honey, I guess it's okay with me."

"It's fine," you repeat. "I'll check in with you when I come up."

"You'd better," says Sasha. "Later, Jett Johnston," he waggles his fingers at you both before descending the stairs and disappearing into the crowd.

Jett turns to you and leans in closely once again. "You look like you could use a drink." He reaches under the table and magically produces a bottle of Dom Pérignon. He gives it a vigorous shake and pulls the cork from the bottle, causing a frothy spray to eject from the bottle all over the crowd below, who cheer and scream for more. He laughs and turns to you—"Your turn"—then tips the bottle into your mouth. You take several long draws, the bubbly sweetness tracking delightfully down your parched throat.

Jett covers the mouth of the bottle with his thumb and gives it few more hard shakes then sprays the remaining contents into the crowd, who respond with a raucous cheer. "Don't worry," he says. "There's more where this came from."

"None for you?" you ask. You can already feel the alcohol hitting your bloodstream, the slight buzz just below the surface.

"Nah, I don't touch the stuff." Jett reaches for a bottle of water and takes a long swig. "Be right back." He jumps down the booth's little staircase in one swift movement. Immediately the crowd is upon him, both women and men screaming his name, snapping selfies, pulling at his shirt, and running their hands over his chest. He weaves his way through to the bar and after a few moments he returns with a tall glass filled with a liquid that fades from a deep gold to white from the top to the bottom of the glass.

He holds it well above his head as he navigates back to the booth. "The bartender invented this in your honor." He hands you the icy glass. "It's been his best seller all weekend. Would have been a shame for you to miss out on trying it."

Jett lowers the music and picks up the mic. "I'd like to propose a toast," he shouts to the crowd. "To our honored guest for the evening, Honey Noble. Honey, thank you for DJ-ing with me tonight. We cannot wait to see your show tomorrow!" He lifts the empty champagne bottle and clinks it with your glass, "To Honey!"

"To Honey!" the crowd echoes, and you take a sip of the sweet liquid. You can taste a hint of ginger, a minty flavor, and a subtle but definite touch of honey. The main ingredient, however, is clearly vodka. It's actually pretty good.

"It's delicious!" you tell Jett.

"Glad you like it. Here," he hands you an unopened bottle of water. "There's a ton of vodka in that drink. I watched him pour it. You're going to need this water."

You are impressed. For a moment you were convinced Jett was doing his best to get you intoxicated. "Thanks," you tell him.

A half hour later, Jett turns the music to autoplay. "That's it for me," he tells you. "Just need to tidy up." He begins coiling wires and cables and packing them into a crate at the back of the booth.

"Can I help you?" you ask.

"No, I've got it. It'll only take minute."

Jett piles the headphones on top of the crate's contents. "Follow me," he tells you, and leads you back down the stairs taking a sharp left at the bottom and through a curtain to a concealed doorway leading into a utilitarian service hallway. The silence in the hallway is an almost deafening contrast to the noise of the club.

"This is my backstage," Jett explains. "Pretty glamorous, huh?"

"Looks a lot like my backstage," you laugh.

Jett leads you to an elevator and presses the button. "I just have to dump this stuff in my room."

Jett's room, as it turns out, is more like an apartment. The enormous suite has been decorated in warm browns and grays. The walls are covered with posters of what you guess are Jett's favorite recording artists. Stacked crates of records tower against one wall. Jett adds tonight's crate to the pile.

"Sorry," he apologizes. "It's a bit of mess. I wasn't expecting company."

"This is nice," you tell him, running a finger along a shelf lined with an assortment of miscellaneous knickknacks ranging from bobble heads to shot glasses to something that looks like an Emmy. "What is all of this?"

"Just stuff I've picked up along the way. Some of it is memorabilia from my old show. See this one?" he lifts a bobble head with a mane of long, dark, curly hair. "Recognize her? You said you were a fan of the show." He shakes the doll gently to set its head bobbling back and forth.

"Ha!" you exclaim as you realize. "Is that Stacey Silversmith?"

"You got it," he tells you.

"Doesn't she want her doll back?" you tease.

"Oh, don't worry, she has several of her own. She sent me this one Christmas with a note saying she hopes it will continue to annoy me as much as she did." He laughs at the memory. "She really was the sister I never had. Endlessly pestering and very moody."

"Are you still in touch?" you ask

"Yeah, all the time. We all still talk. I know it sounds clichéd but we really were like a family, and that didn't end even when the show's run ended." He pauses for a moment lost in thought, his eyes, an otherworldly translucent blue, aglow with his memories. "Anyway, that was then and this is most definitely now." He focuses his full attention on you, and you feel heat rise to your cheeks.

"What happened to your hand?" he asks, noticing the bandage you've artfully covered with fingerless gloves.

"Oh it's nothing," you tell him. You'd almost forgotten all about it. "A stupid accident with a broken vase. A few stitches."

"I thought that was a fashion accessory but I noticed you favoring it."

"Unfortunately more of a fashion disaster," you grimace.

"Bummer," he says. "So, what now?" he asks.

You bite your lip and think for a second. It's a good question. You know you should go back to your room, but you are still buzzing with energy—whether from the club, the alcohol, or meeting this new guy who you think kind of seems to like you, you don't know.

"We could hang here, if you want," Jett offers. "Or we could venture down to the casino. I could show you the ropes. You don't look like much of a gambler."

"Yeah," you agree. "I'm not." But you do feel ready to take a gamble and you're intrigued by DJ Jett. Maybe you should just stay and get to know him better. Plus, he's proved an excellent distraction and you really don't want to be alone with your thoughts right now.

Still, you promised Sasha you would go back to the hotel room after the club. You know he'll worry if you're not there when he returns—and you could use a night of rest. And, what are the chances

you'll even ever see Jett again after this stop in Vegas? There's probably no point in starting something that can't be finished.

What should you do?

To return to your hotel room, turn to page 134.
To go with Jett to the casino, keep reading.

"I'm up for a lesson in gambling," you tell Jett.

"All right!" He cheers. He runs his hand through his spiky hair.
"One sec." He opens a kitchen drawer and rummages for a minute,
then blushes adorably as he sprays two quick spritzes of breath spray
into his mouth. "Ready," he announces.

He leads to you back to the elevator and pushes the button for the
lobby. You catch your reflection in the mirrored elevator doors and
realize you haven't even touched up your makeup since you entered
the DJ booth. You run your finger under each eye to remove any
smudged mascara.

Jett watches you for a moment. "You look perfect," he says, then
takes a small step toward you in the already-close elevator. "Except
for this one little thing." He runs a finger over your hairline and tucks
a strand of hair behind your ear. You feel a thrill run down your spine
as Jett licks his lips, leans close, and whispers, "Even more perfect.
How can that be possible?" He leans his free hand past your shoulder,
pushes you gently against the wall of the elevator, and plants a long,
slow kiss on your lips. His minty breath mingles with the slightly
salty, spicy taste of him.

The elevator dings and Jett pulls away a moment before the door
slides open. You face forward and exit the elevator trying to look as
normal as possible, but you notice Jett has the tiniest smile on his
lips, which makes you smile, too.

The casino is smoky and loud. Men in suits and women in an array
of attire ranging from skimpy skirts and halter tops to formal, floor-
length gowns ring every table.

"Where do you want to start?" Jett asks.

"Um, I have no idea—blackjack?"

Jett looks at you from the corner of his eye. "You know how to
play?"

"Not really," you answer, "Don't you just bet red or black?"

"That's roulette," he answers. "You know what? Let's start there. Probably safer."

"Roulette sounds more dangerous."

Jett laughs, "Only if it's Russian roulette. This is the one with the wheel. No skill involved. I'm not saying that any kind of gambling is safe, but this is about as easy as you can get. One step up from slots."

"I'll take your word for it."

Jett leads you to a crowded table and waits until the current game ends. "Two thousand—one thousand each, please," he tells the croupier, who deftly presents four neat stacks of chips, two stack of black, two of gold.

"Don't you have to pay for those?" you whisper.

Jett laughs. "I have a line of credit with the casino. Don't worry, I'm good for it." He slides the gold chips in your direction.

"No!" you object. "I just want to watch—I have no idea what I'm doing." You slide the chips back.

"Best way to learn is by doing. Jett places a warm hand on top of yours to keep the chips in front of you. "Besides, I'm hoping for some beginner's luck."

All around, players slide stacks of chips of varying colors into squares labeled with numbers, colors, or as "odd" or "even." As they look up after placing their bets, some of the other players at your table begin to whisper to one another. One even takes out her cell phone to snap an unobtrusive photo.

A black-suited man in sunglasses instantly appears and removes the offending guest, presses his finger to the device hidden in his ear, then says something inaudible into what looks like a wristwatch. He nods to the croupier who lifts his head to address the table in general. "There are no photographs allowed at the table," he reminds the remaining players. "Final bets, please."

You have no idea what to do.

"Just go with your gut," Jett tells you.

You pick up a single chip and carefully place it on red. The croupier arches an eyebrow.

"Sorry," Jett picks up three more chips and adds them to the single chip you placed.

"Outside bets are a minimum of one hundred," he explains.

You nod, though you have no idea what that means.

The wheel begins its hypnotizing spin. Little by little, its rotation begins to slow. At last it stops, wavering for a moment before landing on red.

Jett whoops with delight. "Yes!" he yells.

"Did I win?" you ask.

"Yes, you won!"

The croupier slides your chips back to you, along with a smaller stack.

"I won!" You jump up and Jett lifts you, spinning you in a victorious embrace. "Let's do it again!"

This time, you bet on odd and you win again. Your next bet is on 1-18. You win that one, too.

"Should we keep going?" you ask Jett.

"Absolutely, you're on a roll!"

Two more wins begin to draw the attention of the surrounding crowd, and spectators gravitate toward the table to watch. Before you know it there is a tall glass of fizzy champagne in your hand and the crowd is so large you can no longer see through it.

You are about to place your next bet when you feel a light touch on your shoulder. You spin around to see Freddie standing a few feet behind you, an excited gleam in his eyes.

"You are causing quite a stir," he says, over the noise of the crowd. "I had to come see what all the excitement was about. Looks like you're having fun! Don't let me break your streak."

You slide a tall stack of chips onto black. The crowd falls silent, holding its collective breath while the croupier gives the wheel a spin. The wheel slows and the crowd whoops a huge cheer when the wheel lands on black. Your stack of chips has become enormous.

"Place your bets," he says once again.

You look at Jett and then over at Freddie. Freddie smiles and shrugs.

"I really feel like I'm pushing my luck," you say uncertainly. You have no idea how many chips you've accumulated but you're sure the towering piles must represent several thousands of dollars, perhaps even tens of thousands.

"Up to you," Jett says. "It's only money."

"Okay, just a few more spins." You slide two stacks of chips across the table. You win on both bets to the delight of the crowd.

Three more bets and your winning streak still hasn't broken. Two more dark-suited men with earpieces now stand discreetly behind the croupier. You bet again and again, and continue to win, the chips piling up in front of you in a colorful mountain.

At last, you place a simple bet on red, and as the wheel slows you see the little silver ball click into the black slot and catch. The crowd lets out a groan. You don't know how much you've lost, but after the croupier takes his share, the pile of chips that remains still far outweighs what has been removed.

"That's it," you announce, decided.

"Really?" Jett asks. "You can keep going."

"Nope," you rake in the huge pile of chips in front of you. "This is a pretty good haul."

One of the secret service clones says something into his wrist and approaches you as the crowd begins to dissipate. "Congratulations, Ms. Noble."

"Thanks," you answer, a little unnerved that he knows who you are.

Jett takes one white chip from the pile and places it on the table. "For you," he tells the croupier.

"Thank you, sir," the croupier bows, then deftly stacks your winnings by color and slides a single coin of gold, one of gray, one of purple, two of black, and one of blue your direction before removing the other chips from the table.

You are thoroughly confused by the exchange, but gather that your huge pile of smaller chips has just been exchanged for a few chips of greater value. "How much is that?" you ask Jett.

Freddie is still by your side, and trails you as walk to the booth. "Just in case you need a protection," he explains, puffing up his chest.

You present the little stack of six chips to the attendant, who glances up as she notices the gold chip in your stack. "That's fifteen-seven-fifty," she says, spinning to the back wall of the booth, then after a few minutes she spins back around and hands you a check for thirteen thousand, seven hundred, and fifty dollars.

"Holy crap!" you exclaim.

"Holy crap is right," agrees Freddie. "Pretty good for your first time."

"All right!" cheers Jett. "This girl is a lucky charm!"

"That was so much fun! But this is yours," you try to hand the check to Jett, who puts both hands in the air and refuses to take the money.

"That's not mine, you won that fair and square. I only fronted you two grand—and we just paid the marker back. The rest was all you."

"Oh my gosh—thank you!" You certainly don't need the money, but the win feels phenomenal and the payoff is sweet.

The secret service guy, who you didn't notice has been standing a few feet away the entire time you've been at the booth, walks over to you once again. "We'd like to invite you to come back tomorrow evening," he tells you in a deep baritone. "Champagne is on the house."

Freddie looks up at the tall guard and steers you gently away by the elbow. "Of course he would like you to come back tomorrow," he whispers, "so you can lose all the money you just won. Once they get you back in the odds favor the house. Then they give you all free champagne you can drink so you'll bet recklessly. Oldest trick in the book."

Jett laughs appreciatively. "Don't worry," he winks, "I won't let her fall prey to their sinister plans."

You fold the check and tuck it carefully into your bustier. "Safe and sound," you say.

Freddie rolls his eyes. "Well, I think we should call it a night." He stretches and lets out a huge yawn, "I'm beat."

"I can walk her up," Jett offers.

"Nah, I'm going up anyway, so no reason for you to go out of your way."

Are these two really fighting over walking you back to your room?

"Gentlemen," you tell them, "first of all, I am perfectly capable of walking myself back to my room. Second, who said I'm ready to go? I think my win deserves a celebration. Who's up for a drink?"

"Not me," yawns Freddie. "I need my beauty sleep. Plus Sasha has been texting me since he left making sure you are still alive. I promised to keep an eye on you, and I am a man of my word. Let's get you back upstairs before Sasha gets back and I have to explain myself to him again."

"It's still hours before I usually go to bed. Besides, I'm on a total adrenaline rush from that run at the roulette table. I just want to unwind for a few quick minutes then I'll be up. Promise."

Freddie hesitates and looks warily at Jett, who assures him, "I won't leave her side."

"You better not," Freddie warns. "She is already past her curfew."

"Okay, Dad," you tell him, reaching on tiptoe to give him a kiss on the cheek. "Good night. I will see you in the morning."

Freddie points a finger threateningly in Jett's direction before softening into a smile and walking off toward the lobby.

"Wow, your friends are really protective of you," Jett says.

You suddenly feel like a teenager whose chaperone is finally off-duty. "So, about that drink . . ."

Jett smiles and takes your hand. His hand feels wonderful wrapped around yours, warm and strong. As you walk, tiny sparks of electricity fly up your arm.

You find a private booth tucked into the back of the bar, blissfully isolated from the noise and crowds of the casino. A waiter comes over with a frosty bottle of champagne, opens it expertly, fills your glass, and sets it on the table. He fills a second flute with sparkling water for Jett. "Enjoy," he says, then glides away.

"He knows me," Jett says by way of explanation.

"Ah, I see," you tease. "You bring all the girls here."

Jett peers through his thick eyelashes and laughs. "It has actually been quite a while since I brought any girl anywhere," he tells you.

"I find that hard to believe."

"Well, I'm flattered," he clinks his glass to yours. "To beginner's luck," he toasts, "and to the beginning of something wonderful."

"Very poetic." You take a sip of the delicious liquid, feeling the bubbles tickle your throat and warm your stomach.

Jett scoots closer to you in the booth, and presses his leg against yours under the table. You feel a little thrill rising in your stomach and take another sip of the champagne.

"That run was really pretty amazing," Jett says. "And you're a smart player—you quit at exactly the right time."

"Thanks. I had no idea what I was doing so thank you for your guidance—and thank goodness you tipped the dealer. I had no idea you were supposed to do that."

"Yeah, well, that's what I'm here for," Jett tells you. "Very useful knowledge acquired through years of scientific research."

You laugh. "What made you decide to come to Vegas?"

Jett takes another quick sip of his water. "Well, it's a little-known fact that being a DJ was really always my dream. I kind of fell into the TV gig after my mom took me to an audition for a tooth-paste commercial. The director happened to be casting for *The Sil-*

versmiths and the rest is history. But spinning tunes was always my first love. Been doing it almost since I could walk."

"No you have not." You're sure Jett is teasing.

"No, really, I have. Did it every spare chance I got. I made some good industry connections and being on *The Silversmiths* didn't hurt. I got lucky enough to be asked to partner up with the original guy who DJed at the Max and then was invited to cover for him when he started taking other jobs, and then eventually they offered me the gig. One of those things that just worked out. So, that's my story." He pauses and scoots a tiny bit closer. "But I'm more interested in finding out more about you."

His eyes are locked to yours and you feel yourself helplessly pulled in. Suddenly his lips are on yours, soft and warm, and his tongue is in your mouth. His kiss is like a long drink of champagne, sweet and inebriating.

"Now I know how you got the name," he smiles, licking his lips.

"Huh?"

"Honey," he says, "it's what you taste like."

You feel heat rise to your face and you take another sip of champagne in a fruitless attempt to cool down. Jett reaches in for another kiss and this time his lips move to your neck, causing your stomach to clench. You feel your nipples harden under the tight silk of your corset. His lips return to yours and he pulls away for a moment to look at you and smile.

"Come on," he says, "let's get out of here." He reaches into his wallet and throws a hundred dollar bill onto the table then takes your hand and leads you out of the bar. You keep your eyes on the ground and hope you aren't attracting any attention as you make your exit.

Jett leads you back to the bank of elevators, and as you step on, the memory of his first kiss comes flooding back. Two couples and a single man step on with you, and you instantly resent their invasion of your privacy.

The ride to Jett's floor seems endless. The elevator stops to allow each of the couples to exit at floors three and six, and then the last man, swaying slightly in his wingtips, makes an uneven exit on the eighth floor. At last, you and Jett are alone in the elevator once again.

"Jett," you say, taking a step toward him, "about that first kiss . . ." Before you can say more, Jett grabs the back of your neck and pulls you toward him into a rough embrace. His lips are on your lips, your neck, your chest, his hands grasp your buttocks and pull you toward him. You feel the hard bulge of his desire against the top of your leather leggings.

"God, Honey," Jett whispers gruffly into your ear, "you are so hot."

You return his kiss and press against the hot bulge beneath his jeans, then let your hand travel down to reach for him. He groans, and reaches up to gently squeeze your breast, kissing the top of your cleavage where it strains against your bustier.

The knowledge that the elevator could stop again at any moment gives you an even greater thrill. You reach your hand down to feel the tip of him, and run your fingers gently along the smooth, hot shaft of his cock.

Jett stills your hand and pulls away for a moment. "My place?" he asks.

But you don't want to be anywhere but right here, right now with him. You slide your room key from your bustier and insert it into the little slot in the elevator panel, then hold the "close door" button for the count of five. The elevator comes to a gentle stop.

"Right here," you tell him.

"How did you do that?"

"Useful knowledge of my own—acquired through years of research," you answer.

Jett laughs. "I don't think I want to know."

"Too bad," you tell him, "because I'm in the mood to share."

You push Jett back against the opposite wall of the elevator, press your hands against his chest, and kiss him hard, thrusting your tongue into his mouth while your hands travel down to undo his fly. You run your fingers through his hair and then press against him, the cool, smooth leather of your leggings the only barrier between your skin and his. He runs his hands up under your bustier and gently pinches your nipples, making you gasp with pleasure. Your hands find their way under his shirt and you reach up to run your fingers along his firm chest, then back down to find him. You look up with a gleam in your eyes, then kneel down to take him into your mouth.

Jett stops you, pulling you gently back up to him, "Don't," he says. "I'm too close."

The slightly embarrassed look on his face is adorable. Maybe it really has been a while since he's been with anyone.

"That's okay," you kiss him again then lean in close to whisper into his ear. "I'm ready, too."

You take his hand and guide his fingers to find you. Bright sparks of desire dance inside you as his fingers find your most sensitive spot. As he pushes your leggings down, you reach around to grab his bare buttock and pull him toward you. He thrusts, the tip of him insistent and hot against you. You hesitate, realizing you don't have your LV clutch or any protection with you.

"What's wrong?" Jett asks, sensing your hesitation.

"I didn't come, um, prepared," you answer.

"No worries," he replies, reaching into his back pocket. After a moment, he pulls you close once more. Suddenly you can take no more and you throw your arms around his neck and pull yourself up, locking your legs around his waist and lowering yourself onto him.

Jett lets out a huge groan and thrusts inside you as you rock gently back and forth, feeling the length of him fill you. It only takes seconds before you come, burying your head into his neck to muffle your moans. Jett comes too in shuddering gasp, pulling you to him in a long, deep kiss as he does.

At last, he pulls slowly away and sets you gently down. "Honey, that was insane." He smiles.

You smile back at him as you smooth your hair and pull your clothes back into place. "Pretty insane alright," you agree, and wait for him to pull himself together before removing your room card from the slot. The elevator begins to move. You reach the penthouse floor and give Jett a chaste kiss goodnight.

"Maybe I'll see you tomorrow?"

Jett laughs but can't hide his disappointment. "That's it?" he asks.

"For now," you tell him. "Thanks for making sure I got home safely." Then you spin through the doors as they slide open.

On the way to your bedroom you crack open the door to Sasha's bedroom and hear the heavy, even breathing of sleep. You close the door softly, make your way to your comfy hotel bed, and know you'll have a peaceful night's sleep after all.

The bedside clock shows nine fifty-eight a.m. when you finally open your eyes. You feel more rested than you have in months. The busy day goes seamlessly. You have a radio visit, a talk show appearance, and a press conference about your fashion line. Remarkably, no one asks about your hand. Whenever a niggling thought of Crispin pops into your consciousness you are quickly able to cast it out. But thoughts of Jett and your encounter in the elevator spring fresh into your mind at odd moments throughout the day, making your insides melt. You draw upon that energy to add a little more sultriness to your strut as you prowl the stage during the show that night. The audience eats it up. It's a nearly perfect day. Even the peacock costume goes on and off without a hitch.

After the show, Freddie escorts you into the dressing room, which bustles with post-show excitement. Sasha enters pushing the enormous rolling costume rack in front of him, finding plenty of space for it along one of the dressing room walls. Everything about the Vegas venue is top of the line, spacious, luxurious, and professional. You can see why music legends decide to come to Vegas and never leave.

Sasha parks the second rolling rack in a corner then gives you a high-five. "Good job girlfriend. Finally that peacock was not an epic fail."

"I know, right?" You smile as you turn around so Sasha can unhook and unzip the cinching corset of your final costume. "The magic of Vegas. Ahhhh," you sigh as Sasha lowers the zipper. "So much better."

"Ah! Excuse me!" Freddie catches sight of your bare back and does an about-face to walk out the door he's just entered. "I'll wait here," he calls, "let me know when you are decent."

"May be a while," Sasha mutters, brushing glitter from your shoulders.

You grab your robe from the back of the hair-and-makeup chair and wrap it around you. "You can come in," you call to Freddie.

Sasha looks over his shoulder as he carefully hangs the corset beside the rest of your costumes. "Freddie, have you always been such a prude?"

"I am not a prude," Freddie tells him. "I am respectful. You could use a lesson."

There's a knock on the door and Freddie and Sasha answer in unison. "Who is it?"

"It's Jett," echoes the voice from the hall.

"One second," you answer, then quickly run to the mirror and give your hair a quick swipe to smooth it where the extensions have made it snarl.

Sasha arches an eyebrow, "Oh, it's like that, is it?"

"Hush, you," you scowl. Then to Jett, "Come on in!"

Jett walks through the door with an enormous bouquet of yellow roses. "That show," he begins, "was amazing! The lasers at the end—awesome! I need to borrow some of your tricks for the club. Outstanding performance!" he gushes. "And the costumes—incredible! That peacock one especially—just so cool."

You smile and take the bouquet, while Sasha extends his hand to Jett. "Jett. Nice to see you again," he says.

Jett looks at you then back at Sasha. "Uh-oh. I feel like I'm in hot water."

"Noooooo," Sasha gives Jett a penetrating look. "But you did keep Honey out way past curfew."

Jett doesn't seem to know whether Sasha is serious or joking. A nervous silence fills the room.

"I . . ." Jett begins.

Sasha breaks into a slow smile and elbows Jett in the shoulder, "I'm playing with you!" he laughs. "Honey's a big girl. And as I said I am not her bodyguard. Besides, your admiration of my costumes has landed you right back in my good graces."

Jett's shoulders drop several inches as he visibly relaxes.

"But don't let it happen again." Sasha glares.

"Okay, Sasha, that's enough," you tell him.

You give Jett a smile. "Thank you for the flowers. They're gorgeous." You try to remember what yellow signifies. Friendship? You wonder whether Jett is trying to send you a message. Either way, they are beautiful. "Sasha, would you have time to put these in water before you go?"

Sasha spins around to look at you, "Am I going somewhere?" he asks, all innocence.

"I mean, if you are leaving"—you emphasize the word *leaving*—"I wonder whether you could put them in water before you do. Leave, I mean."

Sasha walks over to take the flowers from you. "You don't have to paint me a picture, Henrietta." He removes the bouquet's cellophane wrap and balls it up before tossing it in the trash can. "I know when I am not wanted." He plunks the flowers into a vase and clears his throat to get Freddie's attention. Freddie doesn't get the hint and continues to sit on the sofa and flip through a magazine. "Earth to Mr. Angel," Sasha calls.

Freddie looks up at last.

"You ready to go?" Sasha asks him.

"Oh, oh yeah," Freddie says when he notices you waiting patiently for him to leave. He tosses the magazine onto the table and follows Sasha out the door.

"Sorry." You turn to Jett. "They can be a bit of a handful."

"No worries," he says. "They obviously adore you."

You smile at his empathetic and easygoing response. You're really starting to like this guy. "So," you begin, "I was thinking about making another trip to the casino. You up for it?"

"Um, sure," he answers hesitantly. "But I should warn you that beginner's luck really is often just that. And Freddie was dead-on with his warning. Believe me, I know."

"I'm not expecting to sweep the roulette table again, I just want to unwind a little. That was fun last night."

Jett arches an eyebrow and smiles. "I'll say."

You're not sure whether he is referring to the run at the casino or the elevator ride after, and you don't ask him to clarify.

"I just need a quick shower or else I'll be molting body glitter all night," you tell him, walking to the beautifully-appointed bathroom. "Though I have to tell you this tub is really calling my name. You wouldn't believe what a workout that performance is."

"I do believe it," Jett says. "You are pure energy up there for three hours. It must be exhausting."

"It can be. But actually, it's pretty exhilarating."

Jett follows you into the intimate space and stands behind you, then gently pushes an edge of your robe down off of your shoulder. He plants a single kiss on the soft spot where your neck and shoulder meet, sending a shiver up your spine. "Let me run the bath for you." He reaches down and turns the water on full-force.

You step in and perch on the edge of the tub. The warm water on your sore feet feels divine. Jett reaches for a bottle of complimentary body wash and pours it into the tub, creating a froth of foamy bubbles. Clouds of steam roll off of the water's surface as it begins to rise little by little, engulfing your ankles and inching up your calves.

"Warm enough?" Jett asks.

"It's perfect," you answer.

Jett moves to stand behind you and pushes the robe down farther so that both of your shoulders are now bare. He places a strong hand on each shoulder and begins to knead, working away the tension. He moves to your neck then pushes the robe even lower so that he can work on your upper back. The warmth of the water and the warm strength of Jett's touch is an intoxicating combination.

"That feels so good," you tell him.

"Mmm," Jett replies, then follows the work his hands have done with soft kisses, caressing your neck, moving down to each shoulder, then slowly to your back. When the water nears the lip of the tub, Jett pauses to turn off the water.

You stand slowly, your back still to Jett, and let the robe fall completely from your body before you lower yourself into the water. The bubbles just cover you, the foam surging over your breasts. Your bandaged hand rests on the bathtub's edge.

Jett moves around the tub to take you in, and you break into laughter when you see his smile.

"What's so funny?" he asks.

You stop giggling long enough to answer. "Your lips are all glittery!" you laugh.

Jett spins around to look in the mirror. "Well, we'll have to do something about that."

"Come here," you tell him. You grab his hand to pull him down toward you and attempt to wipe some of the glitter from his lips. He ends up with a foamy beard, which makes you laugh even harder.

"Sorry!" you apologize. "I'm just making it worse."

"Soap and glitter," Jett grimaces. "Not a good look." He reaches for a washcloth.

"No, let me," you tell him, grabbing his hand again. This time, you pull hard and manage to dunk half of Jett's sleeve into the water. "Oops," you say, "Now you're all wet." You shrug your shoulders. "Might as well join me."

Jett grins widely. "You don't have to ask me twice," he says, and quicker than you would think possible he sheds his shirt, skims off his pants and boxers, and slides into the tub with you.

"Mmmm," he moans, "this feels heavenly."

He sloshes bubbles and water as he scoots around behind you and, using the washcloth, begins to scrub your back in slow, sensuous circles. You press against the washcloth, savoring the feel of the slightly abrasive cloth against your skin. He works the cloth along your shoulders and up to the nape of your neck, then back down along your spine, pausing to rub circles along the small of your back.

As he rises to his knees and moves closer, you feel the warm, hard length of his manhood press against your lower back. You press back against him as he kisses your neck. When you turn to face him, he lifts the washcloth again, scooping up a mound of bubbles, and works the soapy cloth in circles around each breast. Your nipples harden in response to the friction and Jett leans in to kiss you, gently at first, then hungrily, pressing your body back against the edge of the tub. Leaning over you, Jett moves down to kiss your neck, along your collarbones, then he lifts each breast and brings it to his mouth, using his tongue to outline your nipple then moving in to suckle. At the same time, Jett takes the washcloth and brings it below the water to stroke your most sensitive area, slowly increasing the intensity of the motion.

A moan escapes you as you give in to the pleasure. Jett fishes into the back pocket of his discarded jeans and after a moment you reach with your good hand to grasp Jett and pull him to you. He enters you in one smooth motion and creates waves in the water as he rocks. You hardly notice the bubbles sliding over the edge of the tub as Jett thrusts deeper, bringing the washcloth back up to stroke one breast as his mouth works on the other. You come in a shuddering wave and Jett joins you, pressing his face into your neck and letting out a long, low moan.

Jett seems to float away from you as he lifts his face to yours and kisses you deeply. He looks into your eyes for a long moment and smiles. "Honey, I—" he begins, then stops short.

"What?" you ask him.

"I, um, think we got water all over the bathroom," he says sheepishly, surveying the soapy floor.

Jett wraps you in a fluffy towel and gets to work mopping up the bathroom floor with every remaining towel available, as you wonder what he was about to say.

When you—and the bathroom—are fully dry, you slip into a thong and a black jumpsuit with a halter top, touch up your lip gloss, and run a brush through your ponytail. The body glitter now mostly gone, you look pretty much presentable, and you feel rejuvenated.

Jett turns to you, buttoning his shirt. "You are absolutely stunning." He smiles.

"Thanks," you say. "You're not so bad yourself."

Jett takes you by the arm and together you walk out the door toward the casino, to try your luck for another night.

"Let's try blackjack this time," you tell him.

"It's a trickier game. You sure you're up for that?"

"No, but I'm hoping my beginner's luck will strike again, since I'm a beginner at blackjack."

"All right," Jett sighs, "but I'm not sure that's how beginner's luck works."

This time, you purchase your own chips. A bottle of champagne and two frosty glasses are placed in a tall stand beside you as you wait for the first deal. "They love nothing more than a second-night high roller," Jett tells you.

Your luck at blackjack isn't as good as it was at roulette. You win the first two games and then begin a solid losing streak. You decide to stop when you've lost what looks like about half of your chips.

"Had enough?" Jett asks.

"Of gambling, yes." You smile. "For now." A wave of exhaustion has come over you and suddenly your injured hand is throbbing again, the natural anesthesia of post-show (and other) endorphins having worn off. "I'm actually pretty tired."

"Let me walk you back to your room," Jett offers, ever the gentleman.

You give him a long kiss goodnight in the elevator before the doors to your suite slide open.

"Will I see you tomorrow?" he asks.

"You better," you tell him.

"Good, then," he says. "Goodnight." As the doors begin to slide shut Jett sticks out a hand to stop them. "Hey, Honey, I just realized I don't even know . . . how long are you here?"

"For the week," you answer. "Then I'm off. To God knows where." You try to laugh off the unexpected tremor in your voice as you realize all at once that you don't even want to think about leaving. The feeling is entirely new.

You head straight for the bathroom and wash your face, then snuggle into your bed under the downy covers.

There's a soft knock on your door, and Sasha enters without waiting to be invited in. He sits gently on the edge of the bed. "Well hello, stranger." He pulls the comforter down so he can see your face.

"Hello yourself," you tell him, reaching out to take his hand, which is warm and familiar. You smile in the dim light, thinking that Sasha is like a best friend and brother rolled into one wonderful, sarcastic package.

"Good night?" he asks you.

"It really was," you tell him. "Jett's pretty great."

"Oh lord, here we go again." Sasha rolls his eyes. "How's the hand."

"It's fine," you laugh and give his hand a gentle squeeze. "Now let me get some rest."

Sasha tucks the comforter snugly under your chin and gives you a light kiss on the forehead. "Sleep well, Henrietta." He rises and is out the door, silk robe swishing behind him as he leaves.

You press your head into the pillow and wait for sleep to come but unnerving thoughts jump into your mind uninvited. You can't help replaying your last phone call with Crispin and you wonder what he and Trixie are doing now, whether they have even stopped to think about you at all. Worse, you worry Crispin's relapse will send him spiraling out of control. Even though he's hurt you terribly, there's still a part of you that cares about him.

Why is it that late at night when you're all alone that your worst fears get the better of you? You know there's nothing you can do about it, but the more you try to sleep, the more you seem unable to escape your mind's anxious wanderings. You flip to your back, roll first to your left side then to your right, all the while trying to avoid looking at the clock. After an hour and a half you've had it. You fling the comforter back and go to find Freddie.

A shushing sound that could be waves, rain, or white noise comes from Freddie's bedside table. You lean down to whisper, "Freddie?" into his ear. He barely stirs.

"Freddie?" you try again, this time a little louder. Still no luck. You put your hand on his shoulder and shake him gently. "Freddie, it's me, Honey."

Freddie smacks his lips and smiles. "Honey," he says without opening his eyes, "what's up?"

"I can't sleep," you tell him.

Freddie sits up sleepily and pushes the covers down.

"No," you say. "You don't need to get up. I just wanted to borrow one more of those sleeping pills you gave me."

"Sleeping pills," Freddie slurs. You wonder whether he might be talking in his sleep, or maybe he's taken a sleeping pill himself. "I don't take sleeping pills."

"Whatever you gave me," you tell him. "Can I have one of those?"

"Sure, Honey." He rubs his hands across his eyes and rolls back into the bed, pulling the comforter up to his chin. "Help yourself. Take whatever you need."

"Thanks," you say glancing around the room. It doesn't take long to locate the little brown bottle of pills tucked behind the noise machine. You shake a single pill into your hand and quietly leave the room.

Out in the kitchen, you examine the pill to make sure it looks the same as the one you took the other night. It does, and it works almost instantly. Your head barely hits the pillow before you're carried off into a dreamless sleep that lasts until morning.

The next day you feel refreshed once again, and like before, your hand feels much improved. You bounce into the kitchen to grab a glass of orange juice. Freddie is seated at the breakfast bar sipping a green smoothie.

"Well good morning, sunshine," Freddie smiles at you around a mouthful of smoothie. Even with emerald teeth, Freddie manages to look dashing first thing in the morning. "How was your night?"

"I slept like a baby. Thank you so much!"

Freddie's smile falls from his lips and he almost drops his smoothie. "What exactly are we talking about?"

Does he really not remember? "I kind of wondered whether you were actually awake." You dip your finger into the bit of residual smoothie still in the blender and grimace as the flavor registers. "You were talking—I thought you were at least a little bit awake."

Freddie sets his glass squarely on the counter and looks at you. "What are you saying? That you were in my room?" he asks carefully.

"You really don't remember, do you?" You rinse your fingers in the sink. "I was having trouble sleeping so I peeked in to see whether you could help. You were pretty out of it but you said I could take another one of those pills. So I took one. And I slept like a baby."

"Oh thank god!" Freddie sighs with immense relief. He picks up the smoothie and takes another sip. "You know those commercials tell you about all kinds of crazy side effects, like talking in your sleep, having no memory of things you did the night before, I was worried for a minute!"

"Now Freddie"—you walk up and playfully ruffle his thick hair— "you know I would never take advantage of you when you were defenseless, or even asleep. Aside from stealing your sleeping pills, I mean."

"Very funny, Honey," he tells you. His tone becomes serious once again. "But you should not take any more of those pills. They are only good for once in a while. It is not healthy to take them too often."

"Don't worry, Dad," you tell him. "I won't."

Freddie pats the barstool beside him, inviting you to sit. "Everything okay with you?" he asks.

"Yeah. I just had a really hard time sleeping last night. I kept thinking about everything. Crispin and all that. I couldn't shake it."

"This too shall pass," he says sagely.

"I know it. It just sucks until it does."

"Indeed," says Freddie. "Eloquently put. But, the good news is"— he rises to rinse the blender and his empty smoothie glass—"you're not going to have time to think about anything today. You've got a full schedule."

"That's right," you remember the call you have in a few hours, a video shoot for a possible documentary about your rise to fame. Now that you've scored the cover of *Rock 'N' Roll*, "M," the Music Entertainment Network, has asked to put together a *Rock Doc* about you. Their signature documentaries have featured every massive music success, and you're honored to have been asked.

"I'm going to go jump in the shower before team M & M arrives. Enjoy your healthy breakfast."

"It grows on you," Freddie tells you, raising his glass as you walk out of the room.

Three hours later, you're back in the venue, sitting in your dressing room and in full hair and makeup. You step out of your robe so Sasha can help you into your first costume.

Freddie escorts you down the hall to the stage. "Pretend it's a real show," he tells you, "but just lip synch. You want your voice rested for tonight."

"Okay," you answer.

"And don't exert yourself too much," he tells you, "You need your energy for the show."

"So just like a real show but don't sing and don't put too much energy into it?"

"Right."

"And no audience."

"Right." Freddie gives you a thumbs-up. "But I'll be cheering for you!"

"Thanks" You smile, and head for the staircase that will take you up to the catwalk.

As usual before the show, your dancers ascend the stairs behind you. Still it feels more like a rehearsal, and everyone is more chatty and casual.

Serge seems more attentive onstage than usual, even spinning you in an unchoreographed dance step at the end of one song. Is it your imagination, or is he making more eye contact and holding your hand a little longer than usual during the routines?

The cameras roll for almost two solid hours as you walk through your performance. Finally, the director yells, "That's a wrap!" He calls for a few still shots and dismisses the dancers. Finally, you walk offstage and make your way to the dressing room area.

That night's show runs perfectly once again. You're constantly impressed by the seamless professionalism of the Vegas venue and its staff.

After the show, you have a scheduled meet-and-greet with a group of VIP fans. They crowd into the Hive outside of your dressing room and pose for photos. You sign autographs and gamely smile for a constant stream of selfies. More than an hour later, you are released to head back to the dressing room.

You're exhausted by the time Jett saunters in. "Hi there," he says.

"Hi yourself," you answer, wiping some residual makeup from your neck and chest.

"You have plans?" he asks.

"I'm probably just going to bed," you tell him. "It feels like I did two shows today. I'm really tired." No matter how much fun you've had hanging out with Jett, the truth is that you'll be on the road in two days and your chances of ever seeing him again are slim. You don't want to lead him on—nor do you want to set yourself up for more heartache.

Jett looks crestfallen. "Oh, okay," he says. "I was just thinking you could maybe join me in the booth for a bit. Then we could go back to the casino, if you'd like, or grab a drink . . . or go back to my place," he arches an eyebrow and smirks suggestively.

You don't know what to say. You are tired, but then again you only have a couple of days left in Vegas. And you can always rest tomorrow, you think. Or did Freddie say you have an interview tomorrow? You really cannot remember.

Taking Jett's hand and looking into his eyes, you feel the immediate and undeniable chemistry. Still, you owe it to yourself to tell him how you are feeling.

"Jett, I've had so much fun with you. I think you are amazing."

"Oh God, here it comes." He swallows and takes a small step back.

"No," you tell him, "it's just, I know you know this but I'm only here for two more days. After that I tour for a solid three months. And that could be extended. I don't know where I'll be after that. I just don't want either of us to get hurt."

Jett squeezes your hand gently and smiles. "I know that, Honey." He looks down at you, an incredible tenderness in his eyes. "It's just that I don't often find a connection with people here. It's rare. And I've connected with you. I'm not kidding myself. I know it will hurt when you leave, but I'm prepared for that. I just want to enjoy the time we have together." He pauses to give you a single, gentle kiss on the lips. "No strings, no expectations. Just this amazing connection for as long as it lasts."

He leans back and strokes your cheek then wraps his arms around the small of your back to pull you to him. You melt immediately and press into his solid chest, running your hand along his strong biceps.

You feel like you could stay like this forever, lost in his embrace. You can't remember ever feeling so immediately connected to someone. What could it hurt to enjoy your time with him while you're here? Still, what is the point of getting in even deeper when you'll be leaving so soon? The more time you spend together, the more difficult it will be to say goodbye, and more heartbreak is the last thing you need right now. You also know that if it's really meant to be, that someday, somehow, fate will put you together again. What should you do?

To end your fling with Jett, turn to page 134.
To stay with Jett, keep reading.

"Okay," you relent. "I'm in."

"You sure about that?" Jett leans in for another kiss, this one long and lingering.

"I'm not sure about anything"—you laugh, then kiss him again—"except for this minute, right now."

"Then let's enjoy it," Jett smiles and leads you out the door into the Vegas night.

The crowd in the club is a throbbing mass of energy, chanting, "Jett, Jett, Jett, Jett!" They go wild as you step up into the DJ booth. Jett puts you in charge this time. When he sees you need help, he reaches around you for the turntable, and his hand brushes your arm, your hand, your bare shoulder as he sets a record spinning or adjusts the mixer. You press back against him, daring him to get closer.

The tension is almost too much to bear as Jett ends the night and puts the music on autoplay.

"Well? What next?" He loads the last of his records and equipment into the crate and hoists it off the ground. "I need to take my stuff upstairs but after that I'm all yours."

Though part of you wants to follow Jett up to his room and hang the Do Not Disturb sign, another part of you is enjoying the delicious build of tension. Plus, you'd love to try your luck at the casino one last time. "Let's hit the casino, just for a little while," you tell him. "I'm feeling lucky."

"Alright, then. Okay if I run upstairs to dump this stuff and take a quick shower?"

"Sure, I'll meet you at the roulette table."

"Why don't you come up with me, it will only take a minute."

You know what a trip to Jett's room will probably lead to, and you want to get a visit to the casino in first.

"I'll be fine. I know my way around the casino now. Plus I can always find one of those big, burly secret service guys if I run into any trouble."

"You sure this is a good idea?"

"Trust me, I'll be fine. And you'll be down in a minute. I'll see you down there."

"Okay, I guess," Jett says uncertainly. "I'll probably be down before you can even place your first bet. But if not, don't put it all on red," he teases.

"Don't worry about me, mister. I know what I'm doing. Kind of. See you soon." You smile as you watch Jett, admiring the view of his firm backside and strong thighs as he walks away.

Feeling like a bit of a pro, you take your marker to the roulette table and exchange it for a massive stack of chips. Your luck isn't any better than last night's and immediately the stack begins to dissipate. Much too soon, you're down to just a few chips. Your gut tells you that a change of luck is just around the corner.

As if he's read your mind, the dark-suited guard you recognize from your winning streak appears at your side. "Would you like to continue to play?"

"Actually, I think I'm going to call it a night," you tell him, gathering the chips into a neat stack. "I'm just going to wait here. For my friend."

"Well, while you wait, the house would like to extend you an open line," says the man in a confidential tone.

"Um, thank you." You aren't sure exactly what that means, but he reaches into his breast pocket and slides out a thin, leather folder that looks like a waiter's cheque. "Please sign here," placing a pen in your hand.

You sign as instructed and the croupier immediately slides another stack of chips equally as large as the first across the table.

"Thank you."

The croupier nods solemnly, "My pleasure."

Despite your gut prediction of a forthcoming win, the wheel stubbornly lands against your bets repeatedly. No matter the strategy or betting combinations, nothing seems to work. At last, your red bet lands and you collect a small pile of chips. Encouraged, you decide to keep going. Besides, Jett still hasn't made an appearance and you have time to kill.

Before you know it, your stack has dwindled once again.

"Would you like to continue playing?" asks the croupier.

"Yes," you tell him, "just a few more games."

"You'd like more chips, then?"

"Yes—the same amount as before I guess."

"Very good," he says, sliding you another stack of chips.

One of the other players at the table is on a winning streak similar to the one you experienced your first night. A small crowd begins to gather to watch her as she excitedly rakes in stack after stack of chips—many of them yours. You notice a few members of the assembled crowd of spectators whisper to each other and glance at your diminishing pile of chips. Soon, you're down to almost none again.

"Will you continue?" the croupier asks.

You have no idea how much time has passed but Jett still hasn't appeared. "Yes, please," you answer. You're sure your luck is about to turn—after all, luck has always been on your side.

The first roll of the roulette wheel brings you a win and so does the second.

Finally, you see Jett weave his way through the crowd to join you.

"Not doing too badly, huh?" he asks, taking note of the tall stack of chips in front of you.

"My luck is finally turning around," you tell him, confident that your comeback can only continue and you'll soon win back the money you've lost.

"Funny!" he laughs. You're not sure what he thinks is funny, but things quickly begin to turn again as the bejeweled woman across the table revives her winning streak and jumps gleefully up and down, her ample cleavage surging with each leap. You give her a strained smile of congratulations.

"Maybe you should quit while you're still ahead?" Jett asks.

"I'm definitely not ahead," you tell him. "I'm trying to win back what I've lost."

"Wait." Jett's expression becomes deadly serious as he turns to look at you. "You were serious about your luck turning around?"

"Yeah. Did you think I was joking?"

"I did think you were joking," he swipes his hand across his chin. "I wasn't gone that long." He looks around the casino. "How much have you lost?"

"This was my third stack of chips."

Jett's face pales. "Your third stack? Do you know how much you started with?"

"Don't worry—I can win it back in a few rounds," you answer.

More color drains from Jett's face.

"What?" you ask.

"No, nothing. Just a little déjà vu," he tells you. "Believe me, it's not a good idea to keep playing."

"What do you mean? My luck is about to change. I can feel it."

"If nothing else, let's take a break and assess the damage."

Back at the booth, you hand the cashier a receipt and the small stack of chips you have left. She looks down at the receipt and then up at you briefly. "Give me a moment please."

She returns with another dark-suited man, but this one isn't as tall, he's a little on the rounder side, and lacks the sunglasses. "Ms. Noble," he bobs up and down on his heels as he speaks, "I'm Martin Connetti, casino manager. We are honored to have you with us." His smile is wide and sympathetic. "Looks like you had bit of a rough night." He folds his hands and tilts his head. "Why don't you come back to my office?"

Your stomach clenches as he pushes open the door to the booth and escorts you back to his office. A sea of screens monitoring the gambling floor from every possible angle fills one wall, while framed photos of Mr. Connetti with an arm around an array of celebrities fills another.

He gestures for you to sit. Jett takes a seat beside you.

"So, it appears you had a bit of a losing streak," he begins.

You feel like you're in an elementary school principal's office about to get slapped on the wrist for pulling someone's hair on the playground. A trickle of sweat makes its way down your back.

The little man teepees his hands below his chin. "Do you have an idea of how much you lost tonight?"

You think for a minute, trying to calculate, and realize you can't begin to figure out what the total might be. "I wasn't finished playing. My luck was just turning. I can win it back, no problem."

"I'm afraid we cannot extend you further credit," Connetti tells you.

"You don't have to. I still have chips left."

"Ms. Noble, it would be nearly impossible for you to win back what you've lost. We can credit you what you have left, but we need to settle the debt."

"Okay, I'm sure that's no problem. How much do I owe you?"

Connetti places his hands palms-down on his desk. "The balance is $712,500."

"What?" You are shocked and baffled. "You mean that's the amount of the credit you gave me?"

"No," he clarifies. "That's the amount you lost tonight."

"That can't possibly be."

"I can do the math for you, I assure you, but take my word for it. I thought it might be something of a shock, which is why I thought it best to bring you back here. Behind the scenes. To avoid any undue embarrassment."

Jett swallows loudly as the casino manager continues.

"I'm sure you understand that we do need to settle the debt, before you leave tonight."

You begin to speak, but your words come out in a stutter and you realize your hands are shaking. You look over at Jett. "I need to call Freddie," you tell him. "And Sasha."

"Okay, no worries." Jett tries to sound calm but his voice sounds strangled.

"Take your time to call whomever you need," Mr. Connetti says.

A half hour later Freddie has joined you in the office and Sasha saunters in sleepily a few minutes later. Both wear identical expressions of shock and drop their heads into their hands as you explain the situation.

"It's fine," you tell them. "It will be fine. I'll pay it back."

"What a nightmare," is all Sasha has to say.

"Thanks," you tell him. "Very comforting."

They both glare at Jett, clearly placing the blame squarely on his shoulders.

"It isn't his fault," you tell them. "This was completely my stupidity. Jett had nothing at all to do with it."

Jett opens his hands in a gesture begging forgiveness, but neither Freddie nor Sasha seems to be in a forgiving mood.

For his part, Jett looks completely crestfallen and beyond exhausted. "You can go back to your place," you tell him. "We'll handle this."

"I'm happy to stay," he begins then notes the unwavering glares still fixed on him from the corner of the room. He rises reluctantly and places a hand on your neck. "If there's anything I can do," he says.

"I wish there were," you tell him. "I got myself into this and I have to get myself out."

"Will I see you tomorrow?" he asks.

"If I'm not in debtors' prison," you answer, only half-joking.

He gives you a smile and your shoulder a squeeze and leaves the office.

Once the door is firmly closed, Freddie leans toward Mr. Connetti, all business. "What are our options?"

It's almost three in the morning by the time a deal is struck. It's not pretty, but it's one you'll have to live with.

Two weeks after your tour ends, you report directly back to Vegas to begin your residency, per your agreement with the Maxamillion Resort and Casino. Your name is in lights on the Vegas Strip and the Max markets you as their headliner on dozens of glowing billboards. The hotel suite they give you is cushy enough—just a notch or two down from the suite you were given when you first visited during the tour.

Freddie is content to come along for the ride and Sasha is happy as a clam to enjoy the Vegas nightlife and friends old and new who call Vegas home.

Some of the dancers have been replaced, and you especially miss Serge, with whom you formed a bit of a friendship, but who, it turns out, is also an accomplished cellist and who has decided to return home to try his hand at being a professional cello soloist.

A few rumors swirl about your swift return to Vegas following the end of your tour, but you quash them by explaining that you loved Vegas the first time around and wanted to be in a place you could feel settled, if only for a few months' time. In fact, Freddie has calculated that a close to sold-out nightly audience should have you out of your indentured servitude after only a few months, and your show will be turning a tidy profit long before your six-month commitment is up. The dedicated venue comes with a built-in audience of resort guests and visitors, ensuring healthy returns every night you perform. Maybe you'll decide to stay. It's a gamble, but you have a feeling luck is on your side this time around.

Somehow, part of you feels perhaps this was all meant to be. Most nights after the show, when you're still surfing an adrenaline buzz from a standing ovation, you seek Jett out, knocking gently at his door. He answers without fail no matter how exhausted he is after DJ-ing for hours. He gently takes you into his arms and guides you to his bed, slowly massaging your aching shoulders, working his way down to your arms, your hands, then back up from your feet to your calves and thighs.

Some nights he holds you close, his chest pressed to your back and his arms wrapped snugly around you, as you fall into a deep and dreamless sleep. Other nights, he turns you over and covers you with tiny kisses, pausing to pay special attention to your breasts before making his way lower, where he uses his tongue to bring you close. You signal him that you are ready and he rises over you, kissing your neck as he enters you. You wrap your arms and legs around him and feel fully satisfied in this moment, in the bed of this man you took a gamble to find, after all.

When your time here comes to an end, perhaps you'll decide to stay. Or maybe you'll take Jett back with you, if he'll come. There's a certain freedom in not knowing what the future holds, an excitement in the uncertainty that forces you to enjoy every day as it comes. You wonder whether there is any such thing as luck, really. You're not so sure. You ponder the question for a long moment then rest your head on Jett's shoulder and bask in the warmth of his embrace. Maybe, you think, just maybe Jett is the real luck Vegas had in store for you all along.

THE END

To take Honey on a new Bedventure, go back and choose a new path.

From page 11...

"Hand over the phone." You reach your hand in Sasha's direction.

"Oh fine." He slaps the phone into your hand. "You're no fun." He bends to pick up the costumes and hauls them back onto the rack. "I've got to get all of these over to the dressing room."

You help him hang the last of the rogue pieces and then pull on your leggings and jacket, sliding Crispin's phone into your pocket.

Sasha pauses, his arms loaded with costumes. "But seriously, Henry, what would you do if something was up with him? You have given him so many chances."

"I don't know," you answer honestly. "It's a difficult situation. He can't help who he is. Besides, I love him."

Sasha looks at you for a long moment and says softly, "And you can't help that. Therein lies the rub." He reaches to open the door and stops once again. "But Henry, no matter what, just remember that I love you, too."

"I know that," you assure him. "And I love you right back."

"Then take care of yourself, girl," he snaps. "And don't think I forgot our pact."

"Yes, I know." You repeat the promise you made to each other long before your sweeping rise to fame began. "If neither of us is married by the time we're thirty-five, it's just you and me and a sperm bank."

He smiles, nods reverently, and glides out the door.

You peek in the mirror and slick back a few errant strands of hair before heading out of the chilly trailer toward the venue's main building. The sun is just beginning to dip toward the horizon and the dry, desert heat feels heavenly against your skin. You stop at the talent entrance to allow yourself a few deep breaths.

Backstage, low music thrums through the long, sterile, tiled corridor and you feel the familiar surge of adrenaline begin to pump through your veins. Freddie intercepts you as you head toward the dressing room.

"Want to take a look?" he asks.

He guides you to the stage, where a frenzy of pre-show activity is in full swing. Cords are being strung, lights adjusted, and mics tested. You walk to center stage, careful not to interrupt the crew, and take a moment to gaze out into the sea of empty seats. In a few hours, you'll be standing right here, the arena bursting at the seams with a rapt audience cheering and calling your name. Right now with the house lights up and the arena empty, it all seems oddly mundane.

You turn to walk off the stage and run smack into the firm chest of your backup dancer, Serge.

"Honey!" he gasps. "I am so sorry! Are you okay?" He asks in a thick accent. "I did not see you there."

"I'm fine," you laugh. "I was just checking out the venue."

"Yes, that is what I am doing." He pushes a lock of black hair back from his forehead and surveys the arena. "It looks very nice."

"Lots of empty seats," you say.

"They will all be filled tonight. Everyone will come to see you." You hadn't noticed how tall Serge is, and how his white teeth shine against his fair skin.

"To see us," you correct him.

He smiles and looks into your eyes, the thick lock of hair falling back just over his brow line. "No, they come to see you," he says. "I have no problem with it. You give us good job, I am happy."

You laugh at his honesty. "Well, I'm glad you are happy." You smile. "I'll see you tonight."

As you walk off the stage you look back to see Serge stretch one long leg in front of him. You can't help but stop to admire his perfect body, every muscle in his arms, legs, and buttocks defined as he strikes a dancer's pose. For a moment you imagine running your hand down along one arm, feeling those sinewy muscles next to your body. Then you shake the thought from your mind and find your dressing room.

The show that night goes almost perfectly, the peacock costume still the only glitch. Even with a third set of hands, provided by Freddie, the costume change takes too long.

You return to your dressing room after the show to find Sasha cursing as he gathers up the reams of costumes and Crispin waiting with a gargantuan bouquet of roses.

"Excellent show, love." He kisses you lightly and places the heavy bouquet into your arms.

"What are these for?" you ask him.

"For you of course," he says. "For putting up with me and sticking by my side. Not everyone would have, I'm well aware."

Sasha lets out a low groan and heads for the door. "That's it for me. Goodnight all."

"Good show, Sasha. Thanks!" you yell as he retreats.

"Don't think he likes me much," Crispin tells you.

"He's fine," you say. "Just a little flustered. You know he's like a big brother to me. Very protective."

"He is, isn't he? But I'm not someone he has to protect you from."

"I tell him that all the time," you assure him. "Oh! I almost forgot!" You grab your jacket to retrieve Crispin's phone. As you slide the phone from your pocket, you see the string of texts on the home screen. You only have time to read, *Did you do it yet?* before you hand the phone to Crispin.

"I wondered where that had got to," he says.

"You left it in the costume trailer. Must have fallen out of your pocket when we had that little run-in with the wardrobe rack."

"Oh that," he takes a step toward you. "I'd almost forgotten about that. We were rudely interrupted, as I recall. Where were we?"

Crispin pulls you into a long kiss, sliding his hands beneath your robe. "Mmmm," he purrs, "this is much better." He reaches around and slides a hand under your buttocks, lifting you into the air and then lowering you gently down onto the furry faux sheepskin rug in the center of the room. He hovers over you for a moment then thinks to bolt the door before joining you on the rug.

"I'm full of stage makeup and glitter," you tell him.

"I could not care less," says Crispin, spreading your robe and burying his head between your breasts. He pulls back for a moment, opens the robe and runs a finger down from the hollow of your neck, between your breasts, and to your belly button. "You are very sparkly," he appraises.

"I told you," you say. "That glitter gets everywhere."

"Everywhere? Are you quite sure?" he asks, a glimmer in his eyes. "I'd better do some investigating."

He lifts one breast and runs his tongue under it. "Nope, none there." Then moves to the other breast and does the same. "Area one is clear," he proclaims. "Time to migrate farther south." He smiles and trails his fingers lightly lower, softly caressing you as he goes. He glances down and blinks. "How in the world did all of this glitter"—he pauses to blow softly, filling the air above your stomach with sparkles—"get all the way"—he blows again, harder this time, and the effect makes you gasp—"down here?"

"That tickles!" you tell him, instinctively lowering your hands.

"No, no," he laughs, pushing your hands back up above your head, "I'm afraid you've got to allow me to clear the area. Else I'm going to look like I fucked a goddamn fairy. Just give me a moment." He leaps up, disappears for a second and returns with a pink feather duster.

"No!" You laugh helplessly as Crispin feather-dusts your body. "I'll brush it off, just let me—" You reach down and Crispin grabs your hand, pushing it back up above your head.

"I'm sorry, I can't let that happen," he tells you. "This is a job for an expert." He reaches to your side and in one swift movement pulls the sash from your robe. "And since you can't seem to help yourself," he reaches above your head and pushes your wrists together, then snugly ties the sash around them so that your wrists are bound above your head, "you leave me no choice." He rises to his knees for a moment. "Much better," he says, "now I can continue my work."

The tickle of the feathers across your most delicate area is instantly stimulating. Crispin brushes until you beg him to stop, then sweeps the duster lightly across your breasts, making your nipples harden. When he finishes there, he turns you over to run the feathers from the bottoms of your feet up your legs, along your thighs, and across your buttocks. When you don't think you can take any more, he puts the feather duster down, then follows with his tongue.

You wriggle back around, yearning to run your hands through the back of his hair and down his washboard stomach, but your hands are literally tied and you have to admit the sensation is thrilling. "Crispin," you say, "I want to touch you."

Crispin looks up, his cheeks and chin sparkling with glitter. "What?" He smiles, clearly well aware he's already covered in sparkles.

You giggle as he continues to lick you. At last he seems to sense that you can barely take another second. "All right"—he smiles up at you—"all clear at last." Unrelenting, he picks up the feather duster again, running it over your abdomen and across your breasts, then back between your legs one last time before rising to his feet. "Won't be minute," he tells you.

He strips off his jeans and tosses them into the corner of the room then reaches up to entwine his fingers with your tethered hands. "Now," he says, hovering over you for a moment, "that bit of housekeeping is done and we can enjoy ourselves." He slides between your legs and thrusts into you, grinding your buttocks into the robe and sheepskin rug beneath. It takes you only seconds before you wrap your legs around his hips and are carried away by waves of pleasure.

Crispin follows in a moment, breathing hard into your neck as he comes. "Sorry," he apologizes, "that's the effect of rehab. My tolerance is nil."

"You don't need to apologize," you tell him. "That was amazing."

"Well, thanks," he says, nuzzling your neck. "Glad you think I've still got it." He rises to find his jeans.

"Uh, Crispin?"

He looks back and remembers your hands, still tied by the sash.

"Oh sorry!" He quickly frees you then gently kisses your wrists where they have slightly reddened.

You wrap your arms around his neck and press your bare body to his, giving him a long, slow kiss and running your fingers through his hair at last. You pull back to look into his golden eyes.

"Crispin, I . . ." You feel an urge to tell him you love him, but at that moment his cell phone buzzes and when he looks away for a second, you lose your nerve.

"Yes?" he asks, waiting patiently.

"I—um, I'm just really glad you're back."

He smiles and plants a little kiss on your lips before turning to skim into his jeans. "So am I," he tells you, checking his cell, "believe me. And I'm here to stay."

The next night is your second and final Albuquerque performance. From here, you're off to Vegas where you'll have a luxuriously long four-night stay and even a bit of down time. You can't wait.

After your final show in Albuquerque, you quickly thank the crew, say an exhausted goodnight to Sasha and Freddie, and head for your tour bus. Once inside, you take a quick shower, towel off, pull on soft yoga pants and a baggy top, and wrap the towel turban-style around your wet head.

You're reaching for a bottle of water from the little row of cabinets when there's a knock at the door. You certainly aren't expecting company at this hour. "Who is it?" you ask.

"Hello? It is me, Serge," comes the deep voice from the other side of the door.

"Serge? Come on in. Are you okay?"

He looks anxious and as he enters the little bus, he removes his soft, felt hat and twists it in his hands. He slouches slightly, apparently aware of how much space he occupies in the confines of the bus.

"I am fine," he says, "I just wonder if I could speak with you . . . for just a moment."

"Okay." You gesture for him to take a seat at the table.

"I was looking for you in your dressing room, but Sasha said I could find you here. I hope it is okay?"

"It's fine," you tell him. "What's up?"

"I am looking for some"—he seems to search for the word for a moment—"advice." He pronounces the "v" like a "w."

"From me?" you ask, not sure how you can help him. "I'm not really a dancer anymore . . ."

"You are a performer," he explains. "I am a performer. Both passionate about what we do."

"You are a really talented dancer," you tell him.

"Thank you," he says, "but I am not looking for compliment. I need to know—did you ever wonder whether there is something else you should be doing with your life?"

"Me?" You stop to think for a second. Music has been your passion for as long as you can remember, and you are fulfilling every dream you've ever had. "I can't really say I did."

"Hmm," Serge replies, laying his hat on the table and grimacing slightly. "For me, dancing is not my passion."

"It isn't?" you ask, wondering whether he's come to tell you he's leaving the tour.

"No, it is not. I very much enjoy dancing, but how would you feel if you knew in your heart you were meant to be a doctor and you ended up as a lawyer instead? Your heart would be yearning for something else. Would it not?"

"Yeah, I think it probably would," you agree, not sure what he is getting at. "Do you want to be a doctor?"

"No, no," He dips his head, causing that handsome lock of jet-black hair to fall across his brow. "My problem is, I have another passion."

"You do?" you ask cautiously.

"I do. I would like to share it with you, if you will allow me."

You have no idea what to think and even though his words are starting to make you a little uncomfortable, the look in his eyes when he glances up from under his thick lashes is one of pure sincerity. "You can tell me."

He looks down at his hands and then back up into your eyes. "I would like to show you. When we are in Vegas. Would you allow me to do that?"

"Um, sure," you tell him.

"That is good." He breathes a sigh of relief. "I will let you know when it is time. Thank you. You are very good to me." He rises and places the hat back atop his head, then turns for a moment and takes your hand. His large hand is warm, the fingertips noticeably thick and solid. A slight tingle rises up your wrist as he rests his other hand atop yours and locks eyes with you. "Goodnight."

With that, he opens the door and is gone. You are both unsettled and intrigued. You momentarily consider opening the door and calling after Serge but the thought of the early morning ahead stops you. It's a long drive to Vegas tomorrow, and you'll have plenty of time there to find out what Serge wants to show you.

Turn to page 85.

From page 36...

You arrive in Vegas early the next evening after a long day en route. Your hand feels a little better but still throbs off and on, and the Tylenol isn't helping at all. You haven't been very good company for Sasha; and Crispin still hasn't returned your texts or calls. He was well aware you were leaving for your next stop, and the fact that he hasn't even bothered to check in has turned your anxiety into irritation.

"I am so ready to get off this bus," Sasha sighs as he exits the highway. Sasha's high-school classmate, Carlie, has become a well-known Vegas showgirl, and Sasha has already prepared you that he is planning to spend every moment he's not working exploring Vegas with her. You're still not entirely clear whether Carlie is a man or a woman—not that it matters. "Carlie's kind of a big deal in Vegas," Sasha tells you. "You've heard of her show—Carlie's Angels?"

"I don't think I have,"

"What? Have you been living under a rock?" Sasha gives you a scolding look. "Carlie's only the headliner. I personally cannot wait to see it."

"Wish I could come along," you say, only half-joking. "My agenda's pretty packed though. Two shows, two appearances, some DJ gig, and a book signing I think."

"Sucks to be you," says Sasha.

Sasha expertly pulls the bus into the huge parking lot of The Maxamillion Resort and Casino. Huge palm trees sway at the hotel's entrance and jets of neon-lit water ring an enormous fountain, dancing to the pulse of the music blasting from hidden speakers. You debark and flip up the hood of your jacket, hoping to navigate the hotel lobby incognito.

As you enter the hotel, you see you have no reason to worry— even Elvis himself would go unnoticed in the mass of blinged-out humanity crisscrossing the lobby in every direction. In the distance, you can hear the *clicks, clangs,* and *chirps* of what must be the casino. The air smells of an intoxicating mix of perfume, cigarette smoke, alcohol, and money.

A bellhop captaining a huge rolling luggage cart appears at your side. Sasha elbows you lightly and tilts his head in the direction of the bellhop's uniformed behind. "Cute right?" he whispers as you step onto the elevator.

"Behave yourself," you whisper back.

Your suite is expansive and glamorous, decorated in gleaming black marble and white leather. The bar is fully stocked and there's even a lit makeup counter in one corner. "Perfect," you exhale, taking it in.

Sasha heads for a bedroom and immediately throws himself atop a downy bed, "Ahhhhh," he sighs.

"Will that be all?" asks the bellhop.

Sasha leaps from the bed and walks casually toward the waiting man.

"I don't know," Sasha arches an eyebrow, "do you offer any other services?"

"The concierge is excellent and can help you with anything else you may need," the bellhop answers, not missing a beat.

"Well, that's no fun," Sasha takes a step toward the bellhop, who holds his ground. "I was hoping you might be able to assist me."

A rosy blush rushes to the bellhop's cherubic cheeks. He bows quickly, and nods as he backs toward the door. "Sir, ma'am. Enjoy your evening."

"Oh hold on," Sasha sighs, pulling a twenty dollar bill from his wallet and handing it to the bellhop.

"Thank you very much, sir," he says, smiling.

"Please, call me Sasha."

The bellhop turns for a moment, the smallest of smiles on his face.

"I'm Gavin," he says, looking Sasha in the eye playfully. "Do feel free to ask for me . . . if there's anything else you need." He winks, tips his hat, and is out the door.

"I knew it!" cries Sasha the minute Gavin closes the door. "My gaydar is totally on fleek. If I don't answer my cell, just ask for Gavin. I do love a man in uniform."

"Down, boy. I thought you were all about spending every free moment with Carlie."

"Oh, don't you worry about my schedule. I can manage my time." Sasha disappears into his room.

Your cell buzzes from your pocket. You pull it out and are enormously relieved to see a text from Crispin:

What's the room number?

Are you here?

Just got here.

Where were you?

What do you mean?

I texted and called. You left me stranded at the ER

Didn't Sasha tell you?

Tell me what?

About Trixie?

What about Trixie?

I had to do two rescues that night

?

She fell spectacularly off the wagon. Ended up with a broken nose. It wasn't pretty. She's back in rehab

Sorry to hear that

No you're not

OK not really

Good news is, I'm off the hook as her R.A. Looks like my ties to Trixie are severed for good

But why didn't you return my texts?

As I said, I thought Sasha told you. He made me promise not to call or text you after I left that night. Said he would take care of you, you needed rest, etc. Plus, my mobile has been on the blink for some reason . . .

Sorry. Are you still upset about that?

There's a brief pause before Crispin replies.

I'll admit I was. But it seems to be working now. And I'm sure
you'll make it up to me. Room number?
    Penthouse A.
    Be right up

From page 82, from page 109 (and continued from above)...

You gaze out the huge picture window down onto the Vegas strip
and drink in the glittering scene that unfolds as far as you can see as
you wait for Crispin to arrive. The sky glows a smoky orange, the
setting sun now just below the ridge of mountains in the distance. In
moments like this, you still can't believe this is your life.

Crispin gives his signature three-rap door knock.

"Coming!" you call.

Crispin breezes into the room and wraps his arms around your
waist, in a better mood than you've ever seen him.

"Hello, gorgeous," he greets you, giving you a long kiss.

"What has gotten into you?" you ask him.

"You know, moonlight, Vegas, sobriety"—he kisses you again—
"and you, of course."

Sasha emerges and greets Crispin as warmly as ever. "Ugh. Here
for two minutes and you two are at it already. Please. Get a room."

Crispin glances around the suite. "Looks like we have one. Or
several." He runs his hand over the marble expanse of the bar. "Not
too shabby."

"Well, steer clear of my room," Sasha says. He hangs a Do Not
Disturb sign on the handle. "I don't want any of your cooties on my
down comforter."

Crispin walks up to Sasha and runs a finger jokingly up Sasha's
chest. "You haven't experienced cooties," he says, "until you've experienced my cooties."

Sasha looks at you in horror.

"It's true," you tell him.

"That's disgusting," he says, easing past Crispin and toward the
door. "I will be out. On the town. Please respect my privacy. And try
to have a little respect for yourselves."

"Have fun." You laugh as Sasha exits the suite.

Crispin walks over to the window to take in the view. "This is pretty amazing," he says.

"Yeah." You stand behind him, wrapping your arms around his waist and leaning your head against his shoulder blade. "I'm glad you're here."

Crispin turns to you and rests his arms on your shoulders, looking down into your eyes, "Me too."

Everything feels so right. You're glad you trusted your instincts. It feels like Crispin has turned a corner, like something is different, back on track. You'd be happy just to stay here and enjoy a quiet night in the room, but Crispin has other ideas.

"Your first time in Vegas. And my first at The Max. Let's go check it out."

You change into a pair of sleek, leather pants and a glittery gold bustier. Your makeup isn't perfect but you add a coat of glossy red lip color and pair of sunglasses to hide your barely made-up eyes.

You decide to explore the casino first. Crispin grabs your hand and leads you onto the casino floor.

"Slow down," you tell him. "I can only walk so fast in these shoes."

He immediately slows his pace. "Sorry, just want to get through this crowd."

"Too late," you tell him. "Two o'clock."

A tiny blonde in a low-cut minidress eagerly approaches, pen and cocktail napkin in hand. Her Southern drawl is so thick it's almost impossible to decipher. "I'm so sorry to bother you, but I just couldn't help myself!" Her extreme level of inebriation is clear. "Can I just get a quick autograph? I just adore your music!"

Neither of you answers, as you wait to see which one of you the enthusiastic fan will give the pen to. It's a little game you and Crispin play when you're together: one point for each autograph, as long as neither of you encourages the request. So far you're winning. Fifty-seven to twenty-three.

"Well, can I?" She holds the napkin up, then thrusts the pen toward Crispin.

Darn! You think to yourself.

"With pleasure." Crispin grins smugly and takes the napkin and pen. He signs with a flourish and hands the napkin back to the woman.

She squints hard at the autograph. "You sure you're not a doctor?

I can barely read this!" she snorts with laughter. "My girlfriends will never believe this says *Justin Timberlake.*"

Crispin reels as if slapped, and you clap you hand over your mouth to stifle your laugh.

"I'm not . . ." Crispin begins, but you grab his arm and pull him away.

"Come on, Justin," you say loudly. "We don't want to keep Lance and JC waiting."

He shoots you a look that could kill.

"Are y'all performing here?" the woman asks, still clearly oblivious.

"It's just me performing, actually," you answer. "Justin and the boys are here for a conference. Kind of like Comic-Con. For boy banders."

"Oh," says the woman, eyes wide. "I had no idea." She looks momentarily perplexed then seems to work through the confusion. "My kids just love you, Honey Noble!" she enthuses. "I didn't even know y'all were friends!" Then she reaches into her brassiere and pulls out her cell phone. "Can I just snap one quick selfie?"

"Of course!" You lean in graciously as she snaps the photo.

She looks at the display and breaks into a wide smile, clearly pleased with the result. "Thank y'all so much! Have a great show!" She waggles her fingers and totters off with her trophies.

"That counts," you tell Crispin. "For me."

"Does not," he retorts. Twenty-four to fifty-seven.

"You do not get a point for that!"

"I should get three for that. Justin Timberlake! I'm horrified."

"I wouldn't be," you tell him. "He's done alright for himself."

"Oh, well if you'd prefer JT to me, I'm sure I can arrange an introduction," he pouts.

"Not a chance." You plant a glossy kiss on his lips. "Where should we start?" The casino floor is a maze of slot machines and gaming tables. You're glad Crispin is with you because he knows his way around.

"Come with me," Crispin leads you to the booth and quickly purchases a tray of chips. "Is Mr. Connetti available please?" he asks the cashier.

She looks up at him, recognition registering on her face. "Of course, sir," she answers.

A moment later, a short, older man in a dark suit rounds the corner. He smiles hugely and claps Crispin on the back, shaking his hand. "Mr. Hershey! And Ms. Noble! Welcome to the Max! Please, follow me."

He slides an electronic key into a slot in an inconspicuous door marked "Employees Only" at the back of the casino and leads you into a private gambling room. Ornate chandeliers cast a glimmering, golden light over an array of low tables. A dark-suited waiter approaches you with two flutes filled with champagne. Mr. Connetti asks for a photo with Crispin and one with you before he leaves, standing as tall as he can to pose for the shots.

You take a seat at one of the tables, joining an aging television star whose name you can't quite remember and a trio of younger players. "Who are they?" you whisper to Crispin as he sits beside you.

"YouTube stars."

"Right."

Crispin is a whiz at blackjack. You're hardly following the game, but you enjoy watching Crispin rake in chips. Somehow your glass seems never to be empty though the fuzziness in your head tells you you've drunk more than you probably should have already. You cheer Crispin on as he wins more than he loses. At last, he lets out a huge sigh and collects the sizeable stack of chips.

"Think I've done enough damage for one night," he announces. Then he leans down and whispers into your ear, "Let's get out of here."

His breath against your ear makes you shiver.

"Sasha says the Max has an amazing lounge," you suggest. "Want to check it out?"

"Why not?" he answers. "When in Vegas . . ."

The doorkeeper escorts you to another discreetly concealed entrance, opening onto a single service elevator. The elevator whisks you up to the VIP entrance, which leads to a dim room with an empty dance floor bordered by low booths upholstered in rich midnight-blue velvet and scattered with pillows and furry throws, and screened by heavy curtains.

"Booths are bottle service only," says the host, a hipster with a pompadour and skinny pants.

"That works," answers Crispin, sliding into a cushy seat.

"This is nice," you say, taking in the surroundings. You're glad for the privacy and for the time alone with Crispin.

A blond bottle service girl who looks like she just stepped of the Victoria's Secret runway appears to take your order.

"Cristal," says Crispin. "And a bottle of Bling."

"Coming right up." She smiles, and saunters away on four-inch stilettos.

"What's the occasion?" you ask.

"I know it's your favorite." Crispin shrugs and takes your hand. "Besides, we're celebrating."

The waitress returns with the champagne and the bejeweled bottle of sparkling water. She pours you each a glass of the Cristal and leaves the water unopened on the table. As soon as she walks away, Crispin slides his champagne flute over to you.

"I'm impressed," you tell him.

"I am serious about my sobriety," he fills his water glass and traces the rim with one finger. "And also about you, in case there was any question."

You smile as he scoots closer to you on the bench and wraps his arm around your waist.

"How is it?" you ask as he sips the pricey water.

"Worth every penny."

You smile. "Crispin," you tell him, "I'm really glad you're here."

"You keep telling me that. Where else would I be?"

You pause for a moment, and Crispin dips his head to look into your eyes. "What's bothering you, Honey?"

"Nothing now," you answer. "Just—it's silly I guess but the whole thing with Trixie had me worried."

"What *whole thing*?"

You take a sip of your champagne. "You know, the rehab partner thing or whatever. It just seems like one thing after another with her. I trust you, you know that. But I don't trust her."

Crispin's lifts the glass of water and watches the bubbles float to the top for a moment before replying. "It's been a bit of a mess with Trixie," he admits. He rubs the back of his neck. "There are some things I haven't told you."

It takes every bit of strength not to visibly recoil. *I knew it*, you think to yourself. You steel yourself for what you are about to hear and take another long sip of champagne, letting the silence spin out until Crispin decides to continue.

"So," Crispin begins, "you know Trixie and I have some, uh, past history."

"Yes, I'm aware."

"Well, there's a little more to it than that."

You place the champagne flute down on the table, clear your throat, and look Crispin squarely in the eye. "Just say it," you tell him.

He breathes in and lays both palms down on the table, never breaking eye contact. "She was my dealer."

"What?"

Crispin flips his palms up but says nothing.

"Are you serious?"

"As a heart attack."

You pause for a moment, with no idea what to say, then drink the rest of your champagne in a single gulp and set the glass down. "Okay then." You think for a minute. "But if she knows you're clean why was she still hanging around?"

Crispin shakes his head. "She'd been acting strangely ever since we got out of rehab. To be honest, I think she may have been dealing even from there. There was this one tech who had a thing for her—I don't know—anyway, she was definitely up to something. Being assigned as her Rehab Advocate, it was pretty much a joke. No way I could succeed in giving her support when I don't think her intent was ever actually to recover. But what was I going to do? Rat her out? I never had any real evidence she was back at it until just recently. I thought I could possibly help her, but now I honestly believe all she's been trying to do is reel me back in. At the same time I think she was worried, since I have a bit of dirt on her, don't I? You know what they say, *Keep your friends, close, keep your enemies closer.* But believe me, I have been crystal clear that I have no interest. I feel better than I ever have. There's no way I would go back to that life."

You scoot a little closer to Crispin and take his hand. He's worked so hard to turn his life around, and you know he's done it for you as well as for himself.

He strokes your fingers. "You know, you're all I thought about while I was in there. All I wanted to do was to get out to be with you again. You're the reason I got through it, Honey. And for the first time in a long time I'm excited about life now, and what the future holds." He pauses and smiles, and tucks a strand of hair behind your ear. "And I want that future to be with you."

You feel a blush rise to your face as he leans in to kiss you, long and deep. "I love you, Honey."

You smile into his gorgeous eyes. "I love you, too."

All at once, Crispin springs from the booth and drops to one knee. You glance around to see whether anyone is watching, but blessedly everyone seems to be in their own little worlds.

"Honey Noble, will you marry me?"

You are caught totally off-guard and don't know what to say.

"Are you serious?"

"More serious than I have ever been about anything in my life."

Suddenly everything around you jumps into acute focus. The bubbles slowly rising from the bottom of your champagne flute and popping gently as they reach the surface. The waxy vanilla and slightly sulfurous scent of the fat candle burning in the center of the table. The amplified beating of your heart, so loud you can hear the *whoosh* of blood pounding in your ears.

You know that in this moment your life is about to change. You do love Crispin, but your relationship with this sober version of Crispin is still new. Still, you've gone through so much together and through it all Crispin has proven himself over and over to be the person you hoped he would be.

Should you go with your head and give it more time, or go with your heart and say "yes"?

To say no to Crispin, turn to page 172.
To say yes to Crispin, keep reading.

From page 219 (and continued from above) . . .

A complete and sudden clarity enters your mind as you focus on Crispin, still on bended knee and gazing hopefully up at you.

"Yes," you tell him, "yes, yes, yes!"

He jumps to his feet, pulls you to him, and kisses you for a long time, his hand on the nape of your neck.

"I'm so sorry," he says between kisses. "I don't have a ring or anything—it just came over me. I can't spend another minute not knowing you are mine. Forever." He quickly slides his wallet from his pocket and places a neat stack of several hundred dollar bills on the table. "Come on."

"Wait, don't you want to celebrate?" you ask, not sure why he's in such a hurry to leave.

"We can celebrate after," he answers. "I want to marry you now."

"What? Tonight?"

"Absolutely," he takes both of your hands gently in his. "Here in Vegas. Tonight."

"But what about having our friends there? Our families?"

"We can do it all again with everyone. I promise. But let's do this just for us. There's so little we get that's just ours. What do you say?"

"You mean not tell anyone?" You're mostly concerned about Sasha and Freddie, who would certainly be hurt if they found out.

"Not a soul," Crispin assures you.

"Okay." You can't believe you're saying it, but for once in your life you are going to go follow your heart and see where it leads. "This is totally crazy, but okay."

Less than a half hour later, you are standing in front of a clerk signing your marriage license.

"You made it just in time," the elderly clerk tells you as you sign your name a little sloppily. "We were getting ready to close."

"Good timing, then, isn't it?" Crispin snaps a selfie with the newly minted license. "For the album."

"Congratulations, kids," the clerk says. "I wish you a lifetime of love and happiness."

"Thank you!" You beam, grateful that she clearly has no idea who either of you are.

You take a taxi to a tiny white chapel just off the strip. YOLO Weddings seems appropriate. A beaming couple dressed in cut-offs, too lost in each other to even notice you, exits the chapel just as you enter.

A tall man in a white suit greets you. Just beyond him, brightly colored stained-glass windows line the walls of the tiny chapel. Three rows of empty wooden pews flank each side of a scarlet-carpeted aisle.

"Y'all here to tie the knot?" asks the man.

"That we are," answers Crispin, proudly holding up the marriage license.

"Splendid," says the man, barely glancing at the license. "Got all your ducks in a row."

A tiny woman in a long, lacy dress comes out of nowhere. A cloud of white hair floats around her head. "I'm Betty." Her bright blue eyes sparkle from a nest of crow's feet, "I'll be your witness." She produces an enormous, ancient-looking camera and aims it at you. "Smile!" she commands, and the camera flashes, momentarily blinding you. "We'll print these out before you leave," she promises. "Now, do you need rings or did you bring your own?"

"I'm afraid all we have with us is ourselves and our license," Crispin tells her.

"Well then, let's get you fixed up."

She leads you a jewelry case. There, behind the glass, sits an assortment of rings ranging from tastefully simple to simply gaudy.

Crispin points to an elegant band.

"Platinum," Betty says. "You have excellent taste." She slides the ring from the case and tries it on Crispin's finger. "It's a little big, but you can get it sized later. Important thing is to have it for the ceremony." She sets the ring on the counter with a clink. "What about you, honey?"

You glance up at her to see whether her face registers recognition, but you guess she's just using the term of endearment since she doesn't seem to know who you are.

"Um"—you peruse the rows of rings—"What about that one?" You point to a slim band encrusted with what look like tiny diamonds. Crispin nods his approval.

"That's a beautiful choice." Betty removes the ring from the case. She slips in onto your finger. It fits perfectly.

Vertigo suddenly washes over you as you gaze down at your hand. You take a stumbling step backward and Crispin grabs your elbow to steady you.

"You all right?" he asks.

The vertigo is gone as quickly as it came on. Crispin's hand on your arm is a sure and steady force.

"Fine," you tell him. "Just too much champagne, I guess."

Crispin presses his forehead to yours and looks you in the eyes. "You are my soul mate, Honey. Never doubt how much I love you."

You smile up at him as Betty shoves a fragrant bouquet of roses and baby's breath into your hands. "This way," she says, and leads you to the front of the little chapel.

The service is a blur. After, you'll clearly remember only a few things: holding the bouquet at just the right height to hide your bare midriff; the use of your legal name, *Do you, Henrietta, take this man, Crispin, to be your lawfully wedded husband*: sliding the too-loose ring onto Crispin's finger: and those two little words: "I do." You have no memory of your return trip to the hotel or saying goodnight to Crispin.

Your next clear memory is the feeling of intense guilt as you slide the slim wedding band into the inside pocket of your travel bag and the odd feeling that everything has changed, and at the same time that nothing is different at all.

Eighteen months later, you are back home in Hollywood noodling on the piano in an attempt to find inspiration for your next single. The label wants "edgy pop" but all you seem to be able to produce are moody ballads. It's not that you are sad exactly—you just don't know how to feel.

At first, your shared secret brought you and Crispin closer together. He came home to you at the end of every day, no matter how late he worked, slid into your bed whispering, "Hello, Mrs. Hershey," into your ear. Something about the sound of his voice made you melt effortlessly, and you enjoyed making love to your husband, your clandestine marriage adding an extra thrill to your time together. You wore your wedding bands only when you were alone, and began a nightly routine that you hoped would never end. The feel of his ring against your bare back sent shivers up your spine every time. Somehow the feeling of security, of solidity, made sex with Crispin seem like something more. You never tired of hearing him call you his wife, telling you how much he loved you over and over as he thrust into you.

After, you lay for hours, arms wrapped around each other, making plans to move in together and then for a real wedding with all of your friends and family present.

But that dream ended suddenly and much too soon the first time Crispin got called away to New York to promote his new single. He returned from that first trip distant, apologizing for being too tired to make love. After the next trip a few weeks later, he returned to his own condo.

"It's only temporary, baby," he still tells you, although it's been close to a month.

When he is in town, Crispin is flaky and aloof, pleading long hours at the studio. You can't help but wonder whether he's come to regret the impulsive Vegas wedding—or whether something more concerning is going on. You know you need to talk, to find out what is really going on, but part of you doesn't want to hear the answer. Plus, every time you try to have a real conversation, Crispin dodges the subject or makes you feel crazy or paranoid for worrying.

"It's just work," he tells you. "You know how it is. As soon as I get this single finished, I'll be all yours."

You want to believe him, but every echoing walk across the expanse of black-and-white tile through the cavernous empty rooms makes you feel more alone. So far Crispin hasn't moved so much as a toothbrush into your house.

Even Sasha has been MIA, in the midst of a new fling. He's probably using his new relationship as an excuse to give you space, still thinking he'll come home to find Crispin there. You want so much to tell him your secret, but you made a promise to Crispin, and you worry that Sasha would never forgive you.

Work is your solace, and you spend as many hours as you can at the piano or in the studio, writing and recording. The hours you don't spend on music you devote to your clothing line. You know you're just being an ostrich, hiding your head in the sand in order to avoid what's right in front of you, but right now you're not ready to face whatever is really going on.

You manage to ignore your suspicions until they surface rudely in front of you in the form of a glossy tabloid headline reading, Is Crispin headed back to rehab? Inside the Singer's Struggles. An ugly photo of Crispin looking like he's recovering from a bender, his bloodshot eyes ringed with black shadows, fills the magazine's cover.

Every fiber of your being wants to toss the tabloid into the trash. Why did you ever subscribe to *WE Weekly* in the first place? But in your experience where there's smoke there's fire, and you know it's time to face the truth. You page through the slim issue until you find the story.

Crispin Hershey seems to be off again—off of his on-again-off-again romance with Honey Noble and off the wagon, the article begins. *Photographed leaving hotspot, Axe, in the wee hours of the night, Hershey stumbled into a waiting car.*

"He reeked of alcohol and couldn't even stand up straight," a source tells WE exclusively. "It's really sad. He just got sober."

Hershey himself seemed ready to celebrate during his night at Axe, reportedly ordering bottle after bottle of Cristal and canoodling with former flame, Trixie Taylor, in a private booth. A blurry photo of what might be Crispin, his head inclined toward a leggy blond who could be Trixie, accompanies the article. A sidebar of photos of Crispin (Crispin with Alien Encounter, his defunct boy band; Crispin smiling after leaving rehab almost two years ago; and several photos of you and Crispin) fills the right side of the page, adding a little substance to the slim article which ends with the sentence, *Reps for Hershey declined to comment.*

You bet they did. You close the magazine and set it gently down on the counter then walk slowly back to the piano. Running your fingers aimlessly across the keyboard, mindlessly assembling unrelated segments of melody, you allow your subconscious to digest what you've just read. When the sun begins to dip below the horizon, you rise from the piano bench to face reality; your suspicions over these past months have to be correct.

Your manager, Freddie, is by your side in an instant, supplying you with the direct line for the attorney he used during his divorce. The attorney arranges to see you the next day. Quietly and confidentially, he draws up the divorce papers. Your hand trembles slightly as you pick up the pen to sign, but the shaking subsides as you put pen to paper and reduce your marriage to a memory.

Three days later, Crispin appears in the foyer unannounced. He looks as though he hasn't slept. His hair sticks up at odd angles and he runs one hand through it constantly as he looks up at you accusingly, a hefty manila envelope in his other hand.

"Honey," he begins, "what is this all about?"

You sigh, more exhausted than you can ever remember feeling. "Crispin, I can't do this."

He looks up at you, an expression of genuine confusion on his beautiful features. "Do what exactly?" he asks.

"You know what I mean, Crispin. This isn't working. It hasn't worked since the beginning. I can't pretend anymore."

"You know what I've been dealing with, Honey." His eyes are desperate, pleading. "My schedule's been insane."

"You don't owe me an explanation," you tell him. "I get it. Believe me, of all people, I get it. But you and I both know this was never a good idea. And now the press is spreading all of those stories about you. I didn't want to believe them for the longest time, I still don't want to. But the more you've been absent the more I don't know what to believe."

Crispin's face reddens and his eyes widen alarmingly. "Those are lies, Honey! You know they are! How can you even believe what you read in those shitty magazines? You should believe me!"

You back up a step. "What about the photos?" you ask quietly.

"Those are shite! None of it's true! Are you telling me you never had a tabloid run a photo of you and tie it to some scandalous fabrication?"

"Crispin, if you've ever been honest with me, I need you to be honest now. Was that you in that bar, with Trixie?"

Crispin is quiet for a moment too long. You feel the weight of the truth hanging between you, creating a chasm you know no words will bridge.

"I mean, just the fact that you would allow those photos to be taken . . ."

Suddenly Crispin explodes. "You know what? You are entirely correct. I don't owe you a fucking explanation! You are not my probation officer!" He takes the thick envelope in both hands and attempts to rip it in half, throwing it on the foyer floor when the papers prove too thick to tear. "And I'm not signing that!"

He turns to leave and pauses by the door. For a moment you have a fleeting sense of hope that he is about to turn around and somehow make everything all right. But instead, he slams his fist into the foyer wall, a final act of violence that seems to serve as an affirmation that you've made the right decision. Chunks of plaster fall to the ground and dust floats in the air as Crispin slams the door.

You stand there, stunned, gazing at the gaping hole in the wall, which oddly feels like a perfect metaphor for the hole in your heart.

Ten years later, you're starting to feel your age. It takes longer to recover from the long nights performing and you find yourself spending more time on the massage table trying to ease your sore muscles and in the dermatologist's office preventing the tiny lines just starting to appear at the edges of your eyes. Still, there's no place you'd rather be than on the stage, basking in the adulation of your audience.

The Crispin disaster, as you fondly refer to that time in your life, took a temporary toll on your public image. You can still taste the alkaline fear and anger that rose like bile to the back of your tongue when the photos from the chapel went public. Your memories of that time are a collage of your own, fragmented recollections mixed with glossy tabloid images and sound bites: Crispin telling *WE Weekly* that the wedding was nothing more than an impulse decision made during a wild Vegas night; telling *Pizzazz* that the success of his single and the comeback that followed was too much for you to handle, and ultimately led to your undoing as a couple. Trixie telling everyone who would listen that she and Crispin forged an unbreakable bond during rehab and were never really apart, that they discovered each other again during their second stint in rehab, that of course she forgave him right away when she realized his hasty wedding was a sham. It was at least a little solace that Crispin and Trixie's relationship went up in flames only weeks later.

One day in a rare moment of boredom, you turn on the TV and flip through channels trying to find something moderately interesting to watch when you come across *Celebrity Relapse*. A familiar voice with an unmistakable accent makes you drop the remote mid-flip. Riveted, you watch as Crispin checks into Malibu Manor, the renowned recovery center of the rich and famous.

You follow the series, rapt, as Crispin suffers through detox, undergoes therapy, and interacts with the other residents. It's like watching some kind of bizarre caricature of the person you once loved. The hurt and anger you pushed aside resurface momentarily, and then are overcome by empathy for Crispin as he struggles with his sobriety. You find yourself rooting for him, praying for his recovery, and more than once impulsively picking up the phone, then just as quickly stopping yourself from contacting him.

By the end of the twelve episodes, Crispin is clean and sober and ready to move out and take another stab at living in the "real world" with all of its temptations. The finale promises a follow-up episode two weeks later. You can't wait to see whether he's succeeded. Depending on what the episode shows, you might just reach out to him after all.

Watching that final episode, you realize you've dodged a major bullet. A self-proclaimed *Celebrity Relapse* success story and *recovery guru,* Crispin has moved back into his home and taken on a bevy of booty-shorts-wearing, midriff-baring *Crispettes.* He inducts the girls into a bizarre boot camp which includes a strict diet and exercise regime, various duties which include alternately fawning over Crispin and catering to his every need, and "classes" taught by Crispin on celebrity comportment, acting, singing, and posing for photographs. The girls sign a contract to live by Crispin's rules in exchange for room, board, and his tutelage.

You have no idea whether he's found a lucrative revenue stream, a way of ensuring companionship (regardless of the quality), whether he's making some kind of strained attempt at reality show fame, or whether he's gone completely insane, but you're grateful you listened to your gut and didn't pick up that phone to text him during the early episodes of the show. You silently wish him well and once and for all release him from your heart.

More than anything, you're grateful for Sasha. Through all of your ups and downs throughout the years, your silly flings and serious heartbreaks, your successes and failures, Sasha has been a constant.

As you prepare for your fourth world tour, you look around your home—at the baby grand in the corner, the comfy sofas and ottomans, the lush gardens bordered by solid privacy walls. Each element so carefully selected. In a rare moment of silence and solitude like this one, you wonder whether you would have spent so much time curating the trappings of perfection if you'd known how little time you'd actually get to spend here. You would never have guessed that, instead, you would find perfection in spite of—and perhaps because of—all of the many messy detours you've taken throughout your journey.

You hear the door click open and shut as Sasha struts into the room, the heels of his boots clicking across the marble tiles, a stack of garment bags slung over his back.

"Hey, Mama!" chirps a high-pitched voice.

Your heart instantly squeezes with joy as a curly, little head pops out from behind Sasha and a compact body comes running into your arms.

"Hi, baby!" You cover Valentine's round, cocoa-colored cheeks with kisses and run your fingers through his springy curls. His huge, green eyes are the color of the ocean on a sunny day. You could look into those eyes forever.

"You ready to get to work?" Sasha asks, unloading the garment bags into the living room sofa. "Val's going to help us pick. Right, V?"

"You got it, Daddy-o." The child nods vigorously, curls bouncing wildly. "Mama's gonna do a fashion show! And then we're gonna go see the Fife-full Tower."

You laugh as Sasha unzips the first of the garment bags and extracts a glittering, fringed bodysuit.

"Woah!" Valentine exclaims, eyes wide.

"We have to go on a long airplane ride first," you remind him for the fifteenth time. "And Mommy has to do some work before we get to go explore. But you and Daddy will be with me the whole time."

"Yay!" Valentine jumps up and down in his Velcro sneakers. "I'm gonna watch movies on my iPad the whole plane ride. And I'm gonna take one million pictures."

Thank goodness for technology you think. At last, Val's old enough to accompany you on the entire tour, and you can worry less about the long flights and train rides that ferry you from venue to venue. He may actually remember some of this trip—especially if he takes one million pictures. Together, you can begin assembling an extraordinary scrapbook that will remind you all of your adventures even long after you stop touring.

The next morning, you board the private plane to London, the first stop on the European leg of your world tour, *Swarm*.

Sasha takes Val's hands as he gamely climbs the "giant" stairway leading to the plane. "Freddie!" he screams with delight, spotting Freddie waiting in the sleek plane. He immediately jumps up on Freddie's lap.

"Oh my goodness," Freddie takes Val's cheeks between his hands. "You are getting too big! Wait a second"—he squints hard at Valentine's face—"are you growing a mustache?"

"Noooo!" Valentine laughs. "That's just some chocolate!"

"Oh, thank goodness! I thought I was going to have to teach you how to shave!" Freddie tickles Valentine, who doubles over with laughter.

As the flight attendant secures the cabin, you feel an overwhelming sense of pride at the life you have created. You gaze with love at your little family: Freddie, who has become like a father to you and a grandfather to Valentine. Sasha, who is the perfect life partner and an incredible parent to your child. And little Valentine, the joy you never knew was missing in your life. One day, you'll tell Valentine how he came into the world, an in vitro baby created out of the pure, platonic love you and Sasha share. For now, you bask in the perfection of this moment, with everything you love in the world right here beside you.

The lightness you feel as the plane ascends matches the lightness in your heart. You watch the world below you growing tinier and tinier until it disappears below a wispy cover of clouds. You smile at Sasha and Freddie, take Valentine's small hand in yours, and know that, at last, you have found your happily-ever-after.

THE END

To take Honey on a new Bedventure, go back and choose a new path.

From page 26 . . .

"So, what exactly is this confidential information you have to share regarding the whereabouts of my mobile?" Crispin asks.

You try to think of a gentle way to tell him but decide to just come out with it. "I have it," you say.

"Have what? My mobile?"

"Yes," you tell him.

"And where might it be?" he asks.

You walk slowly over to the rainbow wig, lift it from the vase on which the wig sits, and reach down into the vat of rice, causing grains to overflow onto the countertop. You fish out the phone, and more grains go spilling onto the floor.

"What?" he asks, confused, brushing rice from the phone and pressing the buttons. After a few long seconds the screen illuminates. "At least it works."

"Thank goodness," you breathe. "Crispin, I'm really sorry."

Crispin looks up at you, genuinely puzzled. "I'm just trying to work it out. I lose my phone, which you know I'm going bonkers trying to find, then somehow it ends up under a wig on your makeup counter in a vat of rice?"

"It's a long story," you say. "Essentially what happened was it slipped out of my hands and ended up getting dunked in water. So we were trying to dry it out."

"We who?"

"What?"

"You said, '*We* were trying to dry it out.' Who is the other party in the aforementioned *we*"?

"Oh, Sasha."

"Mmm," Crispin replies, scrolling through something on the phone. Finally, he looks up at you, apparently satisfied that the phone is operating normally. "But why wouldn't you want to tell me? Not likely I'd be worried about an honest mistake, would I?"

"I know you wouldn't. It was just one of those things that happened so fast, and I didn't have time to think, and then I felt terrible." You reach for Crispin's hand, which he reluctantly lets you take. "I wanted to try to dry it out to be sure it still worked."

"I still don't get why you wouldn't just tell me, Honey."

"Sorry." You really do feel terrible, and there isn't a good explanation. "There's no other reason."

"Okay then. Well, thanks." He lets go of your hand and slides the phone into his pocket, not quite making eye contact as he speaks. "I suppose I should be going. I need to catch up on a few things. Return some texts. Now that I have my mobile."

"Wait, where are you going?"

"S'pose I'll check into a hotel room," Crispin looks past you toward the door. "Got loads to do. E-mails to return. I'll check in with you later."

"Okay," you say. You know he's upset and so you decide not to push it.

Crispin pops a quick kiss onto your cheek and heads out the door.

"Damn," you whisper quietly as you tighten the belt on your robe.

The next morning you leave early for Las Vegas. Sasha listens to you retell the story during the long drive. "He's full-out sketchy, Henrietta. I've been trying to tell you that all along."

"I think he was just reacting to me obviously not telling him the truth. I'm a terrible liar."

"Well, he's a pretty good liar, and that's worse," Sasha huffs.

You stare for a long moment at Sasha's profile as he expertly pilots the huge bus along the interstate. You know he knows you're waiting for him to tell you more, but his eyes remain focused on the road and his lips remain firmly shut.

Finally, you say it. "Tell me what you saw."

He glances over at you for a split second. "Do you really want to know?"

"No, not really." You're suddenly chilly, and you cross your arms over your chest and reposition the air vent. "But I think I have to know."

Sasha pushes back from the steering wheel, stretching his long arms. "All right, Henry. But you're not going to like it."

You wait patiently for him to speak.

"The basic gist of it was, he's still talking to Trixie. Often. A bunch of flirty bullshit. But then some of it reads like some kind of crazy code. There's still definitely something going on. I would not be at all surprised if they aren't doing some kind of contraband together. Or worse." He pauses for a moment to let it sink in. "You need to lose him, Henrietta. I've been trying to tell you."

You sit silently staring out into the glare reflecting from the long stretch of highway and let Sasha's words sink in.

Finally Sasha breaks the silence. "You there?"

"Yeah," you say. "Just processing."

Sasha reaches over to give your hand a squeeze.

"It's fine," you tell him.

"It's not fine. And you don't have to act all tough. But it will be fine." He lets the silence unfurl for several long minutes then yells, "We're going to Vegas, baby!" at the top of his lungs, making you jump out of your seat. "Sorry, but the mood in this bus needed lifting."

You laugh. "You scared me to death!"

"But I made you smile."

"You always do."

"Don't you forget it!" Sasha rolls down his window to let in the dry desert air as you continue down the long road that seems to unfurl endlessly before you.

At last, an array of neon lights blooms into full view against the dark desert sky as you pull into the long, circular drive in front of the Maxamillion Resort and Casino. A monstrous, incandescent fountain dances at the entryway, its water creating a deafening roar as you exit the tour bus.

You instinctively duck your head and push your huge sunglasses up to cover your face as you walk through the hotel's revolving door entry. As it turns out, your attempt to go unnoticed is completely unnecessary. The lobby is so full of glamorous gamblers that not a head turns in your direction, even when the little concierge comes to greet you, dipping and bobbing as he leads you to a bank of elevators that will take you to the penthouse suite.

You hastily dump your luggage and take a quick tour of the opulent penthouse. All glossy black marble and gleaming gold accents, the living room's wall of windows offers a breathtaking view of the glittering Vegas Strip. You can't wait to experience it.

Freddie speeds into the room. "All good?" he asks, nodding at the surroundings.

"It's gorgeous!" you tell him.

"Glad you're happy. Nine p.m. is your guest DJ gig at the Max, the nightclub downstairs. That's all I have lined up for you tonight. After that, you're free to get some rest."

"I've been resting all day." You glance back down at the shimmering lights below you. "I'm planning to find out what everyone's been talking about. It's my first time in Vegas."

"Well, you take it easy, Missy." Freddie turns to leave the room. "Keep an eye on her, will you please?" He points a finger at Sasha, who replies with a mock-salute.

Sasha converts the lone, unused bedroom into a makeshift closet and dressing room. Rolling racks laden with couture line both walls. You skim into the fitted silk bustier and the skintight leather leggings he's laid out on the bed then you walk to the bathroom to check out the finished product. The bustier fits beautifully, allowing you a little breathing room while still lifting your assets just enough to be tempting. The leggings are perfectly tailored to hug every curve without revealing too much. The tip of your ponytail just touches the small of your back when you tilt your chin up slightly. It all works.

Sasha meets you in the great room, a pair of strappy, metal-studded Louboutins slung over one finger. "You look killer," he growls.

"Come on, let's get you down to the club."

"The clock is running and we are not staying one second past the hour mark. I am not missing Carlie's show." Sasha's high-school friend, Carlie, née Carlton, has hit it big in Vegas and headlines a popular burlesque review, Carlie's Angels. "Freddie's coming to see it too."

"What, I'm not invited?" you ask.

"You can come too, don't get your panties in a bunch, Henrietta. I didn't know what you had planned. I was going to extend an invitation."

"Hmm," you respond, annoyed that your inclusion is apparently an afterthought. "I'll see what I feel like after the appearance. Maybe I'll join you."

"Whatever, Miss Thing. Come on."

On the walk to the club, Sasha goes on and on about the DJ you are about to meet. "DJ Jett is only the most famous DJ on the scene right now. Travels all over the world doing gigs. The Max must have given him a pretty sweet deal. Don't tell me you've never heard of him."

"The name sounds kind of familiar."

"Kind of familiar? Girl, you are working too much. Anyway, I'm going to get a selfie. He is H.O.T hot."

The club is a pulsating bath of frenetic energy. Lasers cut across the fog-filled air and bodies merge and separate on the dance floor. Waiters and waitresses in skimpy black uniforms thrust trays of neon-colored drinks above their heads as they deftly make their way through the crowd.

DJ Jett is tall and muscular, and bobs his spiky blond head to the beat as he spins a record on one of two complicated-looking turntables. He pushes a few buttons, adjusts a series of levers, then turns his attention to you.

He lowers his headphones and pushes his sunglasses up onto his head. His eyes are breathtaking, a shade of blue so light as to almost be translucent, and his face is oddly familiar. When he speaks, it all falls into place.

"I'm Jett," he says, the thick Australian accent unmistakable. "Pleasure to meet you." He extends a large, warm hand. "What?" he asks when you stare, dumbstruck. "Is there something in my teeth?"

"No," you laugh, the initial shock wearing off. "I just realized who you are. I'm a little starstruck. *The Silversmiths* was probably my all-time favorite show."

Jett takes a step back and raises his platinum eyebrows. "You are starstruck meeting me?" he marvels. "Well that's a laugh."

An unattainable crush during your formative years, Jett was the adorable teen heartthrob on the popular family sitcom that made him famous. You've probably seen every episode at least five times.

"So you're DJ'ing now?" you ask, immediately embarrassed by the stupid question.

"Seem to be," he answers, giving you a wink and sliding his sunglasses and headphones back into place. As the track ends he takes the mic and introduces you. "Let's make some noise for Honey Noble!" he purrs into the microphone, causing the crowd to erupt into cheers and applause. "She's just arrived in Vegas and her first stop is right here at the Max?" Once again, the crowd goes wild. "Catch her Nobility Tour this weekend—if you can still get tickets!"

You lean in so he can hear you. "Thanks for the plug."

"Not that you need it, I reckon," he replies.

You spend the next hour dancing and helping Jett spin tracks. Sasha manages to snap a few selfies and break out a few crazy dance moves.

It's difficult to talk over the noise of the music and the crowd, but Jett guides your hands, showing you how to move the levers to balance the music. Every touch sends a little shiver through you. You know it's probably the adrenaline and the contagious Vegas vibe, pure pheromones floating through the foggy air, but you're enjoying every moment.

The hour ends much too quickly, and Sasha is at your side the minute ten o'clock arrives. "Alright, Cinderella, you ready to blow this pop stand? Don't want you turning into a pumpkin on me."

"That's a lot of mixed metaphors," you respond, not really ready to leave.

"Not sure those are metaphors," he retorts, arching one eyebrow, "and I think I've enjoyed watching Jett work almost as much as you have. But Carlie's Angels is four blocks down and we still have to navigate our way out of here."

"Okay, just a sec."

You walk back to Jett and lay a hand gently on his arm. Under his shirt, you can feel he's pure muscle. His bicep bulges as he works the soundboard. He holds one finger up then pushes a button and backs away from the board.

"Thanks," you tell him, yelling over the noise of the music and crowd. "This was really fun."

"Glad you enjoyed it," Jett says. He looks out into the crowd as if contemplating something. "Any chance I could convince you to stay?"

"I wish I could," you tell him, then realize it's one of those things everyone says but no one really means. But you mean it. "I really do. But I promised that guy"—you nod toward Sasha—"I'd accompany him to see a friend perform in a show she headlines on the Strip." You feel unaccountably saddened at the thought of disappointing him. "Maybe we could meet up after?" you offer impulsively. You immediately feel a stab of guilt thinking about Crispin, but you immediately quash the feeling as you remember what Sasha told you about Crispin's texts with Trixie.

"Really?" He brightens immediately. "That would be amazing."

"Honey," urges Sasha impatiently from behind your shoulder.

"One second!" you yell.

You slip your phone from inside your bustier. "What's your number?" you ask Jett. He takes your phone and quickly adds himself to your contacts.

The crowd roars a goodbye as Jett announces your departure. You wave goodbye and make your exit.

"What were you doing over there?" Sasha asks. "Did you give that boy your number?"

"Nope," you answer. "But I got his."

"You go girl!" Sasha high-fives you as you walk through the hotel lobby.

You arrive at Carlie's Angels just as the theatre begins to darken.

"I thought you were never gonna get here," Freddie whispers. "Sit."

You slide into a seat at the little candlelit table near the front of the room.

"Well, we're here, so relax," Sasha shushes.

The show opens with a rowdy number. The dancers kick, twist, and writhe their way around the stage. Sasha leaps out of his seat in crazy applause when Carlie makes an appearance. Freddie tugs at his shirt until he settles back into his seat.

"I can't help it!" Sasha gushes. "that's my boo!"

"She may be your boo but your behind is blocking everyone's view."

Sasha scowls at Freddie and sits back down ever so slowly. As he leans back, your eyes slowly adjust to the dim light and you spot the back of a familiar head at the table across from yours. When the head turns, there's no question.

"Oh my god," you mouth.

Sasha and Freddie are too engrossed in the show to notice. You give Sasha a kick under the table.

"Ouch!" he says, reaching down to rub his shin.

You widen your eyes and tilt your head to direct his attention toward the table behind Sasha. Sasha widens his own eyes then shakes his head, not understanding.

You try an exaggerated nod. Sasha turns his palms up, still confused. Meanwhile, Freddie sits utterly oblivious between you, smiling and bobbing his head in time with the music.

Finally, you point your finger in a circular motion, trying to indicate to Sasha that he needs to turn around. The number onstage comes to a close and the audience applauds, hoots, and whistles. Sasha still isn't getting the message and claps with the crowd. There's a sudden quiet moment as the stage darkens before the next song.

"Honey, I have no idea what—" Sasha says too loudly.

You freeze as Han Lee slowly turns in his chair. "Honey?" he asks.

"Hey, Han." You flip your ponytail behind you and cut your eyes at Sasha.

"Oh, lord." Sasha shakes his head. "That's what you were trying to tell me."

Han is out of his chair in an instant to give you a kiss on the cheek, his eyes bright. He squats beside you as the next number starts. "What are you doing here?" he whispers.

"A friend of Sasha's is in the show. And I'm here, touring. Vegas stop. What about you?"

"One of my old backup dancers is in the show too. Small world!" Han tells you, flashing his megawatt smile.

"It certainly is." You can't help but smile back. Han's enthusiasm is instantly disarming. It's one of his biggest assets. He's as boyish and adorable as you remember—and still unbelievable sexy.

Han hangs onto the back of your chair and accidentally brushes a finger against your shoulder as he adjusts his position. His touch sends a wave of familiar pleasure through you. You feel your nipples harden under the silk of your top. "It's so good to see you," he says. "You look gorgeous."

"Thanks. You look really good, too." And he does. Though he's just as you remember him in many ways somehow he looks more mature. His neck has thickened and his biceps bulge beneath his shirt as he steadies himself on your chair.

The music sweeps into full volume and Han leans close so you can hear him. He whispers into your ear, sending a fresh chill to your core. "You want to catch up after the show? Grab a drink or something?"

Out of the corner of your eye, you notice Sasha pretending not to watch your interaction, a disproving smirk on his face.

"Um, maybe," you answer. "Can I text you?"

"Sure," he says, hopping to his feet, then leaning back down to whisper, "I love it that you still have me in your phone."

A familiar heat rises to your cheeks as he returns to his seat.

Sasha shoots you a warning look then returns to watching the show.

You're distracted as you watch, thinking about the crazy turn of events you've experienced in just one night. You knew Vegas would be more than an average tour stop, but you never dreamed you'd run into Han here, or that he would seem so different—but familiar in all the right ways. Or that you'd meet Jett, with his sexy Australian accent and hypnotic eyes. You glance over at Han, his spiky black hair a crazy silhouette against the backdrop of the lighted stage. Still, you can't stop, try as you might, you can't stop thinking about Crispin. Something about the way you left things feels so unsettled. Maybe a night together in Vegas is exactly what you need. You think for a moment, pick up your phone, and hit the message icon.

To text Jett, turn to page 118.
To text Crispin, turn to page 85.
To text Han, keep reading.

Drinks after. Where do you want to go?
The screen remains blank for a few minutes then lights up brilliantly.
I know a fun place. Unless you have somewhere in mind
Nope, your call. Looking forward to catching up
Me2!
You set the phone face down on the table and immediately feel a

knot of unease in your stomach. You attempt to return your attention to the show but images of your past with Han begin to flicker uninvited into your mind: your first kiss on the red carpet at the Platinum Music Awards. That time he sent twenty-three bouquets of roses (one for every day you had been together) to your music video shoot, and the leaked photos the media published right after. His infamous "I'm stuck on Honey," rap on the *Ellie Z. Show*. The tabloids ate it up, making your new romance their cover story of the moment.

Of course Sasha believed Han's grand and very public gestures were nothing but PR stunts, a strategy designed to self-catapult Han to the top. But Sasha wasn't privy to the quiet moments you and Han shared. On your third date, Han bought out the entire Rockefeller Center ice rink so you had the glassy expanse of perfectly smooth ice all to yourselves—just because you'd mentioned once that skating on that rink had been a dream of yours as a child. He was romantic and sweet in so many ways. And he was amazing in bed, generous and attentive. Thinking about it brings on an involuntary chill.

You still feel a little guilty about how it ended. As the weeks went on, the media attention became more than a little grating. You started to find little things about Han that annoyed you—the way he constantly checked his cell phone throughout your dates, the way he loved to tweet a controversial comment or post a photo that caused a media buzz or an online feud with other celebs, the way he caught his reflection in every store or restaurant window you passed when you took a simple walk together. You started to think Sasha was right, that Han was nothing more than a "climber," who wouldn't be nearly as famous had he not dated you. When Crispin came back into the picture and you were about to go on tour, it seemed like a perfect time to make a break. Looking back, you're not entirely sure you gave Han a fair chance. He was devastated when you ended it.

You only notice the show has ended when Sasha jumps to his feet, whistling and clapping like a maniac. You join him, applauding as the cast bows and blows kisses to the audience.

"That was amazing!" Sasha says. "I'm going backstage to find Carlie."

You hesitate a moment too long.

"You coming?" Sasha asks.

"She's your friend. You should go."

Sasha narrows his eyes at you, "That's how you're gonna play it?"

Freddie looks back and forth between you, utterly bewildered. "What did I miss?"

Sasha puts a hand on his hip and leans in toward Freddie. "A blast from Henrietta's past has caught her attention. And we've lost it apparently. That's how highly we rate."

"Sasha, you know it's not like that," you tell him.

"I know exactly what it's like, Henry, and so do you, which makes it all the more disgraceful."

Freddie looks back and forth between you again. "I'm lost," he finally says.

"Well, then, come with me and let's get you found." Sasha links arms with Freddie and leads him off backstage, cutting his eyes at you over his shoulder. "Don't say I didn't warn you," he says as he walks off with Freddie.

You roll your eyes at his drama and turn to find Han at your side.

"What was that all about?" he asks.

"Just Sasha being Sasha," you explain.

"How weird is it that you and I would both be here at the same time? It's crazy! But I'm really glad to see you, Honey."

"Yeah"—you smile up into his warm, dark eyes—"me too." You glance around the room, which is starting to clear, but you have an odd sense you are being watched and want to avoid drawing unwanted attention. "So, should we head out?"

"Totally. What would you think about going back to my place?" Han runs his fingers through his jet-black hair. "I have this sick suite with a hot tub and an amazing view. It's only two blocks away. I have a car waiting outside."

That Han is suggesting a private location, away from prying eyes, is a pleasant surprise. It takes you only a second to answer. "Sounds perfect."

Han's suite is indeed "sick." Like your suite, it boasts a huge wall of windows overlooking the Strip. But unlike yours, it also has a balcony housing a hot tub the size of a small swimming pool. Enclosed in glass on all sides, the balcony appears to float free from the side of the building. The lighting casts an eerily exotic blue-green glow that filters through the glass walls and disappears into the night.

"I'm going to go change," Han says, handing you a robe. "Bathroom's right there. Meet you in the hot tub?"

Han's enthusiasm is contagious, and the hot tub looks inviting.

You slip into the bathroom, skim out of your clothes, and wrap yourself in the thin robe, the silk cool and slick against your warm skin.

Han is already in the hot tub when you walk back out onto the balcony. He pops open a bottle of Cristal, drizzling a froth of champagne into the water.

"Damn! That's like fifty dollars' worth of champagne down the tubes," he laughs.

"It's good for the skin," you tell him, untying your robe and dropping it at your feet.

Han's eyes are immediately on your body, hungrily taking in every inch. "Damn!" he says again. "How do you look better than I even remember? God, Honey, you better get in here before I come over there."

You ease into the water and Han moves toward you, sending a gentle wave of warm water over your breasts.

"Turn around," he tells you. As he goes to work on your shoulders, you remember one of the things you liked best about Han—he gives a fantastic massage. He kneads the tension from your neck and shoulders, working his way down your back with just the right amount of pressure.

"That feels amazing," you say, leaning back into him and feeling the tension of the day beginning to melt away under his expert fingers.

He works his way up from your back to your shoulders, then rubs small circles into your neck with his thumbs. He follows the path of his fingers with kisses, moving your ponytail aside and running his tongue from your earlobe down to the nape of your neck. The chills running down your spine create a delicious contrast to the water's warmth. "This is like fate, don't you think? That we are both here, tonight?" he whispers into your ear.

You turn to look at him. The look on his handsome face is pure enthusiastic joy and infatuation, and it is flattering. "It's definitely an interesting coincidence."

He kisses you, plunging his tongue in and out of your mouth. The chemistry between you is as strong as your remember, and it would be so easy to fall back into his arms.

Kissing Han, you feel an odd mix of the comfort of familiarity and thrill of something new.

The water is warm and soothing, the gentle bubbles tickling every inch of your skin. Han moves his hands to your breasts, which float just below the water's buoyant surface, squeezing them firmly then pinching each nipple before he takes one into his mouth and sucks hungrily. As he does, he moves to position himself over you, and you feel the hard urgency of his erection under the slick skin of his bathing suit. You move your hand to grasp him and he groans. Both the feel of him and the sound of his moan bring back so many memories.

There's a small part of you that wonders whether you should go any farther, but at the same time every ounce of your being wants to give in to this moment. Neither of you have made any promises. You're simply reconnecting, enjoying a chance rendezvous in a place where anything can happen and where secrets are kept.

You run your hands down Han's slick biceps. His muscles bulge as he leans into you. His chest has grown broader and more defined since were last together, and now even his stomach is pure muscle, the washboard ridges visible in the glow of the hot tub lights.

His body against yours, Han's wet swim trunks dig deliciously into you as he thrusts. After a few seconds, you kiss him deeply and you push the bathing suit down. You run one finger down his chiseled abs and then up from the base of his cock to the tip before grasping him again and pulling him toward you. His breath is coming fast and hard, and he has a look of intense desire in his eyes.

"Not yet," he says hoarsely. With a gleam of mischief in his eyes he dives under that water and finds your most sensitive area. He flicks his tongue back and forth then sucks deeply before resurfacing to kiss you again.

"As sweet as I remember," he says. He takes a sip of champagne, then lets the bubbly liquid flow from his mouth into yours.

"You're as crazy as I remember," you laugh.

"Crazy about you," he says, then rises from the water to hover over you. Something about the way the light reflects from his skin makes him appear otherworldly. Every muscle in his arms and chest are defined, glowing blue-green in reflected light. Again, you are overtaken by that odd feeling of familiarity mixed with the feeling of something so different. He lowers you gently, centimeter by centimeter, and pauses for a moment before thrusting powerfully into you.

You move together in the water, making gentle waves in surface of the water, soon echoed by waves of pleasure that roll through your body. Han joins you, moaning into your neck as he comes.

After, he wraps himself around you tenderly and holds you close.

You languish in the warmth of his embrace, the comfort of his familiar scent, and the satiety of your body, as you float together.

At last, Han takes in a big breath of air. "I don't want to let go," he tells you. "I never in a million years thought that this would happen tonight."

You smile. "What happens in Vegas . . ."

Han looks into your eyes. "Does it have to stay in Vegas?"

You're not sure whether he's joking.

Han brushes a strand of hair off of your shoulder. "I'm serious," he says. "I've missed you, Honey."

You don't know how to reply. "What brings you to Vegas, anyway?" you ask him.

"Oh! Right, you don't know. I mean, how would you? I'm actually auditioning—how funny it that? You know the show that gave me my start, *K-Pop*? Colton Powers is developing an American version, *Star Power*. They want me to be a judge. It would be a fun gig, and Powers thinks it's a compelling story, me returning to my roots, and all that."

"Can you make a TV show work with your tour schedule?"

"Believe me, they are bending over backwards to make it work. The audition is just a formality. I'm key to the whole show. They've already pretty much promised me a G6 to get me where I need to be if I'm on tour. The deal is pretty sweet."

"Sounds like it," you say. Han certainly hasn't lost his self-confidence. You wait for him to ask about you.

"Isn't this a ridiculous view?" he asks instead.

"It's spectacular." The glittering Strip below you is breathtaking, the desert lit with neon lights as far as you can see.

Han turns his head and kisses you again. "You're spectacular," he tells you. "What?" he asks when you pull away.

"Nothing," you say. "I just feel kind of strange all of a sudden. Probably overheated."

Han seems to take that as a compliment. "My bad." He smiles.

"I should get going," you tell him, rising from the water and finding a towel and your robe. "But this has been amazing, seeing you again."

Han jumps up, dripping water all over the balcony floor as he does. He wraps a towel quickly around his waist.

"You're not seriously going to run off? After that?"

You squeeze the water from your ponytail and wrap the robe snugly around you.

"I'm not running off," you say lightly. "I just have a lot going on tomorrow. I should get back to the hotel."

"Okay . . ." Han's face falls. "Was it that bad?"

Now you feel terrible. You certainly didn't want to give him the impression that you didn't thoroughly enjoy what just happened. "God, no!" you reassure him. "It was great. It's just—" you hesitate, not sure how much to say. "It's just kind of an odd feeling, being back with you. There's a lot of history. A lot of memories."

"Good memories, right?" he asks hopefully. "Mine are."

You decide to be honest. "Mostly. But things ended kind of awkwardly. You know that."

"Awkwardly?" Han looks thoroughly affronted. "Honey, you totally broke my heart."

You are stunned into silence by the look of genuine despondency on Han's face. "I'm sorry," you say after a moment. "It was a weird time in my life for a lot of reasons that didn't have anything to do with you."

"Yeah, I know," Han says. "But they had everything to do with Crispin Hershey."

"It wasn't like that, Han. I'm sorry if it seemed that way, but honestly you seemed to recover just fine. As I recall, not two minutes after we broke up, you were photographed all over the country with every wannabe actress in town. Plus, if I remember correctly, you spilled some pretty personal details in a million tabloid tell-alls. That didn't look like heartbreak to me."

"Well I'm sorry," he says, a look of genuine pain in his eyes. "I was hurt, Honey. What was I supposed to do?"

"Really?" You sigh, feeling the pull of the familiar argument spiral. It's one you and Han could never seem to escape, and it's exhausting. Verbally or via text, this is the way it always went. And somehow you always came out looking and feeling like the bad guy.

You take a deep breath and step back into the suite. "Han, thank you for tonight. I hope your new show is a success."

"Seriously?" Han asks, following you inside. He grabs another towel to quickly dry his hair. "Is this really how it's going to happen?"

"What's that saying?" you ask. "'Those who do not learn from history are doomed to repeat it.'"

"Right," Han scoffs. He leans against the kitchen counter and looks at you coolly. "Guess I should have seen this coming."

"Han, don't," you say.

"Don't what?"

You blow out a breath. "Nothing," you tell him, disappearing into the bathroom to change. You give Han a quick hug before you leave. "It really was good to see you," you tell him. It's the truth. The night gave you clarity—and closure.

"It's cool," he says as he closes the door behind you. "Good to see you, Honey Noble."

As the tour bus pulls away from the Max and you watch the Strip disappear like a mirage in the rearview mirror, you feel a surprising sadness, as though you've left something behind in the glittering desert. You pull your little notebook from under the dashboard and begin to jot down a string of lyrics.

A few hours into the drive, Sasha pulls into a roadside Quick Mart to refill the gas tanks and your Red Bull supply. As usual, he comes out with a haul of unhealthy snack options, crunching Corn Nuts between his teeth.

This time, though, he's walking with an unusually urgent pace and holding his phone in front of him. He looks both ways before climbing back into the bus, as though afraid someone might catch him in the act.

"I have to show you this," he says, kicking shut the door of the bus. "But I don't want you to freak out."

"About what?" you ask, your heartbeat intensifying in response to Sasha's muted panic.

Sasha plops the plastic bags of snacks onto the seat and hands you his phone. It takes only a second for the cover story to resonate: HONEY NOBLE TOPLESS IN VEGAS! the TMZ headline reads.

"What the hell?" You quickly skim through the brief article. There's a hugely enlarged, extremely grainy photo of you in Han's hotel hot tub. Two blue banners block your breasts from view. Still, you can clearly see that it's you, that you are indeed topless, and that it's Han sitting a few inches away from you, bathed in the balcony's blue-green light.

"Shit," you say. "Shit, shit, shit!"

"I tried to warn you, Henrietta," Sasha begins.

"Please," you snap. "I do not need an 'I told you so' right now." You pace back and forth in the narrow bus and try to think. "This is a total disaster!"

"It could be worse," Sasha says.

"How exactly?"

Sasha is uncharacteristically silent. "I'm trying to think. I can't think of an answer right now. But I'm sure it could be."

"That little bastard," you seethe.

You can see Sasha is dying to say something, but he graciously remains quiet.

You tear your eyes away from the screen and hand the phone back to Sasha. "I guess I should have expected this."

"You gave him the benefit of the doubt," Sasha says, graciously. "It's a good quality, thinking the best of people."

You pick up your phone and start composing a text. *Should have listened to my instincts,* you type, *you never fail to disappoint. Don't ever contact me again.* You pause over the Send button.

Sasha gently pulls your hand away. "He's not even worth it," Sasha tells you.

"You're right." You hit the backspace key until the text disappears.

Six months later, you're lounging by the pool in Orlando, the seventh-to-last stop of your tour. At last, you've become accustomed to the rhythms of the tour and you've learned to take these moments to relax. Freddie is busy working on a plan for a world tour. You don't even want to think about that now—although you have to admit it's pretty exciting.

You flip through a stack of tabloids, amazed to find that blurry photos of that infamous night on Han's balcony still appear in the magazines' glossy pages. *Must be a slow news week,* you think, laughing a little to yourself. Your anger at Han has dissipated. Considering the hugely increased media coverage, the solidly sold-out tour, and the extra buzz the photo has created, maybe you should thank him. Maybe you will, one day.

You laugh out loud as you read *WE*'s latest story about you, linking you to a "mystery man."

"What's funny?" Sasha asks from the chaise next to yours.

"Listen to this: *Honey Noble and her tall, dark, and handsome* date were seen leaving the Tropicana last week, you read. *The pair looked cozy as they walked arm in arm to their waiting car."*

"Let me see that," Sasha grabs the magazine from you and holds the page close to his face. "I look good!"

"Yeah, yeah, tall, dark, and handsome. Now will you do my back?"

"Roll it over," he says. He gives the bottle of high-powered sunblock a shake and expels a sizeable squirt onto your back. The cold liquid is shocking against your warm skin.

"That's freezing!" you squeal.

"Baby," Sasha teases.

You flinch as Sasha spreads the lotion over your lower back.

"Those costumes won't sit well against a sunburn," he says.

You relax and let him finish.

Sasha wipes the excess sunscreen on your thighs, and lies back on his chaise with a satisfied sigh.

"Don't you want me to do your back?" you ask him.

"Maybe when I'm ready to turn over," he answers.

"Well whenever you're ready, I've got your back, Mystery Man." You smile.

"I know you do," he tells you. "And I've got yours."

You take his hand, close your eyes, and enjoy your moment in the sun.

THE END

To take Honey on a new Bedventure, go back and choose a new path.

From page 109...

It's Honey. Show's wrapping up. Would love to get together if you're still free

Jett returns your text instantly.

Absolutely. What did you have in mind?

You up for a night in?

Sounds great to me. Your place or mine?

Ha ha. Same place, isn't it?

Pretty close. Let's check out your suite

Meet you in the lobby in 30

Can't wait

"After you," Jett says, holding the elevator door open as you glide into your suite. With Freddie and Sasha out for at least a few more hours with Carlie, you have the rare luxury of privacy.

"What can I get you?" you ask. "The bar's fully stocked."

"I don't really drink. Not anymore," Jett tells you. "But I'm dying for some water. I'm parched. Too much time in the DJ booth."

"One water, coming right up," you tell him, refreshed at the thought of a man who doesn't drink.

Jett settles into the corner of the huge leather sectional that takes up most of the living room. You join him with two tall glasses of water.

"Water for you, too?" he asks.

"I'm pretty parched myself. Must be the desert air."

"Could be," he agrees. "You need to stay hydrated here. You don't want those pipes failing you in the middle of your tour."

Jett takes a sip of water and swipes the back of his hand across his mouth. You have the sudden urge to reach out to touch the blonde stubble beginning to show just above his jawline.

"So," he stretches out his other arm across the back of the couch, just behind you. You ease back slightly, willing your shoulders to touch his arm. The distance is a little too great. "What brings a nice girl like you to a place like this?"

"You know," you say, "work."

Jett laughs, a lovely, low sound that makes you smile even wider. Something about this man makes you feel instantly comfortable. Could it just be because he feels so familiar from TV?

"No," he says, "I'm serious. I want to know about you. How did you get to be Honey Noble?"

You stretch your legs out in front of you.

"It's a very long story," you laugh.

"I'd like to hear it," Jett says.

You look at him for a moment to gauge whether he's being serious. The earnest look in his eyes tells you all you need to know.

"Well, to begin with, my real name isn't Honey." The moment you say it, you regret it. Why would you tell one of your most closely-held secrets to a complete stranger?

"You're kidding," Jett says with a faux shock and you see that he's kidding, too.

"What, you knew that already?" you ask.

"Well, I assumed," Jett tells you. "I suppose it could be one of those trendy Hollywood names like *Apple* or *Jellyfish.*"

"Jellyfish?" you ask.

"Maybe they only use that one in Australia."

"Maybe." You laugh. "No, mine is a stage name. Sort of. I mean, my parents did call me 'Honey' growing up."

"So, what is your actual name?"

You look at him for a long moment, not sure whether to tell him.

"You've got to tell me!" Jett says. "You started the story, now you've got to finish it."

"It's not something I tell a lot of people," you explain. "Or *any* people for that matter. In fact, Sasha's really the only other person—besides my parents—who knows."

"Sounds like a deep, dark secret," Jett says.

"It's pretty awful."

Jett reaches out to take your hand, sending a cascade of sparks up your forearm. "Your secret's safe with me," he promises.

You take a deep breath. "Okay," you tell him. "Brace yourself."

Jett sits perfectly still and raises his blond eyebrows.

"It's Henrietta," you mutter.

"What?" he asks. "I didn't catch that."

"Don't make me say it again."

Jett leans close and looks you in the eyes. "Just whisper it to me."

You lean in and whisper, "Henrietta."

Jett watches your lips as you say in, then leans in and kisses you, a long, deep kiss that makes your head swirl.

"Henrietta is a beautiful name," he says.

"Now I know you're not telling the truth," you tease. "Which makes everything else you've just said feel kind of suspect."

"I am telling the truth," Jett argues. "Henrietta is kind of a famous name in Australia. There's a city called Henrietta in Tasmania. And have you ever heard of Henrietta Dugdale? She was an Aussie women's rights pioneer. Look it up if you don't believe me."

Jett is so adorable in his earnestness. "I'm impressed," you smile.

"Eh," he says. "Not that impressive. Things every Aussie school kid knows. But I do know one thing," he tells you. "I'd really like to kiss you again. If it's okay with you."

You smile and lean into him. "Totally okay with me," you say.

His kiss is sweet and insistent, sending your head spinning again as he swirls his tongue against yours. You return his kiss completely, enjoying every moment of his embrace. He moves his hand to the back of your neck, squeezing and massaging as you kiss. You feel like you could kiss him forever.

You reach up to tangle Jett's fingers with yours and break away from the kiss for a moment. "Come on," you whisper. As he stands, you can't help but notice his erection straining against his jeans. He sees you notice and blushes.

"Sorry," he says. "Can't quite help myself."

"No need to apologize," you assure him, and lead him to your bedroom.

He stops at the doorway and lets you walk in ahead of him. "Nice," he comments.

"It is," you say. "A little more luxurious than the tour bus."

"I wasn't referring to the room," he says, and you look over your shoulder to see his eyes glued to your backside. He closes the door firmly behind him. Jett leaps onto the bed. "I have a secret to share with you, too. Only fair, since you told me one of yours." He pats the empty spot next to him.

You sit on the edge of the bed. "Okay," you tell him, a little anxious about what he is about to say.

"I know this will also come as an immense shock, but Jett is a stage name, too," he confides.

"Really?" You smile. "I actually thought it could be some kind of cool Australian name."

"No, sadly not. I'm going to tell you my real name, and I promise to never tell anyone yours if you promise to never tell anyone mine. Deal?"

"Deal," you agree.

"My real name is Jethro."

"Jethro?" You stifle a little snort as you try not to laugh.

"It's okay, it is funny. Which is precisely why my manager promptly changed it to Jett the minute I signed on with him. My parents were huge Jethro Tull fans. Hence the name. So, now we're even."

"It's still not as bad as Henrietta," you laugh.

"So, have I lost all appeal now that you know the truth about me? Or can I convince you to join me?" Jett asks, taking your hand.

"I have to take these off first," you say, sitting on the edge of the bed and unstrapping your shoes, which are killing your feet.

"Ahhh," you say, as you toss each strappy, black torture device to the floor. The straps have left indented, red welts on your feet.

"Ouch," Jett says. "Let me see those."

"Not very pretty," you warn him. "Dancer's feet. I was in toe shoes for a few years. No pedicurist can seem to undo the damage."

Jett smiles. "Let me take a look."

He gently picks up one of your aching feet in his hands. "Hold tight," he tells you, then races off to the bathroom. You hear the water running for a few moments. Jett returns with a two steaming towels plus a dry bath towel. "Lie back," he tells you, rolling one of the towels and placing it under your ankles. Next, he wraps a warm, damp, towel snugly around each foot. The sensation is heavenly and you immediately feel your sore feet begin to relax.

"That feels amazing," you tell him.

"Just wait," he answers.

After a few minutes he finds a bottle of lotion in the bathroom and removes the heated wrap from one foot. He uncaps the lotion and pours a generous dollop into his hand, rubs his hands together, then begins to work on your foot. The cool lotion is a perfect counter to the residual heat from the towel.

"Ahhh," you sigh.

Jett starts at the ball of your foot, squeezing gently and massaging, working his thumbs against your sore muscles as he rubs the lotion into your skin. You close your eyes and give in to the relaxation completely, allowing yourself to enjoy every sensation. He finishes the first foot and re-wraps it in the still-warm towel before he moves onto the other.

When he finishes with your other foot, Jett's hands move up to your calves, slowly relaxing the muscles there, then he moves to your lower thighs. His touch ignites a smoldering burn in your core. When he moves to your shoulders, you are slightly disappointed, but his fingers work magic there, too, rubbing the tension away.

"Turn over," he tells you.

You do, managing to keep the towels precariously balanced on your feet as you turn. Jett pauses for a moment then moves his hands back to the top of your shoulders, down your back, and then to your thighs again.

"You are a man of many talents," you tell him.

"A few," he allows, sliding his hands down to your buttocks, massaging each in slow circles.

He emits a low, "Mmmm," as he does.

He finishes with a light stroke up and down your back, then places a single kiss at the nape of your neck, sending shivers down your spine.

"How's that?" he asks. "Better?"

"You have no idea," you tell him. "I'm going to sleep like a baby."

"You're tired? I can let you rest."

"Not on your life." You pull him into a deep kiss. Every inch of your skin is beautifully relaxed and deliciously aroused at the same time, and you don't want the feeling to end.

You strip off his shirt, leaving only a little necklace on a leather cord hanging around his neck. You yearn to feel his muscled chest against your skin.

He seems to pick up on your thoughts and reaches around to unzip your top, moaning as your breasts spill free. His eyes rest there for a moment, but he refrains from reaching out to touch them. Instead, he pulls you close. His skin is hot against yours, and you can feel the rapid beating of his heart.

He eases you back onto the bed so that you recline onto the pillows. He runs a finger down your forehead, pauses to press your bottom lip, then runs his finger down your chin, slowly from your neck, between your breasts, and down your stomach. He lowers his mouth and kisses you there, sending a new set of shivers to your toes.

With a series of small kisses, he moves up to just below your breasts, and lays his palm flat on your belly, gently skimming his fingers over your mound as he does, sending a new set of sparks through your body. With his other hand, he lifts one heavy breast, running his tongue along the low curve to just below your nipple. He moves his other hand up to gently pinch the nipple of the other breast.

You gasp in response, and reflexively push up into him. He smiles a little and begins to suckle your breasts slowly, one at a time, and moves his hand lower. He works his fingers beneath your waistband and finds your most sensitive spot, stroking you gently there. He deftly skims your leggings off and away.

He works rhythmically, and you close your eyes to see strobes of light begin to flash in your mind. You are returned to that first moment in his DJ booth, and you can hear the beat of the music perfectly echoing the rhythm of his strokes as brings you close.

When you grasp his hand to pull him away and reach into the LV clutch on the nightstand to extract a condom, Jett looks into your eyes and kisses you again, making the music pulse louder and lights dance behind your eyelids.

When he enters you, you can hardly breathe. You wrap your legs around his and bury your face in his neck as waves of pleasure pulse over you, in perfect time with the rhythm of the music in your mind.

He pulls back and looks into your eyes, then thrusts into you. You feel him shudder as he kisses you deeply.

You have no memory of falling asleep after, and you wake in the morning to a feeling of complete peace. You gently move out from under Jett's arm to peek at the clock. Seven thirty-six a.m. You rub your eyes and blink until they adjust to the light, then roll back over to watch Jett in his sleep.

His hair is adorably mussed in a wild array of blonde spikes and his face is beginning to show the slightest hint of the need for a morning shave. He seems to sense you watching, and slowly opens his eyes. When he sees you, he breaks into an immediate smile.

"Good morning," he says, his voice still hoarse with sleep.

"A very good morning," you agree, and intertwine his fingers with yours.

Just then, the door to your room swings open.

"Well, well, well," Sasha sashays into the room, wearing a tank top and a pair of zebra-print drawstring pants. "Look what the bee brought home." He makes himself at home, sprawling out at the foot of the bed, stretching his long frame and propping himself up on one elbow. "I guess you do catch more flies with honey!"

You throw a pillow at Sasha's head. "Very funny."

Sasha rolls onto his stomach, kicking his legs into the air behind him and showing off his fuzzy unicorn slippers.

"What are you wearing?" you laugh.

"Didn't realize you had a dress code," he answers, arching an eyebrow in Jett's direction. "This is like some kind of wild dream, being in bed with the two of you," Sasha rolls onto his back. "Not exactly as I imagined it, but still not a bad way to wake up."

To his credit, Jett chuckles as he rubs sleep from his eyes.

Sasha rolls back onto his stomach and pushes up off the bed.

"Well, I will leave you two lovebirds alone. But do invite me next time around. It's always more fun with unicorn slippers."

"I've got to look into getting a pair for myself," Jett laughs.

"Oh, I can hook you up," Sasha winks.

"Goodbye, Sasha," you call, as Sasha glides out of the room, blowing you a kiss before closing the door ever so gently. "I think he likes you," you tell Jett.

Jett blinks his eyes and runs his fingers through your hair. "Is that what that was?"

"Believe me, that was much better than it usually goes when he meets my b—uh, some of my friends."

Jett grins mischievously. "What were you just going to say?"

"What do you mean?" you ask, all innocence.

"It sounded like you were about to say something other than just *friends*."

"No, I wasn't." You smile, roll out of bed, and pull the sheet around you.

You quickly brush your teeth and return to find Jett sitting on the edge of the bed and pulling on his shirt.

"Busy day?" you ask him.

"Not until tonight. But I've got to hit the gym. It's kind of my morning ritual. Care to join me?"

You think for a second, knowing you'll get plenty of exercise on stage tonight, but a little extra cardio—and a little more time with Jett—can't hurt. "Sure," you tell him.

You slip into a sports bra and your Lululemons, slide on a pair of sneakers, and throw your hair into a high ponytail.

Jett clearly knows his way around the gym. He cycles through a series of reps on several machines.

You choose a pair of ten-pound hand weights and work on your triceps.

"Nice form," Jett comments.

"Thanks." You smile.

Jett moves to a bench and loads a bar with a stack of heavy-looking weights.

"Spot me?" he asks.

"Um, sure?"

"Just make sure I don't drop the bar on my neck and suffocate."

"No pressure." You laugh nervously.

"Don't worry. I haven't dropped a bar yet," Jett reassures you.

Jett lies on his back on the narrow bench and places his hands on either end of the heavy bar, just inside the each stack of weights. You stand by his side, not sure what you're supposed to be doing.

"The spotter usually straddles the lifter," Jett directs you.

You look around, glad the gym is empty except for the two of you. "Seriously?" you ask.

"All you have to do is stand over me and give me a hand placing the bar back on the rack when I'm finished with my reps."

You gracefully step over Jett's prone body and stand, legs splayed, over his chest. You feel very silly.

Jett looks up at you and grins. "This is a much better view that I'm used to."

Jett easily lifts the bar from the rack on which it rests and brings it down to his chest in a slow, controlled motion, before heaving it back up. His chest and arms bulge as he lifts. He continues the exercise until a sheen of sweat breaks out on his chest and brow. He heaves the heavy bar up one last time. "Okay," he says.

You stand at the ready as Jett lifts the bar with trembling hands toward the rack. You reach to help him make the final inches, your hands splayed on either side of his, and together you set the bar back into its resting place.

"Thanks," Jett breathes. "Couldn't have done that without you." He moves his hands so that they cover yours, still wrapped around the cool, steel bar. "Come here," he whispers, and you lean in to kiss him, tasting the slightly salty flavor of his workout on your lips.

His hands move to your back as he kisses you, pressing you to him, and you brace yourself against his strong chest.

"God," he says, "you look so good in those pants." He moves his hands to your backside and squeezes gently, then presses you to him. You feel him hard and ready against you through the thin cotton of your workout pants.

Jett rises to sit on the bench, straddling it as he pulls you to him. He runs his hands lightly over your breasts, making your nipples stand out hard against the thin fabric of your sports bra. He pulls you onto his lap and thrusts against you, the slippery fabric of his shorts providing just the right amount of friction. You reach past him and use the weight bar to steady yourself as you move against him.

Your head swims as he kisses you again, and your body is on fire from the mix of adrenaline and pure lust. "Hold on," you say, and break away for a moment to bolt the door so no one walks in on you. You can feel Jett's eyes follow you as you walk toward the door.

As you walk back to join him, he stands. His erection is huge, straining at the elastic of his shorts. He pulls you to him to kiss you, thrusting his tongue in and out of your mouth, takes you by the shoulders to turn you away from him, then bends you over the weight bench. He pulls down just the back of your stretchy bottoms, runs a hand reverently over your backside, and strokes you. He moans as he gauges your readiness. You feel him bare against your buttocks, thrusting gently, then hard as he drives into you, filling you instantly. With one hand he reaches around, sliding his fingers under the elastic bottom edge of your bra to squeeze and caress your nipple as he thrusts. With every thrust, he slides almost completely out and then plunges deeply back in, bringing you quickly to the edge. When he brings his other hand around to stroke you, it is too much to bear, and you succumb to waves of pleasure. Jett quickly joins you, squeezing your breast and burying his head in your shoulder as he comes with a primal growl.

A second later, there's a knock at the door.

"Oh no!" You scramble to pull your pants back up and reposition your bra.

"Coming!" Jett yells, sending you into peals of laughter you stifle with the back of your hand.

"Should I open it?" you whisper.

"Give me a second," Jett says, trying to adjust himself. At last, he gives up and grabs a towel, which he holds as casually as possible over the front of his shorts while he unlocks the door with his other hand.

The muscle-bound weightlifter waiting on the other side of the door gives Jett a suspicious look as he opens the door.

"That wasn't locked, was it?" Jett asks smoothly.

The meathead grunts and pushes past you on his way to the weight rack. You give Jett a look as you both exit hastily.

Jett leaves you at the door to your room, giving you one last kiss. "Thanks for a great workout," he says, making you giggle as you close the door.

Sasha sits on the couch, flipping through a Vegas tourist guide.

"Hey, Sash," you say, attempting to slip past him.

"Not so fast," he stops you in your tracks. "Come sit." He pats the empty spot on the couch, beside him.

"I'm all sweaty," you tell him, trying to escape. "I really need a shower."

"I bet you do," Sasha replies, a droll smirk on his face. "But you can grant me two minutes of your time."

You perch lightly on the edge of the sofa.

"You seem awfully flushed, Henrietta," Sasha says. "I know you didn't work out that hard."

You can feel your face redden as you drop your eyes. You can't help but grin.

"Wow," Sasha observes. "You really like him."

You raise your gaze to meet Sasha's eyes. "I do really like him," you admit. "He's a good guy."

"And he is smoking hot," Sasha adds.

"He's not bad," you admit. "We're having a good time. But what happens in Vegas . . ." You trail off wistfully, painfully aware that tomorrow morning the tour moves on, and that you still haven't officially ended things with Crispin, even if it feels like he's ended things with you.

Sasha takes your hand and squeezes it gently. "For what it's worth, I like him, too." That's high praise from Sasha, and you don't take it lightly. "You never know, maybe your paths will cross again. Or maybe you can convince him to become a groupie if the DJ gig doesn't work out."

"Yeah," you say. "I don't think that's going to happen."

"Well, I'm glad you're having fun. I was beginning to think those frown lines might become permanent."

"What about you?" you ask. "Are you having fun?"

"Honey, Vegas is a gay man's dream. Between the drag queens, Elvis impersonators, and the married men looking for a hookup in almost every public restroom, what is there not to love?"

"Sasha!"

"I love it that I can still shock you, Henrietta." Sasha laughs. "But seriously, if you ever find your way into a residency here, I won't be mad. Then I can have my share of casual sex and you and Jett can live happily ever after."

"It's tempting," you tell him.

"Go get that shower," Sasha says. "I want to go explore the Strip with you on my arm before your appearance this afternoon. Maybe you can invite Jett along."

"Sounds like fun," you say, and make your way to the bathroom.

You spend the day popping in and out of casinos and exploring Vegas's shops, both the high-end boutiques and the tacky tourist stops. Jett takes you to his favorite diner and you share a sinful chocolate milkshake. Sasha seems to genuinely enjoy Jett's company and the repartee of a companion who can keep up with him. You're sure he's enjoying the view, too. Jett's cheeks have picked up a tiny hint of color from his walk outside, making his blue eyes glow against the frame of his dark lashes. Everywhere you go, you're stopped for a selfie or an autograph, and you bask in the adoration of your fans and the burgeoning friendship you feel developing between the man who means so much to you and the man who is beginning to mean more to you with every minute you spend together.

The day goes by too quickly. You say goodbye to Jett as he heads to his room to get ready for work and you go back to your room to prep for your appearance.

That night, the ballads in your set list seem to take on a new meaning. When you sing the opening line to "I Never Knew Love 'Till I Found You," you instantly picture Jett's face. You scan the first few rows of the audience, hoping maybe he's found a way to make it to the show, but he's nowhere to be seen.

You host a hasty meet-and-greet after your final encore and head back to your hotel room, thinking maybe Jett will come to visit when he's finished with work. When he doesn't appear, you shower for the second time that day, wash your face and towel dry your hair, then head to bed.

You wake from a dreamless sleep to feel the covers lift, the bed dip, and someone slide in beside you. The scent of smoky club, subtle cologne, and the signature scent you can only describe as something green, tells you right away that Jett has come to join you.

He presses his body against yours, fitting every angle of his body against the curve of your back. "Sorry to wake you," he says, nestling his head into your neck. "I just had to see you. And Sasha didn't think you would mind."

You roll toward him, unsure whether you are awake or have found yourself lost in a dream. "Sasha was right," you tell him, and pull him into a kiss.

You make love in a sleepy, dream-like state, then curl up against Jett and fall back to sleep feeling safe and satiated, his body wrapped around yours.

The next morning is a bustle of activity as the tour prepares to move on. Jett stays by your side, helping you pack and even bringing your bags to the bus to save Sasha the extra work.

You spend the morning trying not to think about the fact that you are leaving and that you have no idea when you'll see Jett again. You want to remember your time with him as happy, and you don't know why you've even allowed yourself to become so attached when you knew from the start that it could never last.

When the last of the costumes are loaded, Jett walks you to your bus, dragging his feet slightly along the sand-dusted pavement.

Sasha interrupts your goodbye to give Jett an enormous hug. "Thanks for being an excellent host."

"Totally my pleasure," answers Jett. "I'll miss you guys."

"I'll miss you more," smiles Sasha, blowing Jett a kiss and skipping up the stairs to the bus. He turns around with a slight shimmer in his eyes. "You sure you don't want to give up that silly DJ gig and hop aboard?"

Jett laughs. "It's certainly tempting."

"That's exactly what Honey said when I suggested a Vegas residency," Sasha tells him. "Spooky."

"Really?" asks Jett.

"Really," Sasha tells him. "I, for one, think we would make a fabulous threesome. Think about it. It's not too late!" He winks at Jett then disappears into the bus, leaving you and Jett alone at last.

You both begin to speak at once, then look at each other and laugh.

"You go," says Jett.

You look down at the dusty ground then up into his clear, blue eyes. "I was just going to say how much I've enjoyed this," you tell him. "It really has been exactly what I needed."

"Good," Jett says, kissing you softly on the lips. "I feel exactly the same way. You're an amazing woman, Honey. I am so glad to have met you."

"Well, I hope we'll meet again. Someday."

"I know we will, Honey," Jett tells you. "And until then, you've got to promise stay in touch, no matter how busy you get. Will you do that?"

"Yes," you promise.

Jett folds you into a long embrace and kisses the top of your head. "Safe travels," he tells you.

You nod your head, unable to get any more words out around the lump in your throat.

You buckle yourself into your seat, push your sunglasses up onto the bridge of your nose, and try not to look back as the bus pulls away. At the last second, you turn to see Jett standing stationary as he watches you leave. Glimmering waves of heat flash around him and then slowly envelope him until he disappears like a mirage in the distance.

Sasha reaches out and squeezes your leg. "You've still got me, right?" he asks.

"Thank goodness," you tell him, blinking a film of moisture from your eyes.

You rummage under the dashboard until you find the little notepad you have stashed away there for moments like this, and begin to pen the lyrics to "Mirage," which exactly nine months from now will take on a life of its own as your next hit single.

Four grueling months later, the Nobility tour finally wraps. Even though you love touring, it takes a physical toll that requires a lengthy recovery. True to your word, you've kept in as much contact with Jett as you could. As soon as you stopped touring, Jett began traveling internationally to DJ at the hottest clubs all over the world and to do PR for the Max. Lately, you've been texting, even returning his calls via text. Sometimes the sound of his voice brings on a longing and sadness that takes days to shake. You don't mean to push him away and you know you have the habit of closing yourself off when you're afraid you might be vulnerable, but it's a habit that's difficult to break.

When the photos of you and Jett on the Vegas Strip went public, Crispin went ballistic, sending you a string of angry texts that led you to finally decide to make your break permanent. Thinking about it now, you know that everything happens for a reason; Jett came into your life just when you needed him most. You can only imagine what might have happened if you'd tried to resuscitate your unstable relationship with Crispin. Lately, you've heard rumors he's back with Trixie again. You're glad things ended when they did.

Back at home, you spend your days in the cool solace of your house, luxuriating in mostly unscheduled days, the fact that you can choose to cook a meal in your own kitchen or simply curl up on your comfy armchair and write your music. You feel your creativity resurging as the days pass. You find your thoughts returning to Jett over and over again and the ache that is left by what could have been lends inspiration to your songs. You can't believe that after all these months the feelings haven't faded, no matter how hard you try to push them away.

One day, you're sitting at your piano, plinking away at the melody for a new song, when you hear the front door open.

"Hello?" you yell, your voice echoing down the hall.

You hear footsteps approaching and are sure it must be Sasha, the only person besides you who has a security clearance and a key.

Jett steps out of the sunlight, looking more gorgeous than you remember. He seems taller somehow, and his blue eyes shine with the same otherworldly glow you see in your dreams.

"Hi," is all he says, then quickly bridges the distance between you, pulling you into an embrace that feels as though it fills up every empty space inside of your heart.

He looks into your eyes and kisses you, setting off a shimmer of fireworks behind your eyelids.

"Are you really here?" you ask, unsure of your own eyes.

"I really am," he assures you.

"Oh my God," you say, the tears you've held back for so many months spilling down your cheeks. "I missed you. So much."

"Me too," Jett says, kissing you again.

"How did you get in here?" you ask him.

"I have a good friend who happens to have a key."

"You're welcome!" calls Sasha from the direction of the doorway.

You laugh through your tears as you hear the door close behind him.

"I had to see you," Jett tells you, wiping the tears from your cheeks. "Those short little texts were not nearly enough. And you said you would call."

"I tried," you tell him. "It just made me miss you too much."

"Well, no need to miss me now."

You lead Jett to the couch and he fills you in on his news. He's in town to shoot the pilot for a *Silversmiths* reunion series. He'll play the grown-up version of his childhood character, now a successful rock star.

"My acting is a little rusty," he admits, "but with any luck, fans of the original show will forgive me and watch anyway. And if it gets picked up, I'm here to stay. I'm thinking it could be time to settle down."

"I'll be watching—and Sasha will, too, of course," you tell him. Suddenly the light in the room seems brighter, colors more vibrant. "Jett, I'm so glad you're here."

"Me too," he says again. "You have no idea."

Jett stays with you throughout the shoot. You spend your days at the studio while Jett is on set, your evenings in lively conversation or playing silly board games with Jett and Sasha, and your nights in Jett's arms.

You wait on pins and needles to find out whether *The Silver-smiths Shine* will be picked up. The night you get the news, you, Jett and Sasha celebrate together with dinner and champagne. Somehow, your unique little threesome balances one another perfectly.

Club 2000 throws you a private debut party, when your single, "Mirage," drops. All of your friends, your tour cast and many of its crew members, and even your family are present. Jett guests in the DJ booth. When the song comes on, you climb up into the booth and pull him into your arms.

"You know I wrote this about you," you tell him.

"Really?" he asks. "That is so romantic."

He listens to the lyrics as the song plays. "Flattering as it is, though, I need you to know how real this is to me." Jett drops to one knee, causing the crowds to explode into cheers.

"Honey Noble," he says, pulling a huge, sparkling diamond from his pocket. "I've loved you from the moment I laid eyes on you in that smoky DJ booth. Here we are, together in a DJ booth again. Seems fitting." He takes your hand in his, and looks into your eyes. "Would you do be the great honor of marrying me and making me the happiest man alive?" His eyes shine as he holds the glittering ring in front of him.

Music pulses and light strobes through the smoky room. Sasha stands in the distance, phone trained on you to catch the moment. You see your siblings in the crowd, beaming as they wait for you to answer. You pull Jett up to kiss him as he slides the ring onto your finger. "Yes," you tell him. "Yes!"

As the last strains of your song drift into silence, you wonder whether maybe this is all a mirage, maybe just a dream. If so, you hope you'll never wake up.

THE END

To take Honey on a new Bedventure, go back and choose a new path.

From page 49 and page 69...

Jett escorts you to the elevator and pauses before the door slides shut. For a moment you think he's going to lean in for a kiss, but instead he settles for an awkward hug goodnight.

You close the door to your room and are instantly grateful for the silence. "Hello?" you call.

"Hello!" comes Freddie's booming voice from the other side of his bedroom as you enter the suite. He emerges, still dressed in the suit he wore during the day. "Turning in early?" he asks.

"I guess. I was thinking about doing some gambling. When in Vegas, and all that. But my hand is throbbing and my head doesn't feel much better after that noisy club.

"I'm going to take a quick shower," you say. "I smell like smoke."

Ten minutes later, you feel entirely better. You hair and skin feel and smell fresh and you're wrapped in a luxurious hotel robe. Freddie sits on the sofa, paging through a file. His reading glasses make him look even more handsome. You curl up on the other end of the sofa.

"Sasha's not back yet?" you ask.

"Nope. Must be having fun." Freddie tosses the file onto the coffee table and looks at you for a long moment. "You know you look beautiful without any makeup on."

"Thanks," you tell him.

"I don't know whether I've ever told you how lucky I feel to represent you; that you signed on with me. I know you had options."

"Well, Freddie, thank you again. I feel just as lucky. I couldn't think of a better person to represent me."

"Well," Freddie smiles, "since we're in Vegas and I'm not gambling and you're not gambling, we may need to entertain ourselves with something more pedestrian. Did you see that there's a stack of board games under the bar? What do you say to a friendly game of Parcheesi?"

"Parcheesi?" you ask. "I've never played."

"Honey, you haven't lived until you've played Parcheesi!" Freddie rises to grab the game.

You set up at the little table in the corner. You're pretty sure Freddie lets you win the first round but he beats you handily the second time. Freddie brings his final game piece home apologetically.

"It's okay," you tell him. "I can take it."

"Well, you did very well for your first Parcheesi," Freddie says with a grin. "And considering you had to play with your left hand." He boxes up the game and walks back to the bar. "How is it feeling anyway?"

"A little better," you tell him. "Definitely not as sore as it was. But it's a little red around the edge of the bandage. Probably just from pressure. But I'm going to have the doctor look at it when we get to New York."

"Let me take a look," Freddie offers. You gingerly reach out to rest your hand in his. He gently lifts the edge of the bandage to peer at the periphery of the incision. "It is not as red under the bandage," he pronounces. "I think you are going to live."

"Thank you, doctor." You laugh, looking up into Freddie's eyes. Something about the warmth of his smile, the tenderness of his touch, the concern in his face makes you melt. You reach up with your other hand and lay it against his cheek, rough with stubble. "Freddie, I—"

Afterward, you won't remember who initiated the kiss. You'll just remember that it tasted of mint, felt like safety, and made your head swim.

It is Freddie who ends it, pulling away as if from a magnetic force and stepping back blinking, as if coming back to his senses.

"I don't know what came over me, Honey," he stammers. "I'm so sorry!"

You take his hand. "Don't apologize," you tell him. "That wasn't just you."

He runs his hands through his thick, black hair, peppered with just a few strands gray. "I think," he says gravely, "that we should go to bed." He blushes hotly. "Alone, I mean. Of course."

You smile, amused by how discombobulated Freddie is. "I knew what you meant," you assure him.

Now your heart is pounding fast again and your own pulse whooshing in your ears. That kiss was a pure shot of adrenaline and you know it will be hours until you sleep. Unless . . .

"Freddie, do you have any more of those pills you gave me last night."

Freddie's eyebrows draw into a tight line of concern. "That was only a one-time thing," he says.

"So it will be two times," you tell him. "This will be the last one, I promise."

"Hmmm," is all Freddie says, thinking.

You lay a hand on his bicep. "I swear."

Freddie holds up one finger. "Last time," he tells you.

"Last time," you agree. "Scout's honor."

Freddie goes to his room and returns with a single pill, which he deposits into your palm. "Good night, sleeping beauty." He gives you a chaste kiss on the forehead.

Sleep hits you mercifully quickly.

The next morning is a packed day of interviews, appearances, and of course the show with its meet-and-greets before and after. You and Freddie act as though nothing happened. You do your best to push aside thoughts of the night before but every time you have a quiet moment, the confused jumble of emotions springs back to the surface.

On the car ride back from your morning show appearance, Sasha senses your mood. "Okay, Henrietta, spill it," he says, tilting his sunglasses away from his eyes.

"Spill what?"

"Whatever it is," he drawls. "You are unusually quiet today. Something is going on."

So much of you wants to share what happened between you and Freddie, but at the same time you know it could be a very bad idea. You're so glad you decided to not let things go any further with Jett; things are already complicated enough as they are.

"Just thinking, I guess," you tell him.

"About?"

"Just, stuff."

"Henry." Sasha looks you in the eyes over the rims of his shades. "I am not a dentist."

"It's nothing," you tell him, knowing that now that you've hinted that you are thinking about something, Sasha's not going to relent until he has successfully extracted the information. "Well, I have been wondering about Freddie. What do you think of him?"

"What do you mean you've been wondering about Freddie?"

"I mean, what kind of person do you think he is? He's a good guy, right?"

Sasha knits his eyebrows, clearly confused by your line of questioning. "Yes . . . he's a good guy. Why are you asking me this?"

"I don't know. We just spend so much time together, all of us, and I feel like I don't know him that well."

"Freddie is a character," Sasha says, "but you know I love him. Lord knows he gives me good advice when I need it. He's like a father figure to me. To both of us."

"Right," you say, catching Sasha's slight emphasis on the word *father*.

You decide to change the subject, and thankfully Sasha lets it drop.

That night, before the show, you and Freddie are left alone in your dressing room. Sasha has run off to ensure the costumes are in place and crew is making the many last-minute preparations for the production.

The tension between you is palpable. You feel as though there's an imaginary cord running between you, pulling you insistently toward him. This is what magnetism feels like, and it's almost impossible to fight. You do everything you can to avoid making eye contact for the few moments you are alone. You try to think of something to say to bridge the awkward silence, but Freddie carries on as though nothing is awry.

"Ready to go?" he asks.

"Yes, yes, let's do it," you answer then head down the hall to your meet-and-greet.

For the first time on tour, you flub a dance step during your "Waterfalls" routine. You gamely carry on, covering the misstep as smoothly as you can, and hope no one notices. You are relieved when the last number comes to an end. You've felt off all night.

Serge finds you in the dressing room as you are unstrapping your shoes. "You okay, Honey?" he asks you.

"Yeah, fine. Why?"

"I thought maybe you tripped, during "Waterfalls?" he says. It takes you a minute to decipher what he is saying, through his thick accent.

You look up at him, less surprised that he noticed than that he's taken the time to come check whether you are okay. "Yeah, I forgot a step," you admit. "I just blanked."

Serge smiles at you, his shock of dark hair falling over his eyes. "Happens to all of us," he says reassuringly. "You covered it like a pro."

"Thanks, Serge."

He leans against the doorframe, seems about to say something else, then nods his head.

"Well, I'll be going, then. Long day of travel tomorrow."

"Right," you smile. "Goodnight."

Serge turns to leave the dressing room.

"Hey," you stop him.

He turns back to you, an expectant look on his face.

"Thanks for checking in," you tell him.

"Of course," he says, his white teeth flashing as he smiles. "Goodnight."

Moments later, Freddie breezes into the room. Your heart clenches unexpectedly as the scent of his cologne fills the room. What is wrong with you?

You feel a hot blush rise to your cheeks and spin around quickly, away from Freddie.

"Another excellent show," he tells you.

"Thanks," you say, bending to unstrap your other shoe. It's no easy task with your injured hand.

"Can I help?" he offers, and kneels in his suit to help remove your shoe. "Even my big hands are probably more useful than your injured one."

"Ahhhh, that feels a thousand percent better," you sigh, wiggling your toes.

Freddie sets your shoe next to its mate. "Honey, do you have a minute to talk?"

Before you can answer, Sasha rolls into the room, lugging the heavy rack of costumes behind him.

"Whew!" he exhales. "Vegas, check!" He looks around to see Freddie standing awkwardly nearby. "Burning the midnight oil?" he asks.

Freddie straightens up and brushes the front of his slacks with his hands. "Yeah, well, I just need to talk to Honey for a minute before I go back to the hotel."

"Okay . . ." Sasha says. "Henry, let's get you out of that first so I can hang it up," he says, eyeing the costume you are still wearing. He hands you your robe and begins to unhook the elaborate fasteners at the costume's back. "Don't mind me," he says. "Talk amongst yourselves."

Freddie sits on the ottoman, "It is no problem. I can wait."

"What, you can't say what you have to say with me here?" Sasha asks, chuckling slightly.

"Actually no," Freddie replies. "We kind of need to talk privately. You know, business stuff."

"Alrighty then," Sasha catches your eye and you give a little shrug. He expertly drapes the robe around your back while you shimmy out of the costume and skim your stockings past your feet. He scoops up the discarded garments and you tie the robe snugly.

"You don't mind if I meet up with Carlie, do you?" Sasha asks. "Just for drinks. I won't be too late."

"Not at all," you answer.

Sasha hangs up the costume and heads for the door. "Well, I will leave you two to it, then. Ta-ta!"

" 'Night, Sasha," you call after him as he shuts the door to allow you privacy.

You fall into the comfy chair across from Freddie, who politely averts his eyes. "It's okay, I'm decent," you tell him.

He hesitantly brings his gaze to meet yours.

"So, what did you want to talk about?" you ask.

He looks down at his hands before answering. "Did I do something to make you feel uncomfortable? Today, I mean?"

"No," you assure him. "Not at all." You think for a moment before continuing, not sure how much of your feelings you really want to share. "I'm sorry I'm making you feel awkward. It's totally my fault. I wish I could just rewind. I don't know what I was thinking."

Freddie seems to take this in. He lets the silence spin out for a long moment before continuing. "It isn't entirely your fault," he says.

"It takes two to tango, right?" He smiles up at you, his eyes sparkling and the laugh lines around them becoming more pronounced.

"I guess." You smile.

Freddie takes in a deep breath. "Honey, you know how much I care about you, don't you?" he asks, and places his hand lightly on your knee. His touch sends a shimmer to your core, and you pull away ever so slightly, causing Freddie to immediately remove his hand.

"Sorry." Freddie frowns and drops his eyes. "Maybe this wasn't a good idea."

He rises to go, and every fiber of your being wants to stop him in his tracks. Still, part of you knows that he's right, that this is a terrible idea. Isn't it?

"Freddie." You place your hand on his arm. The heat of his skin radiates through the sleeve of his suit jacket.

He turns to look at you, gazing intently into your eyes. Without your shoes on, he seems much taller, and you stand slightly on tiptoe as you kiss him, cupping his deliciously stubbled cheek with your good hand. He kisses you gently then more deeply, patiently savoring every moment. Your head swirls but your thoughts are clear enough to wonder what he would be like in bed.

There's a sharp knock on the door and you pull away quickly.

"Hullo?" comes a raspy voice from the other side of the door.

Freddie looks you in the eyes again and kisses you very lightly before running his fingers over your lips, no doubt correcting your smeared lipstick.

He smiles at you and holds up a finger. "Who is it?" he asks mischievously.

"Is that Freddie?" the voice on the other side of the door asks.

"Maxx, is that you?"

"Open the door, you old coot!"

The door swings open, revealing Maxx Swagger. True to his name, he swaggers into the room, his lanky six-foot, five-inches all legs, gangly arms, and shaggy hair wrapped in a signature head scarf which hangs to his waist. Maxx bounds joyously over to Freddie and they clasp hands, briefly touch chests, and smack each other on the back.

"Maxx," smiles Freddie, "you look fantastic!"

Maxx scowls down at him. "I most certainly do not," he protests.

"Look what they've gone and done to my eyes! Went for a simple eye lift and now I look like a bloody alien!"

Freddie squints at his old friend and assesses the damage. "It is not that bad," he pronounces. "Maybe like an illegal alien, but definitely not an extraterrestrial alien," he teases.

"Bloody hell," Maxx says, "I knew it." He stops, seeming to notice you for the first time.

"Honey Noble!" he cries. He covers the distance between you in one long stride and kisses you on each cheek. "What a sight for sore eyes. Your show was absolutely brilliant! That bit when you floated down from the rafters—glorious! Couldn't have done that in my day, of course. All we had were ropes and pulleys. Would've ended up dropped on my head." He leans back to take a long look at you. "You are just as gorgeous offstage as on, did Freddie ever tell you that? I bet he didn't. And that voice! Like listening to the angels sing. You are going to go places, Honey Noble. Mark my word."

"Well thanks!" you reply, thoroughly entertained by the force that is Maxx Swagger. His presence utterly fills the room. He's a music legend, and now almost equally famous for the staggering number of plastic surgeries he's had. Aside from his signature hair and head scarves, he looks almost nothing like he did in his heyday. The transformation has only made him more famous.

"What are you doing in Vegas?" Freddie asks.

Maxx sighs dramatically. "Another one of my endless benefits. Everyone loves a good botched plastic surgery story. Then I heard Honey was playing, which meant you must be here with her. So here I am. Paying a visit to my old—very old (he gives you a conspiratorial wink when he says this)—friend."

"Okay, I'm ancient, I get the point," Freddie tells him.

"You, my friend, are a legend," Maxx says. "You up for a drink?"

"I think I have a few more hours left in me," Freddie replies.

Maxx turns to you. "Honey Noble, I would be honored if you would join us."

You think for a second, but know you would feel like an awkward third wheel if you took Maxx up on his offer. "Thanks," you answer, "but I'm really exhausted. And I need a shower. You two have fun. I'm going to crash."

"You sure?" Freddie asks, although you can tell from his tone he's only being polite.

"Totally sure," you say. "But thanks."

Back in your room it's blessedly quiet. You pace around the room, head still spinning from your latest encounter with Freddie. You pick up the little odds and ends that decorate the room. A pen emblazoned with the hotel logo. An odd glass paperweight that resembles a blue jellyfish. You walk to the bar and consider pouring yourself a drink, then think the better of it. What you need is sleep.

You walk to your room and strip off your clothes, folding them carefully and placing them in your suitcase. You sit on the edge of the bed and pick up the notebook you keep on your bedside table, in case song lyrics come to you on the threshold of sleep, as they often do. You tap your pencil on the empty page, feeling an idea imminent, just below the veil of conscious thought. When your agitation gets worse and nothing surfaces, you decide a shower might help.

You let the hot water run over your neck and shoulders, willing it to ease the tension you feel. You turn to let the steaming water run over your chest, and you feel your nipples harden. The memory of Freddie's kiss immediately jumps into your mind. You will the thought away, turning your back to the water. As you do, you imagine Freddie's hands kneading your shoulders, the smell of his cologne as he rubs your neck, the tickle of his thick hair as he begins to kiss you . . . what are you thinking?

Frustrated, you turn the water off, quickly towel dry, and get into bed. You lie as still as you can, trying to calm your racing mind. You can't get comfortable so you flip the pillows back and forth, try sleeping on two pillows, then you decide one feels better. You're too hot so you throw the covers off, but then you are immediately too cold. You lie on your back, close your eyes, and practice meditative breathing. After what feels like hours pass, you are still as awake as when you began. You wonder whether Freddie might have left any of those pills lying around.

Though no one else is in the suite, you tiptoe out of your room like a thief and slowly push open the door to Freddie's room. Neat as a pin, it's hard to tell that he has even been in it. Only the bathroom bears any trace of Freddie's existence, a single travel bag lying out on the counter. Could it be so easy? You quietly unzip the bag and bingo! The little pill bottle is lying right on top. You pour a single white pill into the palm of your hand, re-cap the bottle, and place it carefully back in the exact position you found it.

Back in your room, you fill a hotel glass with water and pause as a moment of guilt washes over you. Obviously Freddie trusted you or he would never have left those pills in such an accessible spot. You know it's not right to have breached his trust—nor his privacy—but still you're sure if he knew what a hard time you were having getting to sleep, he would have given you another pill. Wouldn't he? Anyway, there's no way you could be addicted after only taking these things for two days. It's an unusual situation, what happened tonight, and after this you know you'll be back to normal.

You pop the pill into your mouth and down it with a swallow of tepid sink water. Hours later, the morning light wakes you from a solid, dreamless sleep.

It takes you a few minutes to figure out where you are as you open your eyes. Then you remember: today is the day you leave Vegas and end the western portion of your tour. You have three long days of travel ahead of you as you cross the country to head to New York and one of the biggest stops on your journey filled with nonstop appearances and three nights of shows. You're so glad you feel rested. For one guilty moment, you think about what happened last night. But today's a new day, and you jump out of bed feeling ready for your next adventure.

"Well, hello," Sasha greets you as you enter the living room. "Good sleep?"

"The best," you tell him. "How was your night?"

"Un-be-freakin'-lievable," he answers. "You should have come with us. Saw a whole side of Vegas I didn't know existed."

"Do tell," you say.

"I have plenty of time to fill you in on the bus. Checkout is at hand. Why don't you go brush your teeth and put on some clothes."

"Yes, sir," you smile. You look around the room. "Where's Freddie?"

"Wasn't my turn to watch him," Sasha answers.

"You think he's downstairs already?"

"He's probably already downstairs waiting to lead the caravan as usual." Sasha looks at you from the corner of his eye. "Why are you so concerned?"

"Just curious."

As it turns out, Freddie is in fact waiting in his car. For a moment, you consider knocking on his window to check in on him but decide against it and climb onto the bus instead.

The drive to New York seems endless. Sasha regales you with stories of the transgender Vegas "other world" as he calls it, a society unto itself of supportive men in various stages of transition to the female gender, and his friend, Carlie, who is almost through her metamorphosis and loving every minute of her new existence.

"She's like a butterfly breaking free of her chrysalis," he says. "It's a beautiful thing to witness."

That gives you an idea for a song. "Hold that thought," you tell Sasha as you open the glove compartment and begin to scribble lyrics into your little notebook.

Sasha gives you a knowing look and a satisfied smile as he drives east, the sun setting at your backs.

That night the itch for one of Freddie's little white pills is like thirst in the desert. You tell yourself you don't need it, and you will sleep to come. After lying awake for an hour, you finally give up and pour yourself two shots of whisky. You sleep for a few hours but find yourself wide awake at three a.m. You spend the rest of the night jotting down lyrics and melodies. When the sun finally rises, you drag yourself out of bed.

Sasha looks you up and down as he rolls out of his bunk. "You're up early. You pull an all-nighter?"

"Something like that," you say and start a pot of strong coffee.

You nap off and on throughout the day, your sleep restless and peppered with dreams of Freddie.

You arrive in New York on a grey and windy afternoon. Tumbleweeds of trash blow down Broadway as you make your way past Times Square to your hotel, 567 on Broad. The inconspicuous façade, which blends into the background of the surrounding buildings, as well as the incomparable discretion of the staff, makes 567 a popular choice for visiting celebs.

A uniformed doorman whisks you up to the penthouse level and escorts you and Sasha to your suite. Though much smaller than Vegas sprawling apartment, the room is expansive by New York's standards. The furniture is low, sleek leather and the walls are upholstered in what appears to be dark grey velvet. The lighting is dim and moody. It's the quintessential NYC hotel. Sasha pushes the heavy draperies aside to reveal a stunning panorama of Times Square.

"I never get tired of that view," he says, gazing out into the sea of humanity swirling below the dazzling array of electronic billboards and LED displays.

You usually love this view, too, but for some reason the flashing lights and milling crowds makes you edgy today.

"Can you close it?" you ask Sasha.

He looks at you as though you have two heads. "No, I cannot close it. This is what I live for. What is your problem?"

"I'm tired," you tell him, and flop down onto one of the low sofas. "Ow. This is harder than it looks."

"That's what she said," Sasha jokes. "Not even a smile?" he asks when you fail to appreciate his attempt at humor.

"Ha," you manage.

"Go take a nap," Sasha tells you, turning back to gaze down at the lights and crowd below.

There's a knock at a door you hadn't noticed before—the adjoining room's door, set inconspicuously into the wall near the closet.

"Yes?" Sasha asks before opening it.

"It's me," comes Freddie's muffled voice from the other side of the door.

"Me who?"

"Open up, you idiot."

Sasha chuckles and unlatches the door.

"Hmm," Freddie says, looking around the room. "I guess this is the deluxe suite. Not very spacious but it's a palace compared to the tiny cubicle I'm in. Come look."

"That probably would rent for five thousand a month in this city," Sasha says.

"True," Freddie agrees. "I've been on the West Coast for too long. But there is no place like New York City." Freddie turns around and notices you on the sofa. "What's the matter with Honey?" he asks.

"She's tired," Sasha explains. "Three long days of sitting on a bus can be exhausting."

For some reason Sasha's answer triggers your last nerve. "You're right. Three long days in a bus with you can be exhausting," you retort. You regret it the second the words are out of your mouth.

"You do need a nap," Sasha says, drawing his mouth into a thin line. "I think I'll go do some exploring. Catch you later."

"Sasha, I'm sorry," you say as he heads toward the door. "I didn't mean that."

"It's all good, Henrietta," he says, clearly stung. Then he's gone, and you feel awful.

Freddie sits gently down on the sofa beside you. "That is not the Honey Noble I know. What's up?"

"I don't really feel that great. I shouldn't have taken it out on Sasha."

"Well, we all say things we regret. He'll get over it."

"I actually might go take a walk too," you glance over your shoulder at the lights of Times Square. "This is one of the few places I can be out in public without being accosted by hordes of fans and paparazzi."

"Really?" Freddie asks. "Have you tried that lately? I think you may be more famous than you were the last time you were here."

"It's New York. No one even makes eye contact. I'm pretty sure people would still leave me alone."

"I would say we could test your theory, but I wouldn't want to risk your life." Freddie rises from the sofa and gazes out the window. "You're definitely going to want to steer clear of Times Square. Check this out," he says.

"What is it?"

You follow his gaze out the window. "I don't see—"

Freddie takes your shoulders and pivots you in the right direction. Then you see it—the enormous, glittering billboard advertising your show. GET STUNG AT THE BARCLAY CENTER! the billboard reads. The hallmark image of you in your Nobility Tour costume, a glittering, gold gown meant to evoke both the image of a queen bee, complete with a crown and a scepter, dazzles you even though you've seen it in print a thousand times. Something about the vast brilliance of the LED display makes it seems so much more alive. "Wow!" you exhale.

"Wow is right," Freddie's eyes reflect the strobe of the lights as he gazes at the towering billboard. "That's really something. Think you could walk through the city and be left alone now?"

You stare down at the mass of tourists filling the square. Many of them have their phones and cameras pointed at your billboard. "I'm guessing probably not," you admit.

"I'm definitely in agreement," Freddie concurs.

"Well, it's just as well." You turn away from the window and blink away the flashing lights that still echo before your eyes as they readjust to the dim room. "I really would rather stay in."

Freddie walks over to the bar and rifles through the selection of available beverages. He selects a bottle of wine and deftly uncorks it. "Even the bottles of wine are miniature," he observes. He pours two generous glasses then tips the bottle upright to dispense the last few drops. He walks over to sit beside you again and hands you a glass. "I have a feeling you could use this."

"I am definitely in agreement with that." You take a sip. "Not bad, for such a tiny little bottle."

"Well, I guess good things can come in small packages," Freddie swirls the ruby liquid around and savors his first sip. "It is pretty good."

There's an uncomfortable silence while you gaze into your wine glass. You both begin to speak at once.

"Freddie, I—"

"Honey, I—" Freddie says at the same time. "You go first." Freddie's eyes twinkle with warmth and amusement. Looking into those eyes, the thought that you love him jumps unbidden into your mind. Suddenly you're not really sure what you were going to say.

"No, you go first," you tell him.

"Well, I was just going to finish what I started to say in the dressing room the other night." He pauses and takes another sip of his wine.

"Which was?" you ask, looking up at him.

He breaks into a huge smile. "You know it is very hard for me to think clearly when you're looking at me like that."

"Like what?"

"You know, with those huge, beautiful eyes."

"Is this better?" you close your eyes, and feel the tips of your long lashes brush the tops of your cheeks. A moment later, you feel Freddie kiss you gently, his lips soft and warm on yours. An instant heat blooms inside you and you return his kiss, running your hand through his thick hair as you pull him toward you. You move to set your glass down and accidentally graze his crotch, and you feel his hot, hard hunger brush against the back of your hand.

Taking his hand in yours, you rise and lead him to your bedroom. "Honey, I don't think—" Freddie protests.

But you place one finger against his lips. "Don't think," you whisper as you gently close the door behind you.

The minimal twilight filtering through the seam in the heavy curtains is infused with neon flashes from the billboards below. Otherwise, the room is dark, and you have to feel your way back to the bed in the unfamiliar space. When you find the edge of the bed, Freddie pulls you to him and kisses you, running his hands through the hair at the nape of your neck and sending a warm thrill down your spine. Your legs give way and you sit heavily on the edge of the bed, trying to pull Freddie to join you.

He stands still, resistant, so you weave your fingers through his and tug gently. When he still doesn't join you, you decide to take matters into your own hands. You quickly find and undo the button of his pants and pull down the zipper. His huge erection strains against his boxers (silk, you notice, with amusement). You slip your fingers into his fly and release him, running your fingers along the smooth skin. He is thick and hot, and you are surprised by how badly you want him. When you run your tongue along his length, he gasps.

"Honey, don't," he protests.

You answer by taking him into your mouth and sucking gently, while you cup his balls with your hand, working your fingers into the thick, curly hair around the base of his cock. His taste is slightly sweet, his scent clean and warm.

You feel him tense under your touch, and he groans as he rests his hands on your shoulders, then seems to regain his composure, "Honey, I can't." He pulls back gently.

"You can." You smile in the darkness, pulling him back toward you.

You kiss him as you unbutton his shirt and slip it from his arms. You run your hands down his chest and his surprisingly firm stomach. Without thinking, you slip you hand back under the band of his boxers, eliciting a gasp.

"Not yet," Freddie says, pushing you gently back onto the bed. He unbuttons your jeans and deftly slips them off, then slides a finger along the edge of your lace thong and skims it down your legs. He runs his hands back up your legs and along your hipbones, then up your stomach, pulling your shirt over your head. You rise up onto your elbows as he pauses to look at you in the dim light.

"My God," he gazes at you, then cups your breasts in each of his hands. "You are so beautiful."

You've imagined this moment so many times, and now that it's here, it's more than you expected. The feel of his skin on yours, the slight prickle of his chest hair against the swell of your breasts, the strength of his hands on your back as his tongue dances with yours, the taste of his kiss, tinged with the smoky, sweet wine, is like coming home.

Falling back onto the bed, you pull him to you and lift your hips to join his. The silk of his boxers is cool and delicious against you, but is also an obstacle you can't wait to remove. You move your hand down to push them out of the way, but Freddie takes your hand to still it. "Not yet," he says, his voice thick with desire

He kisses your neck, pausing to breathe you in. "You smell so good," he tells you, working his way lower, planting small kisses along the tops of your breasts, then gently taking your nipple between his teeth, grazing it just slightly before he moves lower, kissing you along your stomach and bringing his fingers up to test your most sensitive area. "Mmmm," he groans when he finds you more than ready.

Dropping to his knees at the edge of the bed, he places both hands on your thighs and pulls you decisively toward him. He begins with light kisses then lets his breath fall gently against you before pulling your legs farther apart and using his tongue to explore you.

You are lost as he swirls his tongue against you. Expert and creative, he brings you quickly to the edge. The strobe of the lights bouncing from the walls seems the perfect backdrop for this improbable fantasy. You run your fingers through his thick curls as he works his magic. You are suddenly close. "Come back up," you say.

"I'm enjoying this," he barely pauses before going back to his work.

"I'm too close"—you move your legs slightly together—"and I want you."

This gives him pause, and he finishes with two long, slow strokes of his tongue and after a moment he rises, slips a condom from the bedside table drawer, towers over you, and gazes hungrily into your eyes.

His thrust is immediate and strong, as you arch up to meet him. The feel of his skin against yours is unimaginably erotic. You match every thrust and grasp his strong buttocks to pull him farther into you. Much too soon, waves of ecstasy roll through you, and you grip him with your legs, pressing your face into his neck as you come. "Freddie," you say, as you feel him join you a second later.

"Honey," he moans, kissing you deeply.

You lie together, more satisfied than you have ever felt, and fall asleep wrapped in each other's arms.

A glaring light and sharp noise jars you from your dreamless sleep. Momentarily disoriented, you blink as your eyes adjust to the light. You nearly jump out of the bed when you see Freddie's slumbering form beside you and memories of the night before come flooding back. You pull the sheet up to cover yourself just as Sasha bounds into the room.

"What in the name of all that is holy?" Sasha gasps, horrified. He leaves as quickly as he entered, shutting the door loudly behind him. Somehow Freddie manages to sleep through it. You slip from the bed as quietly as possible, pausing to cover Freddie's bare torso with the comforter. You quickly pull on your clothes.

A second later, Sasha bursts back into the room. "Okay, I thought I was having some kind of waking nightmare, but clearly that is not the case. Do you care to tell me what in the name of insanity is going on here?"

"Shhh!" You glare at Sasha and glance over at Freddie, shocked that the commotion hasn't awakened him. You shut the door gently behind you and lead Sasha from the room.

Sasha begins to pace the length of the suite wildly.

"Relax, Sasha, it's not what it looks like."

"Not what it looks like? Not what it looks like? Because I cannot even begin to imagine what else it could be. Unless the two of you decided to play naked Twister and somehow fell asleep during the game. Except there was no game board that I could see. And you were in the same bed. And usually Twister is not played in a bed. At least not that kind of Twister. Tell me you are going to lie to my face, Henrietta. What do you mean it is not what it looks like?"

"Just . . ." you begin, but then realize you don't know how you can explain what happened last night. You look up at Sasha, and see total confusion mingled with hurt and betrayal in his eyes.

"I'm waiting." He stops mid-pace and folds his hands across his chest.

"I don't know how to explain it." You fall back onto the sofa and sit with your head in your hands. "I need some time to think."

"I would bet that you do," Sasha walks toward his room then stops and turns around. "Were you going to tell me at some point?"

"Sasha, it just happened. I haven't been hiding anything from you."

"Okay," he snaps. "Best keep it that way."

Mercifully, you, Freddie, and Sasha have no reason to interact for most of the day. You can only imagine how awkward that would be. The day is filled with appearances and meetings for your fledgling fashion line. You are shuttled around the city endlessly and exhausted when you return.

The packed schedule leaves you little time to think, but when you do your mind returns to your night with Freddie. Somehow it was exactly what you needed at exactly the right moment. And you're incredibly grateful that you were able to fall asleep on your own, without the help of any of Freddie's pills. Maybe the warmth of his arms was the perfect antidote.

You jump almost directly from your last appearance, a hasty interview over a salad and coffee, into prep for your show. Your driver deposits you at the Barclay Center's performers' entrance. Freddie meets you at the door, not letting on for a moment that anything has changed between you, though every time your eyes meet, you burn with a desire you hope the people around you cannot sense. Your stomach clenches at the thought of having Freddie and Sasha cross paths—and at the fact that as far as you know, Freddie is blissfully unaware that Sasha knows what he knows.

After the show, Freddie quickly retreats to the hotel. The second the dressing room is empty, Sasha starts. "So?"

"So what?"

"You know what," he huffs, heaving an armful of costumes onto the hanging rack. "You going to tell me what is going on or not?"

"Sasha." You sigh, pulling on your stretchy yoga pants and comfy sweatshirt. "I am exhausted. This has been the longest day, and I really just need to decompress. No offense but I don't really want to talk about it right now."

Sasha hangs the rest of the costumes. "That's fine," he says, clattering the hangers more loudly than necessary. "You just let me know when you're ready to be honest with me. Your best friend. Or is that no longer the case?"

"Sasha, don't be an idiot." Suddenly you are just too tired to deal with any additional nonsense.

Sasha draws himself up to his full height and pushes the rack of costumes roughly back into the corner of the room. "Now I'm an idiot? Whatever, Henrietta. You need to get over yourself. Or at least be honest with yourself, if you're not going to be honest with me."

He flicks the light off and locks the dressing room door. The ride back to the hotel is totally silent.

Back in the suite, you busy yourself with social media updates and tweet a note of gratitude to your NYC audience, which really was amazing. You push thoughts of your friction with Sasha out of your mind and wait for him to lock himself in his room, then tiptoe to the door adjoining your suite with Freddie's. You knock softly until he answers.

He is dressed in dark jeans and a soft, cashmere sweater over an oxford shirt. He pulls the glasses from his face and sets his book down on the bedside table when you enter the room. You close the door and bolt the lock.

"Honey, we shouldn't," he begins, but you stop him with a kiss, which he returns reluctantly at first, then with more gusto as you pull him to you.

"My heart is beating so fast," you tell him, lifting his hand and placing it against the swell of your breast.

"It is," he says, stroking your hair. "See, this is making you nervous."

"No, I'm just happy," you tell him, smiling. "I want to be with you." You take his hand and lead him to the bed, pulling his sweater over his head and running your hands over his chest.

He takes both of your hands in his, careful with your injured hand, and looks you in the eyes. "You know how very much I care about you," he begins.

"I do." You smile.

"So you have to understand that this is not an easy thing for me. You are one of the most special people in my life, Honey. I want to be sure we get this right. I would not be able to live with myself if I were to hurt you, or to disappoint you."

You smile up at him, the sincerity in his eyes warming your heart. "You couldn't disappoint me if you tried," you tell him.

He leads you to the little loveseat by the window and sits down beside you. "Even if that's true, it is part of my job to protect you. You know that, don't you?"

"You don't need to protect me." You take his hand and rub small circles into his palm with your thumb. "I can take care of myself."

Freddie lifts your hand to his lips, kissing your palm gently. "I know you can, you are one of the toughest women I've ever met. And very capable. But I want to take this slowly. For me if not for you. You can understand that, right?"

"Of course." You are immediately relieved. A second before you'd been certain he was going to tell you to go back to your room, that this couldn't possibly go on.

"Good." Freddie sighs, rising and pulling you into his arms. "Then we will move at my pace."

True to his word, he takes it very slowly, deliciously slowly, exploring every inch of your body with his hands and his lips before bringing you expertly to ecstasy.

After, you lie in Freddie's arms and wait for sleep to come. He snores softly beside you, one arm draped around your waist. For some reason, the thoughts of your argument with Sasha run endlessly through your mind. You resolve to find a way to talk to him tomorrow, but then you obsessively consider every possible outcome of your confession. What if he tells you he thinks you are delusional, or acting out some kind of father-figure fantasy? You imagine each argument, playing out your responses. Before you know it, hours have gone by and sleep still eludes you. You shift out from under Freddie's heavy arm and try to lie facing the other direction, sure that a little space or cooler air will allow you to sleep.

When another half hour passes, you begin to worry. Tomorrow—well, today, now—promises another grueling schedule. You can't bear to think about how you will be able to function without any sleep. You slip deftly from under the sheets and quietly steal into Freddie's bathroom. Once again, the little travel kit sits open on the counter. You know the exact location of the pill bottle and silently open the cap and slide a little pill from the plastic container. You pop it into your mouth and swallow it dry, then creep back into the bed. Sleep is upon you in seconds.

Your time in the city passes in a New York minute and before you know it you're on the road again. Sasha gradually accepts your burgeoning affair with Freddie, and even seems to begin to enjoy the time the three of you spend together. Somewhere between New Hampshire and Maine, Freddie moves onto the tour bus with you. He makes sure you have coffee in the morning and even pulls down your bedsheets at night.

"We are going to have to start calling you Princess Henrietta," Sasha laughs and shakes his head as he watches Freddie spoil you.

Freddie stays by your side at each new tour venue, rescheduling appearances when you need an extra hour of sleep or have trouble making your meet-and-greets. For some reason, you seem to need more sleep than ever before. You find yourself feeling edgy and irritable during the long days and though physically exhausted after each show, sleep takes longer and longer to come. Freddie still hasn't noticed his dwindling supply of sleeping pills.

One morning on the long ride to Chicago, you find you've run out of Red Bulls—the only thing that seems able to give you enough energy to function in the morning. You notice Freddie and Sasha exchange looks when you insist that the caravan pull off at the next gas station to restock your supply. While you are there, you sneak a bottle of Seven Hour Spark, an over-the-counter pill that advertises energy all day. True to its promise, the pills are better than Red Bull and you are practically bouncing off the walls of the bus as you make your way to Chicago. Your heart beats hard and fast, and you feel like you could run a marathon.

The day you arrive in Chicago is packed with interviews and appearances, and you pop another energy pill to wake up and get through the day, then top it off with a mid-afternoon Red Bull.

That night, sleep takes even longer to come. You cuddle up to Freddie and resist the urge to sneak a second sleeping pill.

Freddie shakes you awake as daylight slashes harshly through the gap in the hotel room blinds. "Honey? Honey? I need you to wake up."

You roll over and blink at him, bleary-eyed. "I probably only got about four hours of sleep, if that. I'm so tired." You pull the thick comforter over your head.

"Come on, it's already late. I'll get you some strong coffee," Freddie tugs the comforter down and kisses you on the forehead.

As soon as he leaves the room, you rummage through the side pocket of your travel bag to find the energy pills hidden there. You pop one into your mouth and know that it will help—and that the coffee will wake you up completely.

The first few hours of your day fly by. You have boundless energy for your mini-concert on the *Hello Chicago* show and you're carted from interview to appearance in a haze of happy excitement. It's four p.m. when the crash comes. The back seat of the black SUV is suddenly stifling and claustrophobic, and you feel like you can't get enough air.

Freddie sits beside you, scrolling through e-mails on his phone. The overwhelming need to sleep washes over you like an ocean wave, pulling you into an undertow you cannot escape. You're asleep on Freddie's shoulder before you know it, and awaken only when the car makes a jolting stop in front of your last appearance of the day, an album signing you don't think you have the energy to do.

"Good morning," Freddie says, brushing your hair away from your face.

"I'm exhausted." You yawn. "I honestly don't know how I'm going to get through this thing."

"I can see that," Freddie says. "But I know you. You'll get in there and you will be fine. You'll see."

You're not so sure, then you remember the energy pill you stashed in your jacket pocket this morning. You wait until Freddie turns to exit the car then you quickly swallow the pill. The effect is almost immediate. Your heartbeat quickens and you feel your spirits lift as you walk into the packed atrium and are handed a Sharpie.

The show that night is one of the best you can remember. You are totally on and even engage the audience in some ad lib dialogue. Afterward, you high-five the dancers and crew and invite them back to your dressing room for an impromptu celebration.

Back in the hotel room, you quickly brush your teeth and climb into bed beside Freddie. You fit yourself to his back, cuddling up against him as you wait for sleep to come.

You try to calm your breathing and slow your galloping heart. After an hour, you creep out of bed and sneak another of Freddie's pills, then return to the bed and close your eyes. Your heartbeat begins to regulate but you still feel wide awake. Song lyrics and melodies run incessantly through your mind—you're in full-on creative mode, in the middle of the night.

Tiptoeing out of the room, you grab the little notebook you keep for moments of inspiration and furiously jot down strings of lyrics until they are fully expunged. At last you look up, refocus your vision, and spot a bottle of merlot resting on the counter of the makeshift bar. You quietly uncork the bottle and pour a glass, hoping the wine will help you relax enough to sleep. Returning to the stiff sofa, you take a few swallows and scribble some simple melodies.

A rough shaking wakes you what feels like minutes later. You try to rise, but your head feels like it's trapped in a vise. You crack your eyes open, but shut them immediately when the light shoots a piercing pain directly through your brain.

"Oh my God. Did she drink the whole bottle?" Sasha's voice sounds genuinely concerned and you want to tell him you are okay, but your mouth feels like it's stuffed full of cotton. The feeling is far and away worse than any hangover you've ever had.

"I do not know," Freddie's voice disappears into the distance. "No, not even half. Maybe she's sick?"

"Honey, can you sit up?"

Using all of your effort, you push yourself into a sitting position. The motion makes you feel like someone has struck you between the eyes with a ball-peen hammer. Your stomach lurches and you run unsteadily to the bathroom, where you are immediately and violently sick.

Freddie rushes to your side and pulls your hair back from your neck. Sasha wets a washcloth and hands it to you.

"Sorry," you say, as you rise shakily to your feet. "I'm okay." But you're not, and you make it to the sofa just as your legs go out from under you. Freddie and Sasha catch you by the arms and exchange anxious looks.

You lie back on the sofa and close your eyes. You can feel Freddie and Sasha hovering around you, but their voices fade into unintelligible mumbles as you drift off. What feels like moments later, you hear Freddie say, "He should be here in about ten minutes."

"Who should be here?" you mumble.

"The doctor," Freddie answers.

"I don't need a doctor," you protest. "I'm fine." You wave your hand, then place it on your forehead, which feels as though it is throbbing in painful, rhythmic waves.

Time has taken on a soupy, liquid quality. You close your eyes for what feels like a second then are startled awake by a cold hand grasping your wrist. A gravelly voice echoes through the cottony scrim that seems to have descended over your ears. "Pulse is slightly weak," the voice says. You force your eyes to open against the glaring light and see the doctor, orange-tanned, and leathery-skinned. "Honey, I'm Doctor Childs. Can you sit up?" he asks.

"Mmmhmm," you push yourself up slowly, careful not to recreate the typhoon in your stomach.

"How are you feeling?"

"I've been better," you manage to answer.

He slips a plastic-sleeved thermometer between your lips. "Under your tongue," he instructs.

The little instrument beeps a few times. "Slight fever," he pronounces. "Probably from dehydration." He addresses Sasha and Freddie, who both continue to hover nervously. "I'll get some fluids in her and I think you'll see she'll be good as new."

He rustles around in his bag and returns with a needle and an IV bag. "Boys, get her some pillows?"

A moment later, two fluffy bed pillows are thrust behind your back and Freddie helps you recline—much more comfortably now—onto the sofa. The doctor takes your hand and extends your arm, cleaning it with an alcohol pad. "Little prick," he says, making Sasha snort.

"Something funny?" the doctor asks.

"Nope," Sasha says, extinguishing his grin, which makes you giggle.

"Humor," Doctor Childs observes drolly when you don't even flinch, "the best anesthesia."

He extracts the needle and connects the catheter to the tube dangling from the fluids bag.

"Just relax, now," he instructs.

Despite the odd sensation of the cool liquid running into your vein just under the skin of your arm, you soon find yourself dozing again. When you awaken, Freddie and Sasha sit nearby, Freddie by your feet and Sasha perched on the adjacent chair.

You blink your eyes and are relieved that the light filtering between your eyelids is no longer as painful. "How are you feeling?" Freddie asks.

"So much better," you answer. The throbbing in your head has disappeared and your stomach has steadied.

The doctor strolls over and removes the empty IV bag, then hangs a new bag, full of liquid. "Just for good measure," he explains.

"What is in that?" you ask, amazed that it had such an immediate effect.

"Just fluids," he deftly hooks the new bag to your IV line.

An hour later, two full IV bags in your system, you feel like yourself again.

Sitting in the hair-and-makeup chair before the show that night, exhaustion hits you like a ton of bricks. You have no choice but to pop an energy pill before you take the stage. You know you'll need another one of Freddie's pills at bedtime, but this time you'll know better than to mix it with alcohol.

Freddie and Sasha continue to check on you every few hours for the next day, which you find extremely aggravating. "I'm fine," you tell them. "It was probably just a twenty-four-hour bug."

Your final morning in New York and you're packed and ready to go. You feel full of creative energy and look forward to the uninterrupted hours on the bus to finally write out all of the lyrics and music that is in your head.

Freddie joins you on the five-hour drive to D.C. Between manic scribbling in your notebook, you remove your headphones to chat with Freddie and Sasha.

"One thing I want to do in D.C. is go see the cherry blossoms," you tell them. "We're arriving right in time for them to be at peak bloom. Who's going with me?"

Freddie and Sasha glance nervously at each other.

"What?" you ask them.

"I'll go," Sasha says. "We can be tourists for a day. It'll be fun."

"What about you?" you ask Freddie.

He gazes out the window, apparently deep in thought.

"Ah, Honey," he says, a wistful smile on his face. "Springtime is a young person's season."

"What is that supposed to mean?" you ask.

"Let's get settled in and make plans after that," is his non-answer.

"Okay . . ." You put your headphones back on and resume writing.

The D.C. hotel suite is three times the size of your NYC digs and has a beautiful view of the Potomac. Airplanes descend low over the water, and the trees on the far bank are just beginning to show signs of life. The hopeful energy of spring is all around you.

Freddie comes up behind you as you gaze out the picture window. He wraps his arms around you from behind and kisses the top of your head. After a long moment he says, "Honey, we need to talk."

You feel your stomach drop when you see the grave expression on his handsome face. "About what?" Then you notice Sasha standing in the doorway, hands folded patiently. "What's up, Sasha?"

"He means we both need to talk with you," he explains.

"Okay." You walk out into the living room, and take a seat in a wingback chair. You fold your arms across your chest. "So, let's talk."

Freddie sits beside Sasha on a loveseat separated from you by a huge, oriental rug. "Honey, please know this isn't easy," he says, running his hands nervously up and down his legs as he speaks.

"And we are doing this because we care about you," Sasha adds.

You wait, mystified.

Freddie looks at Sasha, who gives him a little nod.

"Honey, we know it was not the stomach flu that made you so sick in New York."

"Really?" you ask, immediately aggravated. "What was it then, doctor?"

"We would be happy to call the doctor, if you really don't remember," Sasha looks at you coolly.

"It cannot come as such a surprise, Honey," Freddie says. "That mixing chemicals with alcohol would be dangerous."

"Chemicals?" But you know what he is probably referring to, and you feel your heart start to beat triple-time.

"How long have you been stealing Freddie's pills?" Sasha asks, his mouth pursed in a thin line.

"Sasha," Freddie looks at him in alarm. "Don't. This isn't what we—"

"No, it's okay"—you look from one of them to the other—"you can go off-script. I wasn't stealing your pills, Freddie. You gave them to me."

"I gave you one, Honey," Freddie gently corrects you. "Now the bottle is almost empty."

"Well, I'm so sorry," you lash out. "I work my ass off, if you didn't notice, and I need to be able to sleep. You have no idea what it's like coming off the stage pumped full of energy and trying to unwind night after night. And then to have to try to function after a sleepless night, and to have to do it over and over and over again, day in and day out. With thousands of people coming to see you, expecting you to be perfect, and hundreds of people relying on you for their paychecks. Stressful does not even come close to describing it."

"We realize how hard you work, Honey, believe me." Freddie rises and walks toward your chair. "But you are right, I will never completely understand how it feels. I'm sorry you have been so stressed. And I'm sorry I ever gave you that first pill. In many ways, this is my fault."

"It's no one's fault," you say quietly. You feel tears beginning to spring to your eyes. You quickly blink them away.

Sasha sits perfectly still. You can feel the anger coming off of him in waves.

"What are you so livid about?" you ask him through the tears now streaming down your face.

He cocks his head and looks at you. "I just thought I knew you better than this, I guess."

"Look"—Freddie moves to stand between you and Sasha—"when something like this happens people have all kinds of reactions, fear, sadness, anger sometimes. It is all completely normal. The important thing is that we are here for you, Honey"—he pauses to look at Sasha—"both of us. And we are going to help you get through this."

Sasha's expression remains unchanged. The hard set of his jaw and the coldness in his eyes hurts more than any words he could say.

You rise to leave the room, feeling a mix of a thousand emotions. "I don't need your help, guys, but thanks. Really. Your concern is touching."

"Well, you're getting help, whether you like it or not." Sasha rises from the loveseat and stands, arms folded, between you and the bedroom door.

You push past him and close the door in his face. You grab your sunglasses, a baseball cap, and a light jacket and rush out of the suite, moving too quickly for Sasha or Freddie to stop you.

"Honey, Honey!" You hear Freddie yell behind you, but you take the stairs and are out into the city before he can catch you.

You've been to D.C. enough times to know that the nearest Metro stop will lead you downtown. You join the hurried crowd pushing its way through the automated stiles and board a train for the short trip to the Smithsonian Station. You emerge into the sunlight and make a beeline for the Tidal Basin.

Throngs of tourists crowd the pathway along the Basin. Cotton-candy pink trees laden with blossoms line the Basin and reflect their mirror-images in the water's still surface. The fragile petals are just beginning to release their grip on the reedy branches and snow lightly down upon you as walk the path beneath them. You find a spot under a tree, look up between its branches at the light blue sky, and feel a sense of peace descend upon you as realize what you have to do.

To accept Freddie and Sasha's help, turn to page 166.
**To call Freddie and Sasha and tell them you don't need
their help, keep reading.**

You pull your phone from your pocket. You've missed five calls from Sasha and three from Freddie. You close your eyes and turn your face to the sun as you tap Sasha's number. He picks up on the first ring.

"Henrietta, where are you?" He sounds angry, but you couldn't care less.

An odd sense of slowly warping time overtakes you as you speak the next words, "Sasha, you're fired."

"I don't know what you are trying to do, Henrietta, but whatever it is, it is not at all amusing." Sasha spits out the words rapid-fire.

When he finishes, you let a few moments of silence spin out between you before speaking. "Did I not make myself clear? You. Are. Fired."

Sasha laughs incredulously. "You cannot be serious."

"I am serious as a heart attack," you answer coldly. "I want you and Freddie out when I get back to the hotel. Take your time. I'll be gone for a few hours."

"Henry," Sasha pleads, "come back to the room. Let's talk about this."

"There's nothing to talk about."

"Henry," Sasha's voice is low, choked.

You feel a sense of perfect calm as you move the phone away from your ear and gaze at the display for a long second. Hitting End feels satisfying, like hurling a glass against a wall and watching it shatter, the tiny shards raining down into a million pieces.

The next steps suddenly lay themselves out before you in a clearly visible path. You make another call, this time to one of the most recognized and high-powered talent managers in the business. "May I please speak to Colton Powers? This is Honey Noble."

Powers agrees to fly in to meet with you immediately. He is more than happy to offer you representation, He promises to help you get out of your existing contract and to keep the tour running as scheduled. "You just worry about what you do best, and let me do what I do best. The legal stuff, piece of cake."

It turns out that Powers and Dr. Childs, the same doctor who treated you in New York, have a long-standing relationship. When you explain that part of the reason you want to make a change is that your previous team had you running ragged and you haven't had solid sleep in months, he calls Childs in to help. "I've seen it a million times," Powers tells you. "Classic performer's anxiety. Completely normal and completely manageable. Dr. Childs is a miracle worker, you'll see."

At first Sasha attempts to contact you daily, and you are riddled with guilt about the way you ended things. You tell Dr. Childs about your feelings and he brings in a renowned therapist who guides you through what he describes as a perfectly natural period of mourning. When you have trouble sleeping at night, thinking about the sound of Sasha's voice as you ended that last call with him, or you wake up in a cold sweat sure that Freddie is beside you only to find an empty bed, Dr. Childs is right there with an IV of some sort of soothing medicine that helps you fall into a solid, dreamless sleep. Every morning, Dr. Childs administers a "holistic" concoction of antioxidants, herbs, and hydration that keeps you bright-eyed and full of energy all day. Sasha eventually stops calling.

True to form, Freddie sends you a handwritten letter; its tone is tender and respectful. "When the time is right, I hope you will allow me back into your life," the letter concludes. "For my part in what's happened, I can only say how very sorry I am. I hope you never forget how very deeply I care about you." You fold the letter into a tiny square and fold it between the pages of one of your used notebooks.

Four months later, you feel better than you have since before New York. You've kicked both the sleeping pill and the energy pill habits and you feel like a new person. You've hired a new driver who respects your privacy, never pries into your personal affairs, and lets you write and rest on your drives from stop to stop. The media celebrates your revamped tour look, oblivious to the behind-the-scenes drama and personal toll it took to get you here. Powers has done a fantastic job of smoothing over the rough edges and spinning the story in the right direction, and he keeps your schedule so full that it's easy not to think about your past—or anything else, really.

Your career grows even hotter, and you release platinum album after platinum album. You sell your house in Hollywood, opting instead for the carefree luxury of hotel living when you are on tour, which is most of the time. When you have a rare week or two off, you rent villas in Europe or on a Caribbean island. You lose track of how much money you have, and instead quantify your success by how many sold-out tours you have under your belt and how many platinum albums you have to your name.

Serge, the backup dancer you had a mini-crush on when he first started on the tour, has become dance captain and your backup romance. He's more than happy to be seen on your arm at industry events, eager and energetic in bed, and just as content to give you your space when you need it. The tabloids have a field day speculating about the nature of your relationship, so he's useful in keeping you relevant, too. Things really have worked out pretty well, when you stop to think about it.

Following your eighth world tour and ninth album, you are stunned and honored to be nominated for a lifetime achievement award. The day before the Grammys, you attend a pre-show party filled with celebrities, music icons, and industry heavyweights. You do your best to socialize, but you're feeling a little off, and you want to escape the event and head home as soon as you can tactfully make an exit. You pull out your phone to text Dr. Childs.

Going to need a little something extra when I get home. Headed out shortly.

Maxx Swagger intercepts you as you begin to make your way to the door. He's as tall and wiry as you remember and doesn't appear to have aged a day. His leathery skin pulls back into a wide grin as he drapes his long arm around your shoulders.

"Honey Noble," he croons, his accent exaggeratedly rounding the "O's" in your name. "This is a blast from the past, isn't it?"

"Maxx." You smile up at him. "It has been too long."

"How've you been?" He takes a step back, extracts a shiny silver flask from his jacket pocket, and takes a long draw. "Well, I hear. Career's *en feugo* and all that jazz."

"Thanks." You laugh. "I can't complain. I've been lucky."

"Ah, we make our own luck, don't we, love?" He winks.

"I guess you could say that."

"I could say a lot of things. But I want to hear what you have to say." He pauses to take another swig from his flask. "Specifically, about what happened with Freddie."

You're stunned into silence for a moment. It's been so long since you've even thought about Freddie, you don't know how to respond.

"You do remember, he's a good friend. An old friend."

"How is Freddie?" you ask.

"Ah, he's a tough old bird," Maxx looks up at the ceiling and smiles at some memory. "He's found his happiness again. Can't keep Freddie down, you know." His smile becomes solemn. "But you threw him for a loop, Honey Noble, you did."

You feel heat rise to your cheeks while you do your best to repress the fragments of memory you've tried so hard to forget. You feel an urge to bolt from the room, but you fight it and stay glued to the spot.

"You know he only ever wanted the best for you. He was only trying to help." Maxx finishes.

"It wasn't easy for me, either," you say, "but I needed to make a clean break. For my own reasons."

Maxx smiles widely again, but some of the warmth has left his eyes. "Your own reasons. Well. I expect you did have your own set of reasons. And it's really none of my business. I just wanted to let you know that Freddie holds a tender spot for you. Does to this day. And he forgives you. He'd tell you himself, if you'd let him."

You feel the sting of unexpected tears. "Thank you, Maxx. I appreciate you telling me."

You give him a hug and walk out of the room, silently vowing to call Freddie when you get a spare moment tomorrow.

Back at the hotel, you eagerly strip out of your constricting gown, wash the makeup from your face, and bundle into a cozy robe. You smile at the bodyguard lounging on the couch outside your room, and gently close the door to begin your evening ritual of recording the music and lyrics eternally swirling through your mind in the pages of the tiny notebooks you still keep by your bedside. You pull one from your bedside table and notice a square of folded paper drop to the floor. Before you can bend to pick it up, there's a knock at the door.

Dr. Childs's low voice soothes you as he gently inserts the little needle and catheter into your arm. "Don't worry, I got your text. You'll sleep well tonight. You'll feel like new again before you know it, I promise."

The last thing you see before your eyes close is the slow drip, drip, drip of the liquid in the IV bag filtering endlessly into your veins.

You awaken to find yourself floating somewhere over your body. There is perfect, black stillness all around you and profound silence as you gaze down upon your own sleeping form. You reach toward your body, trapped helplessly on the bed below you, but the blackness pulls you away too soon.

You drift for what feels like hours, weightless and totally at peace. You hover high above the city, glimpses of diffuse light just reaching you from below. Through a shroud of filmy clouds you see throngs of people crying, thrusting armfuls of sunflowers and bee-shaped balloons at the red-carpeted entrance to a theater. When you see that the marquis reads THE GRAMMY AWARDS, you try to swim down through the clouds but you are sucked back up into the blackness again.

Then you catch sight of Dr. Childs fighting his way through a press of flashing cameras and microphones. His head is down, and he's pushing away the accosting media, who yell his name from every direction. You see Serge's face, then Sasha's face, and Freddie's. Then the faces of your family, which flash before you then fade into darkness one by one.

In the distance, you hear music. It's a song you recognize, though it's one you haven't yet written. You let yourself drift toward the melody until you are one with it. And then you are nothing.

THE END

To take Honey on a new Bedventure, go back and choose a new path.

From page 161 . . .

A single tear slides down your cheek as you lift the phone and dial Sasha's number. He picks up on the first ring.

"Henry?" His voice is a mixture of alarm and relief. "Where are you?"

"I'm at the Tidal Basin." You close your eyes against the sun. "Can you come get me?"

"Yes, of course . . ." Sasha hesitates for a second. "Where exactly is the Tidal Basin?"

Freddie's voice cuts through the silence in the background. "We'll figure it out." You can hear a shift as he grabs the phone from Sasha.

"Stay put, Honey," he instructs. "We'll be there as soon as we can."

"Thanks," you tell him, and stand up to brush the fallen blossoms from your jeans.

Two laps around the Tidal Basin with Freddie and Sasha and you have it all figured out. Freddie will arrange a hiatus and puts a call into a center he knows in Arizona that offers complete confidentiality and privacy. You link your arms with your two best friends, the loves of your life, and know everything will be alright.

It's Christmas Day ten years later. Looking back, you can barely remember that day in D.C. Everything that has happened since seems like a dream. You look up at the framed photos that adorn the piano's top. The centerpiece is the gorgeous wedding photo from that day you will never forget, when you stood in front of hundreds of Hollywood industry heavyweights, all of your closest friends, and of course your family, who filled the front rows. The sweet scent of the honeysuckle that adorned the arbor, the sound of helicopters circling overhead to try to snap a photo, and the love in Freddie's eyes as you joined your life to his.

You ruffle the hair of the little boy sitting next to you and scooch over to make room for his sister.

"Mom!" yells Sebastian, "show me how to play it!"

"I'll show you how," Camille grabs her brother's hand and places it on the keys, spreading his fingers wide.

"Ouch!" he yanks his hand away. "You're hurting me!"

Freddie puts down his newspaper and rises from his chair. You exchange a knowing look. "She's not trying to hurt you, Sebbie, she's trying to help."

"I want Mama to show me, not Cammie!"

"We can both show you, okay?" You glance over at your daughter, her hands perfectly poised above the keyboard. "Then you can try it."

Camille is a natural musician and picks up melodies with an uncanny effortlessness. Her ability brings you an immeasurable amount of joy. Her twin brother doesn't seem to have been graced with Camille's knack for instrumental music, but he's both a comedian and a fantastic little singer. Together they are like a two-man variety show, and keep you endlessly entertained.

Camille plunks out the first few notes of "Rudolph the Red-Nosed Reindeer" and Sebastian adds the vocals. Freddie rests his hands on your shoulders as you accompany your daughter. Your heart could not be more full, and you vow to commit this moment of pure domestic bliss to memory so that you can call upon it anytime. You never dreamed you could be so happy.

Sasha's voice drifts into the room, first gently overlaying Sebastian's and then adding an irreverent lyrical twist.

"Then one froggy Christmas Eve, Santa came to say, Croak, croak, croak," he sings in a froggy voice, sending the twins into peals of laughter.

"That's not it!" Sebastian howls, "It's soggy, not froggy!"

"Oh, that's what I meant!" Sasha plays along. "Then one soggy Christmas Eve, Santa splashed through the rain . . ."

A pro at five years old, Cammie literally doesn't miss a beat, deftly replaying the verse as Sasha rewinds the lyrics.

Freddie laughs and does his best to sing along.

"Daddy,"—Sebastian frowns up at him—"do you have to sing?"

"I do have to sing," Freddie answers. "If Uncle Sasha can sing, then so can I!" Freddie sings even louder, making Sebastian groan.

The song ends and Sebastian moves to the piano, waggling his fingers dramatically over the keys. He lifts his hands and pauses. "No," he says, "I have decided the piano is not for me. I think I'll stick to singing."

Cammie looks over sweetly and gives her brother a squeeze, then leans in and whispers, "I think you made a good choice."

This sends you, Freddie, and Sasha into another round of laughter. "Come on." You rise from the piano bench and stretch your back, which is just beginning to feel the strain from the extra weight of the new little family member you are expecting in the spring. "Let's go have some fruitcake!"

"No!" your family yells, laughing, as they follow you into the kitchen.

The new baby comes early, almost two weeks before your due date. Sasha rushes you from the studio, and tracks down Freddie, who is off playing golf. Freddie grabs the twins from school early so that they can be there when the baby arrives.

Freddie hurries into the room, his brow sweaty and a look of panic in his eyes. "It's fine," you tell him, "I probably still have hours to go."

"Daddy picked us up early." Cammie tentatively enters the room, nervously observing the cords and wires monitoring your contractions and the baby's heart rate. Sebastian hangs back, holding onto Freddie's arm.

"It's okay," you assure them. "It's just hospital stuff. Want to see?" You point to a long ream of graph paper spitting out of the monitor and piling onto the floor.

Cammie wrinkles her nose and shrugs her shoulders. "Does it hurt?" she asks shyly.

"It just squeezes," you explain, resting her little hand on your belly. A sharp kick from the baby makes her jump.

"Whoa!" she exclaims, her eyes wide. "I think she's ready to come out!"

"I think so too." You smile and squeeze her hand.

A nurse briskly ushers the kids out of the room. "Doctor's on his way in to check you," she explains. "You kids can wait right on the other side of the curtain, okay?" Then she catches sight of Freddie. "Sir, are you feeling alright?"

You've been so caught up in the kids that you haven't even glanced at Freddie since he first entered the room. Now that you look at him, you can see that the sheen of sweat on his brow has worsened and his color isn't quite right. In fact, he looks alarmingly pale.

"Freddie?" you sit up slightly, causing the belt velcroed around your belly to shift and the monitor's alarm to sound. "Sorry."

The nurse hurries over to readjust you. "Just relax," she tells you, pushing you gently back down onto the bed. "We'll take care of your husband." She reaches into the rolling cart and extracts a blood pressure monitor, strapping it around Freddie's bicep. You can't read her face, but her words are terse.

"Mr. Angel, I'd like to get a doctor to take a look at you."

"I'm fine," he protests, but as he does, he staggers a step.

"Freddie!" you yell as the nurse catches him by the elbow and eases him down into a chair in the corner of the room.

"Daddy?" Sebastian's voice calls through the thin curtain.

"I'm fine." But his voice is strained.

The next few minutes are a blur. Later, you'll remember a frenzy of doctors and nurses, the children confused and alternately scurrying to try to be with you, to stay out of the way, and to go with Freddie as the nurse wheels him away. You manage to roll over far enough to text Sasha, who arrives in seconds to restore order and to distract the kids by taking them down to the gift shop.

The nurse returns with an oxygen mask and brusquely straps it over your nose and mouth. "Deep breaths," she tells you, grasping your hand as the contractions begin to come hard and fast and you bear down.

"How is he?" you ask, desperate for any news.

The nurse avoids eye contact as she tightens the mask's elastic straps. "It's his heart. We're doing all we can."

Suddenly, you cannot breathe. The suffocating scent of honeysuckle fills the oxygen mask, and you pull it from your face.

"I need you to calm down," the nurse tells you, pushing the mask firmly back into place. "Deep breaths. Let's bring this baby into the world safely."

The baby emerges eerily quiet, finally letting out a lusty cry when the doctor cuts her umbilical cord. You smile through the flood of tears soaking your flimsy hospital gown.

Sasha returns with the twins once the baby is cleaned up and bundled into your arms. The look on his face is one you haven't seen before. Every trace of mirth and sarcasm is erased, and he looks far older than his years. The kids cling to each of his hands, their eyes huge, frightened saucers.

At last, a doctor enters the room, walking slowly and purposefully. He looks down at the kids and the baby in your arms. "Perhaps they should wait outside?" he suggests.

"No, they can hear whatever you have to tell me." You hold the baby closer, bundling her up under your chin.

"I'm very sorry, Mrs. Angel." His face is grave, his voice low. "We did everything we could."

Cammie locks eyes with Sebastian and seems to confirm something she sees there. "Noooooooooo!" Her scream echoes through the room and pierces your heart.

Sasha drops to his knees and presses their little faces into his chest as they sob. He manages to work one hand out of the embrace and reaches up to take your hand in his. He squeezes your hand, warming your heart. "I'm here," he says. "I'm here."

A year later the pain is still fresh. There are nights you awake in a cold sweat, sure you hear Cammie's scream echo through the empty room. Still, every morning you awake to count your blessings. The twins have come through the tragedy admirably, Cammie throwing all of her energy into helping with the new baby, and Sebbie mustering his strength to become the little man of the house. Little Freddie is growing quickly, already taking her first steps and beginning to babble her first words. "Mama," warmed your heart and "Dada" almost broke it. She toddles around the house holding a finger on each of her big brother's and sister's hands.

Sasha has been a lifesaver, standing by you every second of the grueling memorial service you were forced to endure just days after baby Freddie was born. He took care of every detail, helping you make both the big decisions and the smaller ones, and helping with the kids any time you needed him.

You've finally found the strength to return to the studio and are working on your next album, which has a distinctly different feel from the sweeter pop that came before. You hope your fans will enjoy it—but whether they do or not, it's immensely cathartic to pour your emotions into your art. Colton Powers has taken over as your manager and is working on plans for your next tour, convinced your fans will come out in droves to support you and to witness your evolution.

It's hard to believe it's been a year. You still sometimes feel a biting guilt at the moments of joy you experience, but your heart is beginning to thaw as the weather begins to warm and buds begin to emerge on the trees. The little cherry tree you've planted in the front yard is the first to bloom, which you think is a sign from Freddie that life must go on. "Spring is a young person's season," you remember him saying. And he was right. You know now he meant that you should enjoy it, live in it, and let the kids grow in the love and light he left behind.

That afternoon you decide to set up a little picnic in the grass beneath the cherry tree. You sip a glass of wine with Sasha while the kids drink pink lemonade and bask in the sun. Little Freddie's dark curls shine in the sunlight. "Cha-cha," she waves her chubby fist and squints up at Sasha, the sun in her bright blue eyes.

Sebbie begins to giggle, sending a spray of lemonade through his nose.

"Gross!" Cammie laughs. "That's disgusting!"

"Did you hear what she called him?" He dries his nose on a napkin. "Cha-cha!"

Sasha thinks for a minute, then breaks into a wide grin. He puts a finger on Freddie's button nose. "Cha-cha." He smiles. "I like it!"

"Cha-cha, cha-cha," Freddie repeats, sending you all into helpless laughter.

"I'm gonna call you Cha-Cha, too!" Cammie squeals.

"I'm not," Sebbie says stubbornly, folding his arms across his chest and making Sasha laugh even harder.

You look up at the tiny pink buds just beginning to form on the tree. Beyond it, the sky is a perfect blue. You catch a subtle scent of honeysuckle on the wind, and know that Freddie is near. The filtered sunlight warms your face, and you feel Freddie's kiss in its warmth, a benediction.

You whisper a private *thank you* to Freddie, then turn your attention back to your little family to bask in their love and in the promise of the new season.

THE END

To take Honey on a new Bedventure, go back and choose a new path.

From page 91...

The walls seem to close in around you and suddenly you cannot breathe. You notice curious stares in your direction and a few raised cell phones, their users surely snapping as many candid photos as they can. The room begins to swim in and out of focus and you hear an incessant buzzing in your ears. You manage to pull Crispin to his feet as you topple into the booth in back of you.

Crispin looks crestfallen but maintains his composure. "Honey, are you all right?"

"I don't know. I feel like I can't catch my breath."

"Just try to relax," Crispin tells you, gently rubbing your back.

At last, your heart begins to slow and your breathing regulates. You look up to see that the room has come back into focus and the curious crowd that had gathered is beginning to return to their drinks or to the dance floor.

Crispin sits down next to you. "You all right?"

"I'm fine. I'm so sorry. I don't know what just happened. That was the strangest feeling."

"Being asked to marry me, you mean?" Crispin asks with a self-deprecating laugh.

"Crispin, of course that's not what I meant."

Crispin's lips are drawn into a line of disappointment and the hurt is visible in his eyes.

"That was a total surprise," you explain. "Maybe I was a little overwhelmed for a second."

His expression instantaneously turns hopeful. "And now?" he asks.

You sigh and look down at your hands.

"Guess I should take that as a no," he says, looking away from you.

Taking Crispin's hand in yours, you respond as honestly as you can. "It's not a no, Crispin. It's a not yet. Not here. We're just starting to figure this out again. Don't you think we should give it some time?"

Crispin gazes at the dance floor, packed with writhing bodies, and seems to think for a long while before answering. Finally, he straightens up and looks at you. "I know what I want, Honey. I don't need to give it any more time. I've worked hard for this, and I've done much of it for you. But if you're waiting for me to prove myself . . ."

"That's not what I'm saying."

"It's okay," Crispin tells you. He quickly swallows the remaining water in his glass. "It really is. I get it." He pulls out his wallet and tosses two crisp hundred dollar bills on the table. "I think it's best we call it a night, isn't it?" His words are clipped and cool.

"Crispin . . ." You put your hand on his arm but he pulls away as if burnt.

"Really, it's fine." He moves aside, ever the gentleman, so that you can exit the booth first.

As you leave, he walks a couple of strides ahead of you, never taking your hand. Back at the hotel, he wishes you goodnight outside of your door and plants a quick, cold kiss on your cheek, never once making eye contact before he is gone into the Las Vegas night.

You lie awake that night, wondering whether the damage you've caused can be repaired.

The glaring desert sun gleams through the tour bus windshield as you settle in for the long ride to your next stop in New York City. The bustle of getting the tour back on the road has distracted you from thoughts of Crispin, but now that you are back on the bus you find yourself replaying Crispin's proposal in your mind, remembering the devastated look on his face when you failed to say yes, the coldness in his eyes when he left you last night.

Sasha pulls you from your reverie. "What has you so quiet, Henrietta?" he asks as he pilots the bus onto the long stretch of highway that unfurls in an endless black ribbon before you.

"I'm just thinking," you answer evasively.

"You don't have that silly notebook in your hand so I know it ain't song lyrics you're thinking about. You know you're going to tell me sooner or later so it might as well be now."

"It's about Crispin," you begin.

"Of course it is," Sasha mutters under his breath.

"Do you want me to tell you or not?"

"Sorry," Sasha apologizes, glancing in the rearview mirror. "Knee-jerk reaction. Please proceed. I won't say another word."

You look over to gauge whether he seems sarcastic or serious, but his profile appears totally benign. "So, this is crazy and you cannot overreact. I know you will but I'm going to tell you anyway."

Sasha remains silent, true to his word.

"Last night, at the club, totally out of the blue, Crispin dropped to one knee and proposed to me."

You wait for Sasha to react but he remains stoic. A few moments pass before you ask, "Did you hear me?"

"I did hear you, yes. I'm just waiting for the rest of the story. I haven't noticed a ring on your finger so either he's a cheap bastard or you said no. Am I right?"

"Well, he's not a cheap bastard," you answer.

"That's my girl!" Sasha holds up his hand for a high-five, which you do not return.

"I'm not celebrating it."

"Well I will celebrate silently with myself then." He does a little wiggling dance in his seat while keeping his eyes on the road.

"That's kind of mean, Sasha. He was pretty upset."

"Well, what did he expect, blindsiding you like that when the two of you just got back on track two seconds ago?"

"I think he expected me to say yes," you answer simply.

"Sounds like you're feeling a little guilty," Sasha says, reading you precisely, as he often does. "You shouldn't."

"I don't know what to feel," you fold your arms across your chest and direct the suddenly too-chilly air conditioning vent away from you. "It was a sweet gesture. Totally spontaneous and genuine. But it was so strange. The minute he asked me I felt like all of the air was sucked out of the room. My heart was beating a mile a minute and I felt like I couldn't breathe. I actually thought I was going to pass out."

"Mmm hmm. Classic panic attack," Sasha diagnoses.

"No, I've never had a panic attack," you argue.

"Well, you have now," Sasha tells you with certainty. "It happens when your body is trying to tell you to take a minute. It's good you listened."

"I didn't have much choice."

"So how did you leave things with Crispin?"

"When I didn't say yes, he pretty much wouldn't even look at me. It was awkward."

Sasha is quiet for a long moment.

"What?" you ask him.

"I'm just listening. And noticing you said you didn't say yes, right? Does that mean you didn't say no?"

"I didn't say yes. But no. I didn't say no."

"Hmm. Well, I guess that's better than the alternative." He reaches over and takes your hand, giving it a little squeeze. "Don't worry, he'll get over it. Rejection stings. Or lack of acceptance in this case. And I know it hurts to have to do it. But you did do the right thing, Henrietta. One hundred percent."

"Thanks, Sasha. You always know what to say."

"That's why you keep me around, right?"

"Right," you tell him. "That and a million other reasons."

The sudden inspiration for a song strikes you. You gently pull your hand away from Sasha's, extract your notebook from the glove compartment, and feel instantly calmer as you begin to write.

By day three of your journey across the country, the raw pain of your goodbye with Crispin has faded to a dull ache. You try not to think about the look on his face, the coldness in his eyes when he said goodbye. Unsure even where he went after you parted ways, you've texted him several times, but so far he hasn't returned a single text. Maybe you'll call him when you get to New York, but you don't want to have an unpredictable conversation in the confines of the tour bus within earshot of Sasha.

You pull into New York on a gloomy morning. What little sunlight the clouds don't obscure, the skyscrapers kill completely. It feels like Gotham, and a sense of foreboding washes over you. As you unplug your phone from the dashboard charger, you notice a series of texts from Crispin lighting up the screen:

WTF?

Have you looked at TMZ?

Brilliant it's all over Twitter too

Hello?

Your stomach clenches as you read the texts.

"Shit," you say. You're not sure whether to answer the texts or look at TMZ or Twitter.

"What?" Sasha asks, blaring his horn as a yellow cab cuts him off. "This city has the worst drivers!"

"Hold on," you answer, typing a quick reply to Crispin.

Just seeing this. What is it?

You don't even want to know

"Great," you mutter, then type "TMZ" into the Internet search bar.

The second the screen comes up you gasp. Sasha swerves the bus, almost careening into a bicyclist weaving illegally in and out of traffic.

"Jesus, Henry. You almost made me commit manslaughter! What the hell is going on?"

"This." You hold the phone up so Sasha can see the screen.

"I can't look at that! Do you see the chaos I'm attempting to navigate?" Sasha slams on the brakes and you hear something slide off the counter in the little kitchen area. "Just tell me!"

You stare at the photos for a moment longer, and feel a fresh sear of pain through your heart. Though the quality of the photo is less than stellar, the photographer managed to catch you at the moment you pulled Crispin up from bended knee. The look on his face is complete devastation.

"It's a TMZ story," you tell Sasha. "Their top news story, to be exact. Listen to this." You quote the headline that glows in bold, red lettering just under a photo of you and Crispin that night at the club. HONEY SAYS NO! CRISPIN HERSHEY HUMILIATED IN PUBLIC. IS THEIR ROMANCE OFF AGAIN? CLICK FOR EXCLUSIVE PHOTOS!

"Ouch," Sasha says.

"Yeah," you agree. "Let me reply to Crispin."

Just saw the TMZ story. Total BS. I am so sorry.

The bubble filled with a series of dots hovers at the bottom of the screen as Crispin responds.

Not total BS. Guess I'm the idiot for thinking that was a good idea

You're not an idiot. Please don't worry about this. It's just one story

It's not just one story. Google our names. See what happens

Your stomach drops afresh. You know you shouldn't, but you Google your names anyway. The results fill the entire first page, all variations on the same theme: HONEY NO-BLE. WHY THERE WON'T BE WEDDING BELLS FOR HONEY AND CRISPIN. COLD-AS-ICE HONEY NOBLE

REFUSES CRISPIN'S SWEET PROPOSAL. WHAT HAPPENS NOW? FRESH OUT
OF REHAB, CRISPIN POPS THE QUESTION. WILL HONEY'S REFUSAL SEND
HIM BACK OFF THE DEEP END? And worst of all, CRISPIN ON A CRAZY
BENDER PROPOSES TO HONEY IN VEGAS. HONEY REPLIES WITH A RE-
SOUNDING, "NO WAY!"

You feel terrible that the press is spinning the story the way they
are, but you aren't surprised. "What a disaster," you say.

"They say all PR is good PR," Sasha waxes sagely.

"I'm not sure that's the case this time," you tell him.

A new text pops up on the screen:

Did you look?

Yes

And?

What can I say? I feel awful

Not as awful as I feel, I'd wager

Crispin . . .

*Don't worry. It's all good. I've had worse things said about me
than that I'm an unlovable addict loser*

That's not what they're saying

That's just what I'm feeling, I guess

I'm really sorry

No, don't apologize. All you were was honest

Where are you?

*Flew to London for a couple of days. Checking in with the family.
They will be delighted with my news I'm sure*

I'm glad you're with them. You're relieved that he has a support
network around him.

Not exactly what I was hoping to have to deal with while there

I know

Do you?

*Crispin, what do you want me to say? I've said I'm sorry over
and over*

The screen sits stagnant, without a response for several minutes.
At last, the text appears

There's was just one word I wanted you to say

A new text bubble appears a moment later

But you couldn't bring yourself to say it, could you?

Another stab of pain slices you to your core. You know there's no
good answer, and nothing you can do to make this better.

After several more minutes, Crispin sends another text:

So I guess there's really nothing more to say. I'm going to check out for a while. Take a break. From everything

You mean take a break from me?

I mean from everything. I need some time. You can give me that much, can you not?

If that's what you want

It's what I need

OK then. Be safe

You too. Enjoy the rest of your tour

The rest of your tour? The tour isn't over for months. You sit back and gaze at the ceiling, letting this sink in. You feel the sting of tears at the corners of your eyes.

"So?" Sasha asks, sensing your mood.

"I think Crispin just broke up with me."

"Again?"

You look over at Sasha, who has a tiny smirk on his face.

"Seriously?" you ask him, though suddenly you feel laughter bubbling up through your tears. "You really are a heartless bastard."

"But I'm *your* heartless bastard." The sky brightens with the artificial glow of the towering billboards of Times Square. "And we're not in Vegas anymore, Dorothy." Sasha pulls the bus around the corner and slides it into the inconspicuous lot behind your hotel. "Now that we are officially in NYC," he says, flipping his sunglasses up onto his head, "we are going to have some fun!"

You glance at the screen of your phone, slide it into your pocket, and feel your mood brighten as you step out of the bus into the sultry New York air.

After you settle into your suite, Freddie calls a car to take you to visit the venue in which you'll be performing that night. After a quick sound check, you walk offstage to head to the dressing room area.

As you do, you hear low music coming from the wings. It's somber and beautiful and evolves from a slow, haunting melody to a faster, upbeat tempo. You walk around to the back of the stage to find the source. There you see Serge, your backup dancer, straddling a cello, sawing the bow slowly back and forth. He appears completely lost in the melody, his eyes closed, hair swinging in front of his face as his head sways to the rhythm, muscular thighs grasping the instrument from either side. You lean back against the wall to watch him. Something about the passion in his playing is riveting. The tendons in his hand stand out as he fingers the strings, every muscle in his shoulders and arms defined as he plays.

Before long, a small audience of stage crew and facility staff have assembled and watch in awe as Serge plays faster and faster, broken bow strings now whipping wildly back and forth as he saws the bow across the cello in an ever-increasing rhythm. The music is like nothing you've ever heard. It builds to a fevered crescendo and ends abruptly as Serge swings the bow in final arc and opens his eyes.

The little crowd breaks into spontaneous applause. Serge glances shyly around and blushes handsomely, pushing his hair back from his face. "Thank you," he says, then rises from the chair, gives a little bow, and gently places the cello back into its case.

As the crowd disperses, you walk closer to examine the broken bow strings. "Serge, that was unbelievable," you tell him. "I had no idea you were a musician." Though now that you've seen him play, the little you know about Serge suddenly seems to make sense.

"Yes, well." He shrugs, then sheepishly addresses a staff member standing politely off to the side. "I will bring your cellist a new bow."

"Eh," the staff member replies, "we got a million of 'em."

"I am always doing that," Serge tells you. "Breaking the bow-strings."

"What was that song you were playing?"

"It is nothing," Serge shrugs. "Just fooling around. A little of this, a little of that."

"It was a lot of amazing. Have you ever thought of playing professionally?"

"Yes," he tells you, "I have thought of it. I have even tried it, for a time. The pay is not so good. And the music—it will put you to sleep. I am not a traditionalist. But"—he leans back, stretching—"nobody wants a rock-and-roll cellist. Thank goodness I am a very good dancer. So, I can play my music for myself, and I can dance for my pay. It all works out."

"I guess," you tell him. But you wonder. "Are you sure there's not an audience for a rock-and-roll cellist? You certainly attracted an audience just now."

"Yes, they were bored," he says.

"They weren't bored, Serge." You place a hand lightly on his shoulder, the muscle still warm and bulging from his playing. "They were entranced."

Serge looks up at you and smiles, one errant lock of hair falling across his eyes. You've never noticed before how beautiful his eyes are, deep-set, outlined by thick, black lashes, and a startling shade of dove grey against his porcelain skin. "Thank you for the compliment," he says.

"You're welcome." You reluctantly begin to head back to the dressing room. "I'll see you tonight."

"I will see you, *Sladkaya*."

"What?"

"*Sladkaya*. It is Russian for Honey," Serge explains, taking the word "Honey" slowly. "It is not easy for me to pronounce your name—for some reason it does not exactly roll off the tongue."

"Oh." In all this time Serge has been on the tour, you've never had a real conversation with him. He's instantly warm and endearing. "I'm not sure I can pronounce that, but that's sweet."

"Yes, it also means sweet. Very good," he winks.

You walk through the door to the backstage hall, surprised at just how sweet Serge seems to be.

Margot awaits in the dressing room, makeup at the ready.

"Are you feeling well?" she asks as you take a seat in the makeup chair.

"Yes, why?"

"You look a little flushed."

"Do I? I'm fine," you laugh.

"Not to worry, nothing my magic can't take care of." She begins to wipe foundation across the bridge of your nose, and you sit back, close your eyes, and allow yourself to dream.

That night, you think you see something extra in Serge's eyes. He seems to hold your gaze a little longer, to squeeze your hand a little tighter than the choreography calls for, but you could be imagining things.

You decide to throw an impromptu NYC opening night party in your suite after the show. The rush of adrenaline still hums through your body as your cast and crew stream into your suite and you pop open a bottle of champagne. Everyone's in a fantastic mood and even Freddie, normally not a night owl, has decided to join you.

Sasha has the music blaring and the lights dimmed. You join a circle of dancers showing off their moves and are slightly disappointed that Serge isn't among them. When the song ends, you leave the circle to look for Serge amid the bodies. An assortment of crew members lounge on various pieces of furniture, a bottle of beer or glass of champagne in their hands. You don't see Serge among them, either. Finally you spot him on the balcony, talking with one of the crew members.

"May I join you?" The unusually warm spring day has cooled to a perfect temperature and a subtle breeze brushes past the maze of skyscrapers and finds its way to you.

"Of course." The two men turn around in synchrony.

"You know Niko, yes?" Serge asks as you slide between their two hulking bodies. The air is still warm from the day's heat, and the lights of the city twinkle like thousands of terrestrial stars.

"Of course I know Niko," you answer—though in truth you didn't actually know his name. He's one of the two men who meet you at the top of the catwalk every night; Niko is the one who straps you safely into your harness before your descent to the stage.

Niko gazes out across the rooftops. "One can almost imagine that the lights from all of these millions of windows are stars," he observes poetically. His accent is almost identical to Serge's.

"That is something I used to imagine as a child, as well," Serge says. "That all of the city lights were stars."

"Did you two grow up near each other?" you ask, intrigued.

Serge turns to face you, locking those gorgeous grey eyes with yours. "You could say that. In fact, we studied together."

"You went to the same school?"

Niko smiles, his face lighting up in the glow of the myriad lights. "Not exactly. We studied music together."

"You studied music too?" you ask Niko. I had no idea."

"Yes, well. Why would you know?"

"Do you still play?"

"A little." Niko smiles.

"A little," Serge repeats, laughing. "That is like saying the Pope goes to church once in a while. Niko is very talented."

"Do not exaggerate," Niko says, but you think you see a slight blush on his already ruddy cheeks.

"I am not exaggerating. You know I am telling the truth."

You laugh at their back-and-forth, enjoying the obvious closeness you had no idea existed between them.

"What do you play?"

They answer in unison, "Cello."

"Wait, you both play cello?"

"Yes," they say together, again.

You narrow your eyes. "Are you two twins?"

Serge laughs and flexes his muscles, which are not unsubstantial. "Yes. Can't you see the resemblance? He just takes more steroids."

"Serge! I have never touched that poison!" Niko is clearly aghast.

"Relax, I am kidding you," Serge reaches across you to give his friend a thump on the chest.

You snort with laughter. You had no idea Serge was so funny, and the two men fighting like a couple of school boys is hilarious.

"That is not a laughing matter," Niko scowls.

Serge is doubled over in laughter now. "Oh, do not be so sensitive. I was joking!"

Niko continues to scowl, glowering at Serge. "I am going to go inside to cool down. You two stay out here and have your laughter at my expense. Don't worry about me."

"Oh, I'm worried about you, all right," Serge continues to guffaw as Niko walks off. "Come back when you are in a better mood."

Niko glares at him one last time then slides the door open, ducking to clear the threshold.

"He is such a baby," Serge wipes tears of laughter from his eyes.

"I had no idea you two were such good friends."

"Yes, well, we have known each other for a very long time." Serge moves imperceptibly closer to you. Your shoulders almost brush his biceps, and you feel a tingle of electricity between you.

"I feel bad. Maybe we shouldn't have teased him."

"Don't worry, he can take it. One good thing about Niko is that even though his feathers get ruffled easily, he gets over his things very quickly. He will be fine."

"Sounds like you know him really well." You gaze out across the rooftops once again, and feel the energy of the city pulse through you. You feel like anything could be possible here. "That's pretty amazing that you both play cello. Did you ever play together?"

"Yes, we did," Serge answers simply.

"Do you still?"

"On occasion. He is more classically oriented than I am. But he can hang with me a little."

"You mean he can play like you were playing this morning?"

"Was that just this morning? It feels like days ago." Serge moves his hand just slightly, bringing it to rest against yours. The zing of electricity is instantaneous. "Yes, he can. Sometimes."

The image of the two huge men sitting side by side, frenetically sawing their bows back and forth plays in your mind. "Will you show me?" you ask excitedly.

Serge turns to face you, and you feel yourself melt as he smiles, his white teeth flashing against the dark night. "I will show you," he says quietly, gently cupping your cheek in his hand, tipping your chin up with one finger, and leaning in for a long, slow kiss.

Suddenly, your body is tingling with the current running between you. You return the kiss in full, leaning into his solid chest.

Serge runs his hand along your jawline and through your hair. Everywhere he touches instantaneously ignites. Much too soon, he pulls away, rests his palm on your cheek again, and looks into your eyes. "*Sladkaya*," he sighs.

You smile, enjoying the way the moniker sounds on his tongue.

"You don't mind, do you?" Serge asks, never taking his eyes off of yours.

You're not sure whether he's referring to the kiss or the name, but either way, the answer is the same. "No, Serge, I don't mind at all."

Serge kisses you again, a gentle kiss that lasts only a moment. "I suppose we should go back inside to join the party." But he doesn't move, and continues to look into your eyes. "It is rude, keeping you all to myself, no?"

You peer through the balcony door. Your guests are talking and dancing, oblivious to anything outside of their circles. "I don't think anyone has even noticed I'm gone."

"Well, they will soon. And then you will have to explain."

You look up at Serge, a mischievous glint in your eye. "I never explain anything."

Serge laughs, and kisses you one last time, holding you close, his strong hands on your shoulders. "Well that is too bad, because I was going to ask you to explain this effect you are having on me, *Sladkaya*."

Niko slides the door open, making you jump away from Serge. "Am I interrupting something?" he asks with a sideways grin.

Serge diverts him elegantly. "Ah, I knew you would not be able to stay angry for long."

"Yes, as usual I decided to be the bigger person."

Serge gives him an affectionate thump on the back and makes a show of looking up at his towering friend. "You are most definitely the bigger person."

You run your finger around your lips, hopefully removing any smudged lip color.

"Are you two going to stay out here all night long?" Niko asks.

"Actually, we were just coming back inside. I promised to give this lovely lady here a show and I'm going to need your help."

Niko raises one eyebrow, making him look comically suspicious and perplexed at once.

Serge clarifies quickly. "I'm afraid our secret is out of the bag, my friend. Go and get your cello."

"Serge," Niko protests, "these people are trying to have a party. They do not want to hear our amateur efforts."

"I highly doubt anyone would describe your playing as *amateur*," you tell him. "You have your cello here, in the hotel?"

"Yes of course. I travel with it always."

"Of course you do," you say. "What else would I expect?"

"Well, it is certainly not what your party guests are going to expect, either," Niko frowns.

"That's what makes it so great," you say, smiling up at him. "Just one song, please?"

"Oh fine, if you are going to twist my arm I suppose we can play one piece."

"Yay!" You clap your hands and run inside, instructing Sasha to kill the music when Sasha and Niko return.

Even in their huge cases, the cellos appear smaller than you would expect in the hands of the pair of large men. As they set up in the center of the room, the crowd quiets and trades curious looks. The instruments are impressive and well-cared-for, their glossy finishes burnished to a glowing shine and the bows precisely strung. The room falls silent as the pair pulls their bows slowly across the strings to warm up.

Serge and Niko sit side-by-side and look straight ahead, never even glancing at one another as they begin to play in unison. The song begins slowly, a dirge that sounds vaguely Russian. Niko plucks a low rhythm while Serge draws the bow across the bridge of his instrument. Serge's movements quicken as Niko's pace increases. Now Niko draws his bow across the strings of his cello, joining Serge as they play the melody together, the pace of the music growing faster and the notes becoming higher as they play. Their fingers move expertly from note to note, their bows in perfect synchrony.

Soon the two are playing a frenetic pace, heads swaying and bodies jolting from side to side, punctuating the music. Their focus is complete, their eyes far away, a lock of dark hair swinging across Serge's forehead as he plays. The crowd is transfixed and begins to clap and sway to the rhythm. As the music grows even faster, bowstrings begin to break as the men saw the bows so fast they become a blur. At last, with a final pull of the bows across the cellos, the men stop as suddenly as they began, bringing the crowd to their feet. Applause and whistles fill the room and Serge and Niko smile and wipe their sweating brows.

"Where did that come from?" Sasha asks, clearly impressed.

"I know, right? I knew Serge could play, but I had no idea about Niko."

"I'm not a fan of instrumental music, but I would pay to see that," Sasha says, which gives you an idea.

The next morning brings an early start and a visit to the *Sunrise* show, where you'll perform with your dancers on the famed plaza to a crowd of waiting fans. You sip your Red Bull carefully through a straw and try not to smudge your lipstick as you wait with the dancers in the green room.

"We have a drink like that in my country," Serge tells you as he watches you sip. "It is called Revo. It is very similar to Red Bull, but it has alcohol in it, believe it or not."

"That makes my daily habit seem a little less bad," you smile. "I need a little help waking up after last night." Though in truth you feel wide awake, a feeling of excited optimism lifting your mood. "It was really incredible watching you two last night playing in that style—I don't know what you call it."

"It does not have a formal name. We call it *burya.*" The word sounds strong and exotic as he says it, the R slightly rolled. His voice seems deeper and his accent heavier in the confined space of the room.

"What does that mean?"

"It is Russian for *storm.*"

"That's perfect," you tell him. And it is. You take out your phone to make note of the word. "Do you think you would ever want to play like that on a regular basis, for a larger audience?"

"What are you suggesting?"

"I have an idea, and it's just in the very early stages, but I did run it by Freddie and he actually liked it."

"Which is?"

"Which is that you and Niko would make a great opening act."

Serge leans back in the seat and laughs. "For your show?"

"Is that so funny?"

"I do not think we are what your audience would be expecting. Or that they would really enjoy our music."

"I think you might be surprised," you say. "Would you be willing to give it a try?"

"But you already have an opening act."

"I know. Technically you would be opening for their act. We were thinking two or three songs, to start off."

Serge looks at you for a long time, his eyebrows slightly knit. "You are serious?" he finally asks.

"Yes, I'm serious!"

"I would have to talk with Niko."

"Yay!" You give him a quick hug.

"I did not say yes." He looks at you with what you think is mock-seriousness.

"But you didn't say no."

Serge gives you a crooked smile, his eyes sparkling. "You can be very persuasive, do you know that?"

You give him a smile. "I've been told that from time to time."

Freddie signs the duo under his management company. You don't ask for details, but you imagine he's sold them on exposure, future tours, and a possible recording deal to offset a minimal or possibly nonexistent paycheck, since the tour budget has already been cemented.

From New York, it's an easy drive down to D.C., the next stop on your tour. Serge and Niko are so accustomed to playing together that they need almost no rehearsal. The tour's musical director and the head choreographer provide some feedback, encouraging as much intensity, synchronization of body movement, and as many broken bowstrings as possible. Their costumes are simple: dark jeans topped with plain, white button-down shirts, slim ties, and fitted leather jackets. They look killer and sound phenomenal. They debut their act on the first night of the D.C. tour and the audience watches, riveted, springing to their feet in a standing ovation at the end of the duo's performance.

Serge high-fives Niko as he walks off the stage. His brow is sweaty and his face is aglow, eyes shining with joy. Niko retreats to the wings but Serge makes a beeline to you, grabs you by the waist, and tosses you into the air, spinning in a triumphant circle. Your heart leaps in your chest and then steadies as he sets you gently back down.

"You were amazing!" you tell him, looking up into his sparkling eyes. "They loved you!"

"Thank you for this." He beams. "I cannot describe what it was like, playing in front of that audience. I have never felt anything like it!"

"Not even when you are dancing?"

"No, that feeling does not even come close. It was like . . . I can only think of one way to describe it."

Serge takes a purposeful step toward you, places his hand firmly at the nape of your neck, and pulls you to him. He kisses you forcefully, and you taste the salty tang of his adrenaline as his swirls his tongue against yours. You stand on tiptoe to meet him, teetering dizzily as fireworks flash behind your eyelids.

When he finally releases you, your head swims and your body aches for him as you gaze into his eyes.

"Yes, it was like that," he says, his voice rough.

"Wow." You smile up at him, biting your lower lip. "That good?"

"Well, close." He grins and leans down to whisper into your ear, "I am not finished telling you all about it, *Sladkaya.*" His whisper sends fresh chills up and down your spine. He straightens up, looks around, and tugs at the hem of his jacket. "But right now, I have to go change."

"Oh right," you say, blinking back the stars that are still in your eyes. In a half hour, Serge resumes his role as backup dancer. You wonder whether the audience will notice.

Sasha brings you your mic and earpiece and does a double-take when he sees your face.

"What happened to you?" he asks, eyes wide.

"What do you mean?" Is it that obvious that you are transformed, still filled with the electric current of your last kiss.

"Your lips are all smudged and your hair . . ." he spins you around by your shoulders and smooths the hair by the nape of your neck. "Hold on," he says, returning with a bobby pin and a can of hairspray, making "tsk" sounds as he puts you back together.

"Sorry," you apologize as he works. "Must have gotten caught in my zipper."

"You can lie to yourself but you cannot lie to your best friend," Sasha says, not missing a beat. He gives your hair a final shot of spray. "Besides, how were you going to try to explain the mess you've made of your lipstick?"

"Um, water bottle?" you try.

"Water bottle, my ass." Sasha smirks. "We will discuss this later." With that, he sashays off into the darkness, leaving you blushing and smiling to yourself.

After the show, you sign autographs for a steady stream of VIP guests. It seems like every politician in town has pulled strings to get their kids and families backstage. At last, the line dwindles and you escape to your dressing room. Serge is waiting at the door with a huge bouquet of roses. You leap into his arms the moment you see him. Standing on tiptoe to embrace him, you see Sasha over his shoulder, leaning back against the counter with a satisfied smile.

"These are gorgeous!" You take the deep red flowers, each bud perfectly formed. "Thank you!"

Sasha finds a vase and fills it with water, and sets it on the counter. "I'll take care of these." He takes the bouquet from you. "You go ahead and get changed." He turns to Serge and winks, "Nice choice."

Thrilled with Sasha's tacit approval, you slip into the bathroom and skim out of your costume. You shower off quickly, just long enough to remove the surface layer of makeup and body glitter, then slide into the figure-hugging minidress Sasha has thoughtfully hung on the back of the door for you. You glance in the mirror, swiftly swipe a finger under each eye to remove smudged eyeliner then apply a quick swipe of lip gloss. You purse you lips together, widen your huge eyes, and smile.

Serge and Sasha stand conspiratorially side-by-side against the counter as you walk back into the room. "So, what's the plan, boys?" you ask, stepping into a pair of strappy heels that instantly bring you three inches closer to Serge's height.

"What makes you think there's a plan?" Sasha asks, all innocent.

"Oh, nothing." You smirk, waiting for them to come clean.

Serge straightens up and takes a step in your direction. "I was thinking about taking one of those moonlight monument tours. Would anyone like to join me?"

Sasha yawns hugely. "Not me," he says, stretching his arms above his head, theatrically. "I'm beat. But you two go ahead."

"*Sladkaya*?" Serge offers you his hand, a look of hopeful joy on his handsome face.

"I'd love to," you tell him. "And you"—you look over your shoulder at Sasha's smiling face as you exit the room—"should not quit your day job."

"Have fun," Sasha mouths, and blows you a kiss as you walk out the door.

A sleek black Escalade waits at the curb. Serge bundles you into the car, a total gentleman, opening and closing the door as you slide into the soft, leather seat. The driver glides off into the night without a word from Serge. Clearly, he has been informed of the destination ahead of time.

The night is clear, a sprinkling of stars visible despite the diffuse light of the city. The driver takes you slowly past the White House, by the majestic Lincoln Memorial, through the World War I and World War II Memorials with their cascading fountains aglow, and around the soaring Washington Monument. The crescent moon hangs just above the structure's narrow point.

"The first time I came to this city when I was very young, my mother told me that people call that the pencil building," Serge says, leaning into you slightly as the car take a curve. "In the same conversation she told me about the U.S. Constitution. For years, I believed that was the giant pencil used to sign the Constitution."

"That's adorable." You laugh.

"Yes," Serge says. "I was a very cute child."

You laugh again, enchanted by the city, with the moonlight, and with this man who keeps surprising you with his warmth and now with his humor.

"How long have you lived in the US?" Suddenly you are all too aware how little you know about Serge, and you want to know more.

"Seventeen years," he tells you. "Almost two-thirds of my life."

You also had no idea how old he was—so that's one question answered.

"I feel silly even asking this, but where are you from, originally? Russia?"

"Do not feel silly. I am from Ukraine. Close enough."

"Oh, I just thought, since you were speaking a little Russian that must be where you grew up."

"Most people do not realize, in Ukraine we use both Ukrainian and Russian. At home we speak mostly Russian, though."

"What is it like there? Do you remember it?"

"Oh yes. I remember it very well, and I have been back many times." Serge pauses, pensive for a moment. "It is very different in many ways, and in many ways not very different at all." He looks at you for a long moment. "I know that is a terrible answer"—he scoots closer to you—"but it is difficult to describe. I would like to take you there one day, to show you what I mean."

You are drawn to him like a magnet, his energy pulling you irresistibly toward him. Before you can think, your lips are on his, one hand pressing against his strong chest while your other hand finds his thigh. The car hits a bump, jolting you closer together, and as you move your hand to brace yourself, you brush against his desire.

Serge sucks in his breath and kisses you harder, pressing one hand against the nape of your neck as he pulls you to him.

The car comes to a stop and the driver politely clears his throat. "Sir, this is the Tidal Basin." He is a consummate professional, discreetly averting his eyes from the rearview mirror as he speaks.

You come up for air, your lips feeling deliciously bruised. Your heart beats double-time and you feel slightly dizzy but energized and intoxicated at the same time, a combination of the way you feel before you go onstage and the way you feel just after a performance.

Serge quickly exits the car and offers his hand to help you step down. "What are we doing?" you ask him.

"Come and see," Serge says, leading you down a little path toward the water.

You gasp as you take in the scene before you. The Tidal Basin's waters, mirror-still, reflect the crescent moon and the light of the city, casting an almost-eerie glow through the white-pink cherry blossom trees that encircle the Basin. The path, though virtually empty of tourists, is coated with thousands of delicate, individual petals, which fall like flakes of snow from the canopy of trees. The Washington Monument rises in the distance, its top visible past the seemingly endless ring of trees.

"This is beautiful," you say, giving Serge's hand a little squeeze as he guides you along the path.

"I hoped they would still be in bloom when we arrived." He brushes a petal from your hair. "They bloom at different times every year."

"Really?" You've heard about the cherry blossoms, maybe learned about them in school, but you had no idea they were so gorgeous.

"Do you know the history of these trees?" Serge asks as you walk.

"I don't think I do."

"They were originally a gift from Japan, from the Mayor of Tokyo. He gave the US three thousand trees to celebrate the friendship of the two countries."

"Quite a gift." You are impressed by Serge's knowledge and touched that he wants to share it with you.

"It was. And look how they have been cared for and how much joy they bring to the people who see them." He stops talking for a moment as you make your way past a couple embracing under the trees near the water's edge. The darkness provides an intimate privacy you wouldn't have thought possible in this busy city.

"They really are breathtaking," you whisper.

"In exchange, the US gave Japan a gift of flowering dogwood trees, also very beautiful."

"I can't imagine anything prettier than this." Gazing across the water, you see the graceful dome of the Jefferson Memorial coming into view.

"And, did you know, almost seventy years later, Japan suffered a terrible flood and a loss of many of its most beautiful cherry trees. The US was able to give Japanese horticulturists cuttings from these trees, the same trees they had originally gifted to the US, to replace the trees they lost."

You stop to smile up at Serge. "How do you know all of this?"

"Oh, I am a bit of a history buff." Serge laughs, brushing several fallen petals from your hair and shoulders. "And I have a special affinity for cherry blossoms. We used to have them not far from where I grew up, in Uzhgorod. They bloomed the same time that these trees do, in very early springtime, along some of the streets and sidewalks of Pushkin Square. We called it *Sakura Alley.* I used to walk through those streets with my mother, feeling like I must be in the Garden of Eden. Then when I came here many years later, it brought back memories of home, but at the same time it was like nothing I had ever seen. I thought this must be what heaven will look like."

As Serge speaks, his voice becomes low and musical. You can almost see the trees of his childhood as he describes them, the manicured square and orderly pathways lined with a sudden profusion of unruly blooms. It must have been magical.

"Come, let me show you this." Serge quickens his pace, leading you along the path until the Jefferson Memorial looms larger as you grow closer to it, its stone columns bathed in white light.

As you near a fork in the path, Serge takes his phone from his pocket and turns on the flashlight, searching among the trees.

"Ah here!" Serge says, stopping near a large holly tree. "This is it." He lays a hand reverently on the trunks of a gnarled and weathered-looking tree that stands beside the holly. This tree is devoid of petals and its trunk is twisted, limbs amputated in several spots.

"What kind of tree is this?"

"This," Serge says, gazing at the tree with admiration, "is the indicator tree."

"The indicator tree?"

"Yes, it is the most amazing cherry tree of them all. Every year this tree blooms about ten days ahead of the rest of the trees. So, it indicates when all of the other trees will bloom."

"That is very cool." You place your hand gently on the tree's trunk, your palm pressing lightly against the thick bark.

"It is not the most handsome tree," Serge leans back, looking up through its branches. "But it is the most important. It has an ability none of the other trees have. It is very strong. And it is the most reliable." Serge smiles, wrapping his arms around your waist.

"I can see why you like this tree," you smile, gazing up at him. His eyes reflect the moonlight as he locks his gaze with yours.

"That is good, *Sladkaya,*" he says leaning down to kiss you again.

As he does, a swooping sense of vertigo spins through your body again, and you hold on tightly to Serge, knowing he is exactly the balance you need.

The car awaits you at the top of the path. You hold tight to Serge's hand, fingers intertwined, on the ride back to the hotel. Serge tips the driver and opens your door, helping you out onto the street. You have no idea what time it is and want the night to go on forever.

At the door to your suite, Serge is a total gentleman. "This was a wonderful night," he says, glancing both ways down the hall before planting a gentle kiss on your lips.

"It really was," you tell him. "I loved every second. And I loved getting to know you. You really are an amazing person, do you know that?"

Serge blushes adorably, ruddy color rising just above the edges of his five-o'clock shadow.

"The feeling is mutual, Honey Noble," Serge says, struggling with the moniker.

"What happened to *Sladkaya*?" The word sounds much less sexy coming from your lips.

"I will save that," Serge says, lightly brushing your cheek with his thumb, "for when we are not in public."

You look down at the floor for a moment. "Well, maybe we should find some privacy then." Sliding the key into the door, you lead Serge into your suite. Luckily, the room is empty, the lights low, and Sasha's door is firmly shut.

A hot blush rises to your cheeks as Serge dips his head to kiss you. "*Sladkaya,*" Serge breathes, moving to kiss your neck, your shoulders, then returning to your mouth. He pulls you to him hard, and you feel the solid urgency of him pressing against you. "*Ya uvlechion toboy,*" he breathes into your ear.

Though you don't know what the words mean, they have an immediate effect, and you feel yourself melting, your limbs becoming liquid as Serge holds you in his arms. Everything about him feels so unexpected but at the same time so right. You pull away for a moment to lead him to your room.

You tumble onto the bed together, desperately hungry for one another. Now that he has you to himself, he is less inhibited, pulling you to him as he presses into you, kissing you fiercely. He turns you to face away from him and makes quick work of the laces at the back of your dress, pulling it down past your hips and hooking your panties with his finger to fling them aside. He hungrily kisses the back of your neck, then pulls the band from your hair so that it falls thick and free down your back. He groans as he reaches around to take your breasts into each hand, kneading them as he thrusts against you from behind.

You reach around to find him, and run your hand across the hot bulge of his desire. He takes in a sharp breath before taking your hand and entwining his fingers with yours. He pauses and you feel him pull away for a moment before he finds you with his fingers, then you gasp as you feel his tongue move between your legs from behind, quickly finding your most sensitive area. He thrusts his tongue in and out, then flickering just the tip of it against your clit.

All too soon, you are ready, and you reach for a condom then back around to pull him to you again. The smooth length of him presses urgently against your ass, sliding deliciously back and forth against you. Then, in one quick motion, Serge puts his hands on your hips, pulls you backward to him, and thrusts into you.

You cry out as he fills every inch of you, then again as he slides back and thrusts deeply once more.

"Are you okay?" he whispers gruffly into your ear.

"Yes," you breathe, pressing back into him, feeling sparks ignite as he thrusts.

Suddenly, you have to see him, to look into his eyes, and so you pull away and turn quickly. His shirt is still on, so you make quick work of the buttons and he pulls it roughly over his head when enough are undone.

You gasp again when you see him fully naked, his pale, smooth skin like marble illuminated by the diffuse light of the city. Every muscle is beautifully pronounced, his abs chiseled, his arms strong and sinewy. You lie back on the bed, your hair spread around you, and you look into his eyes. "You are so sexy," you tell him.

Serge holds your gaze for a long moment and smiles, white teeth flashing and eyes sparkling. "*Ya tebya lyublyu,*" he says, and kisses you deeply.

You reach to take his strong buttocks in each hand, the muscles stunningly powerful, and you pull him to you. Slowly, he drives into you, and you arch up into him, delighting in pleasure as he fills you. It takes only seconds before you come, pressing your face into his neck as you drown in waves of pleasure.

"Oh, *Sladkaya,*" Serge groans as he comes.

He holds you for a long time, catching his breath and moving slightly inside you, making you tremble. "Sorry," he says. He rolls to your side, wraps his arms around you, and kisses your hair.

You lie like that for what feels like hours, fully connected, skin-to-skin, fulfilled by the simple whisper of one another's breath, soothed by the steadily slowing beating of one another's hearts.

"*Ya tebya lyublyu,*" Serge whispers again, softly.

You wish you knew what his words meant, what to say in return. Maybe you'll remember to ask him in the morning, but right now it feels as though dreams and reality are beginning to mesh. Serge's arms are wrapped around you, his strong chest pressed firmly against your back and you are suddenly very, very sleepy. After a few moments, you drift off into sleep.

The bright sun wakes you early the next morning. You crack your eyes open slowly, and before you are even completely awake you are aware of the sense of complete and utter satiety that fills your body. You lift your head the tiniest bit to peek at Serge. In his slumber, sheets tangled around his waist, he looks every bit the Greek god. His dancer's body is beyond flawless, one perfect buttock and one muscled leg fully visible. Even his foot is handsome, the arch impeccable. You take a moment to drink him in and feel suddenly giddy that this man is in your bed. You stifle a joyful giggle, burying your head in your pillow.

Serge's thick lashes flutter and he cracks one eye open, blinking at you sleepily. Without moving anything but his arm, he pulls you to him, pressing you into a long, drowsy kiss. He pulls away, smacking his lips. "Still sweet," he pronounces, which makes you giggle again. "What is funny?" he asks.

"Nothing," you say. "I'm just happy."

Serge sits up and smiles. "Me too." He grabs you by the waist and flings you back onto the bed, pressing himself into you. "Very happy."

You let out a huge laugh, then stifle it with your hand, aware that

Sasha, who shares your suite, is likely awake and having his morning coffee. A few moments later, you hear a light knock at your door, followed by Sasha's voice.

"You okay in there, Henrietta?" Sasha calls.

This makes you laugh even harder. Now Serge is laughing, too, though he's doing a better job of being quiet than you are.

"Yes," you answer. "I'm fine."

"Fine?" Serge asks in a whisper. "No"—he thrusts against you, making your insides sing with desire—"you are much more than fine."

You widen your eyes at Serge as Sasha calls through the door again.

"You don't sound fine, Henrietta. You sound downright funny. Is something going on in there?"

"Um, sort of," you say, giggling into Serge's neck.

"Oh lord." Sasha sighs. "I'll set another place for breakfast. You're lucky I have my robe on."

Serge falls back onto the bed laughing.

"Busted." You giggle, climbing on top of him and kissing him before rolling just out of his reach.

"That is not fair!" he whispers.

You place your finger on his handsome lips. "To be continued," you promise.

After a quick shower, Serge joins you and Sasha at the table. Serge looks impossibly sexy, dressed in last night's jeans and white button-down, his hair still wet and his five-o'clock shadow highlighting his chiseled features.

"Welcome," drawls Sasha, clearly impressed. "Coffee?" he offers.

"Please," Serge answers.

"Well," Sasha takes a sip and gazes over at you. "This is certainly unexpected."

You tilt your head at Sasha, remembering his shameless setup the night before. "Not entirely unexpected, I don't think," you tell him.

Serge pulls his chair closer to yours and puts his arm around you.

"How was that moonlight tour, anyway?" Sasha asks, taking a bite of his toast.

"It was perfect. Very romantic. Did you have something to do with setting that up?"

Sasha looks aghast. "Give the man some credit. I only helped arrange the driver. The rest was all Serge."

You smile at these two men, one who cares about you so deeply he would do anything to make you happy, and one who might be beginning to feel that way, too. "Thank you," you say. "It was just what I needed."

Serge spends more and more time with you as you travel down the East Coast. Ever the gentleman, he is respectful of Sasha's relationship with you, and he has not yet asked about Crispin, though surely he must have seen the two of you together at some point. When Serge isn't with you, he spends his time rehearsing with Niko, coming up with new stunts to throw into their performances, adding drama by spinning or tossing their cellos in synch.

Serge, Niko, and Sasha even strike up an unexpected friendship, spending hours backstage or on the bus playing cards together. The sight of the two hulking men flanking the equally tall but thin and wiry Sasha never fails to amuse you.

On the first day of your Miami stop, Sasha busily hangs costumes in order and rolls them backstage. Serge, a calm energy in the frenetic venue, sits in the corner reading.

"Hello?" Freddie calls out as he enters the dressing room.

Serge looks up from the book, a giant tome focused on early Roman history.

"Ah!" Freddie announces when he sees Serge. "Just the person I was looking for. You and Niko have attracted quite a following. Your groupies are already lined up outside," he says, referring to the mass of screaming female fans, self-titled "*Burya* Babes," that now follow the duo from venue to venue. "And check out Twitter," Freddie flips his phone around to show Serge the *Burya* page. "Look at that!" he barks. "You just broke seven million followers!"

"Wow! It took me three years to break five million!" You are impressed, but not surprised. Serge and Niko have had almost as many requests for talk show appearances and magazine photo shoots as you have over the past month.

"Very impressive," Freddie slips his phone back into his pocket.

"That is very exciting. Thank you, Freddie," Serge says.

"I have more good news." Freddie smiles. "We have a record-deal offer from none other than Colton Powers. And that's not all. You boys have been invited to serve as grand marshals of the Ukrainian Independence Day Parade. Your home town wants to honor its heroes. The timing would dovetail perfectly with the projected drop date of your first single. Looks like your days as backup dancer and catwalk crew member are numbered." He pauses, waiting for Serge to respond. "So, what do you think?"

Serge looks pensive, taking it all in. "I have to talk with Niko, of course."

"That's it?" Freddie folds his arms across his chest. "Most people would be jumping up and down for this kind of opportunity."

"No, no, I am honored, of course," Serge rises and runs his hand through his hair. "It is a lot to consider." Serge looks over at you. "We would have to take a break from the tour, correct?"

Freddie looks thoroughly confused. "This is what you wanted, what we've been working for, right? To take this thing to the next level?"

Serge takes a long moment before answering him. "Please, allow me to speak with Niko, after the show," is all he says.

Freddie blinks a few times, throws his hands into the air. "Okay, speak with Niko!" He turns on his heel to walk out of the room, clearly exasperated. "You know where to find me," he calls before shutting the door behind him.

Serge turns to you, his eyes greyer than usual and full of an anxiety you haven't seen before.

"It's okay." You smile, going to him and placing your hand on his strong shoulders. "You should be excited. You have worked so hard—this is an amazing opportunity. Don't even worry about me. I'll be right here when you get back. Well, not right here. I'll be in some other city somewhere. But you know what I mean."

Serge sits back down heavily. "Thank you, *Sladkaya.* Of course I do not want to leave you. But it is not just that." He sighs and runs his hand through his hair. "There is so much you do not know yet. It is difficult to understand."

You take Serge's hand. "Will you tell me?"

Sasha chooses that moment to barge back into the room, making you and Serge jump. Sasha uncharacteristically fails to pick up on the mood. "What am I interrupting this time?" he teases. "Haven't you two lovebirds gotten enough of each other yet?"

Sasha's face falls when neither of you cracks a smile. "Uh-oh. Or have you actually gotten enough of each other, after all?" he asks slowly.

You look him in the eye, trying to shoot him a meaningful glare. "Actually, Serge just got some good news. He and Niko have a possible record deal in the works."

Sasha looks from you to Serge then back again. "So why do you look like someone died?"

"No, no." Serge straightens up, manages a smile, and brushes it off. "It is very good news." Serge looks at you wistfully.

"Ohh." Sasha nods his head knowingly. "I get it. Don't worry, you two will be so busy you'll hardly have time to miss each other. And I'll keep a close eye on Henrietta for you," Sasha assures Serge. "And Niko will have his marching orders."

"Thanks," you tell him, genuinely grateful for his incorrect assumption.

Sasha bats his eyes at you before returning to the remaining rack of costumes. "Young love." He sighs, "is there anything sweeter?"

You smile reassuringly at Serge and reach up on tiptoe to kiss him on the cheek. "Let's talk about this more later, okay?" you whisper into his ear.

"Later, yes," he answers distractedly, then walks off to prepare for his performance.

That night, Serge makes love to you with a silent urgency, his mouth on yours as he pulls the robe from your body and pushes you to the bed, using his hand to be sure you are ready, then driving into you powerfully. His breathing quickens almost instantly, his whole weight pressing you into the soft bed in release as he shudders against you.

After, he rolls onto his back, gazing up at the ceiling as he catches his breath.

"You okay?" you ask after a few minutes.

"Yes. I am just thinking."

You roll onto your stomach and run a finger down Serge's abs, ridges noticeably defined even in the dim light. "Care to tell me what about?"

Serge's stomach rises and falls as he thinks. "All this about a single, and an album, and the Independence Day Parade. It is a little stressful."

You rest your head on his chest and watch him as he speaks. You can see the anxiety on his face.

"It's a lot," you say. "I remember how overwhelmed I felt when I started getting some traction."

"I am very happy with the success," Serge says, glancing down at you, a flicker of a smile on his face. "It is all because of you and I am very grateful." His expression becomes solemn again. "But things are complicated with me. And with Niko."

"Oh." You had just assumed Niko would be on board. You hadn't stopped to think that maybe the resistance was coming from him. "He isn't so excited about all of this?"

"No, it is not that. He is excited, too. But there are things I have not told you, *Sladkaya*. Things that I did not think were important anymore."

Serge strokes your hair, sending a shiver down your spine. You wait in silence for him to continue.

After a long moment, Serge takes in a breath. He rests his hand against your arm and gazes into the shadows as he speaks.

"You remember that Niko and I told you we studied music together."

"Yes."

"And you asked whether we grew up near one another."

"Right, and you didn't really answer."

"Correct. To answer your question, we did grow up very near one another. In the same house in fact."

You startle a little then settle back down, wanting Serge to go on.

"It is a very complicated story, but I will give you the short version. Niko's father was Nikolas Zinckenko."

"The bodybuilder?" You know the name well. Almost as famous for his physique as he is for is strong accent, a popular subject of late-night show parodies, you also remember that Niki Z., as he was known, had some sort of short-lived political career after his run in Hollywood ended.

"Yes, that is the one. Nikolas was very famous in my country, very rich. He became a popular movie star and lived in an enormous two-story penthouse in Kiev. The ceilings were so high it felt like a palace. Everybody knew Niki Z. when I was growing up. My mother started out as his house cleaner and then later became his assistant."

Serge shifts his position before he goes on. "There were always whispers when we went out together, Niki, Niko, Niko's mother, and I. Very rarely did my mother come along. She always explained that she had some errand or other to do. But I did not understand until I was much older. All I knew was that I got to live in the grandest building in all of Kiev, possibly in all of Ukraine, and that my best friend, Niko, only four months older than I, was always by my side."

You begin to understand, but wait for him to continue his story.

"Of course, I wondered where my father was, I asked my mother about him constantly. She told me the story of the handsome prince with whom she had shared one romantic night under a majestic willow tree, that she ran from him at the stroke of midnight, and that she never saw him again. But she promised that one day he would find us, reveal himself to me, and that finally I would know who my father was."

Serge smiles to himself, having told the too-familiar tale.

"Well, one day I was playing war with Niko—we must have been about six years old —chasing him around the house when Niki yelled at us both for making too much noise and ripped the weapons we had crafted from sticks and cardboard right out of our hands, and breaking them over his knee. Niko and I retreated to his bedroom in tears, stung by Niki's anger. I sobbed, telling Niko my own father would never be so cruel, and that one day when he returned he would stand up to Niki and take us all away to live in his castle. I shared the tale my mother had told me so many times, and Niko's tears turned to laughter.

"With the unabashed cruelty only a child can have, Niko had opened my eyes to what had been before us all along. 'That story, the one your mother has told you over and over again,' he said, 'it's a nursery tale. It is called *The Golden Slipper*. It is not about your mother and father. It's not even true.'

"I managed to scream, 'You're lying!' before running off to find my mother . . . I remember her holding me in her arms as though I was still a baby, stroking my cheek and drying my tears, rocking me back and forth while she told me the truth. I had been living with her handsome prince, Nikolas Zinchenko, all along. He was my father. That fictitious night under the willow tree happened when Niko's mother, Anya, was four month's pregnant with Niko. And best and worst of all, Niko was my half-brother.

"My mother made me promise to keep what she had told me a secret, even from Niko, and told me that when it was time, my father would tell me the truth himself."

"I knew that my mother would not ask me for such a confidence unless it was very important. And even at such a young age I knew that we had a good life. I had seen children out on the street, children in my school who had holes in their shoes or ate nothing more than a boiled egg or a crust of bread for lunch."

You stretch your arm to lay it across Serge's chest, running your fingers lightly over his muscles, gazing at his handsome face as he speaks.

"Suddenly I understood why Niko and I attended different schools yet shared a music instructor, why Anya seemed at times affectionate and kind and at other times icy and distant, why my mother rarely accompanied us on outings, and when she did why she trailed behind us by at least several meters. In some ways, that day changed everything. And in many ways it changed nothing at all." Serge blows out a long breath, and you sense that he has finished speaking.

You wait a few minutes before asking, "When did your father finally tell you?"

"Not until several years later. Nikolas became a well-known politician, then the Ukrainian Ambassador to the U.S. It was at that time that we moved to Washington D.C., to the Ukrainian Embassy there. It was a big change for our family. Even though Niko and I were tutored in English since we were small, the new country still felt very foreign. It helped that Niko and I had each another."

"Eventually the States grew to feel more like home. We spent hours exploring the city, on hot days we would wander through the museums, or sit in the shadows of the monuments. And we would take long walks along the Tidal Basin in the spring, counting the days until the trees would be in bloom. It reminded us of home, a little."

"That's why you love the cherry blossoms so much." You smile.

"Yes, they hold many memories. And now a new memory, as well," Serge takes your hand in his, kissing your palm.

"And you managed to keep your secret, even from Niko? That had to be difficult."

"Yes, but not as difficult as what happened next, something none of us expected." Serge sighs, his eyes distant. "Anya became very ill soon after we moved to the States. Niko and I knew she was in and out of doctor's offices frequently, but no one told us the truth until she had been ill for months. She died almost one year to the day after we moved into the Embassy. Pancreatic cancer. It was very quick."

"I'm so sorry," you tell him, feeling the sting of tears in your eyes. "That must have been devastating."

"Yes, for Niko especially. I still remember her funeral so vividly. I stood in line behind Niko to kneel at her casket. His back was so straight and so still as he knelt. When he rose to face me his eyes were dry, his face stoic. He was ten years old, already taller than I was, but still had the face of a boy. He grasped my arm as he walked past me. '*Brat*,' he said. And I knew then that he knew."

"He called you a brat?" you ask, incredulous.

"No, no." Serge laughs. "It means *brother*."

Suddenly you feel hot tears track down your cheeks. "Oh," you say, quickly swiping at your eyes.

"That night, Nikolas sat us both down together and told us the truth I already knew. 'You are brothers,' he said. He looked much older all of a sudden, I remember, and he had such sadness in his eyes. 'You have always been brothers. This is more important now than ever before. You must always support one another.'

"Niko looked at me solemnly and I at him. In that moment we made a silent pact. From then on we never spoke about any of it. We just adapted, as children do. And we grew even closer. All of the anger, the fear, even the joy we had we poured into our music. We communicated most openly, most genuinely, when we played our cellos together. We did not need words. To this day, we do not."

You gaze at him softly. "That's a beautiful story," you say. "Thank you for sharing it with me."

Serge smiles. "Of course, *Sladkaya*."

"Does he still live in the States, your father?"

"No, no. Nikolas and my mother moved back to Kiev many years ago. Of course, they have asked us many times to come back, just for a visit. Every holiday season, it is the same. And every time we have a reason not to return. We keep ourselves busy. Kiev is a place that holds many memories, but also much sadness . . . but now it looks like we are going to go back, after all of this time."

Serge is quiet for a few minutes, thoughtful, giving you time to absorb all he has told you. A part of you wants to offer to accompany him, to help him navigate what is sure to be uncertain territory. But part of you also knows it's a journey he needs to make on his own.

"If nothing else, maybe it will bring you some closure," you offer.

"I guess I am going to find out," Serge says, running his fingers through your hair and pulling you into his strong embrace.

Three weeks later, Serge and Niko play their final opening act in Atlanta and head to the airport for their flight to Kiev. The August air is thick and hot as you embrace outside the terminal. Serge gives you a long, slow kiss.

Niko clears his throat loudly. "I am melting out here," he says impatiently. "What do you think this is, Casablanca?"

Serge laughs, giving you one more kiss.

As Serge and Niko walk through the terminal doors, cello cases strapped across their backs and luggage dragging behind them, a draft of frigid air escapes, sending a chill across your skin. Serge turns to look at you one more time and gives you a brave smile before the doors slide shut behind him. You shiver slightly despite the hot day, then slide back into the waiting car, unsettled and missing Serge already.

The tour drags without Serge there to keep you company. You knew you would miss him, but you had no idea how much you had come to look forward to little things, like his kiss in the wings when he and Niko finished their set, his playful whispers as he accompanied you up the stairway to the catwalk, a walk he refused to give up even when a backup dancer was found to take his place, the way he would lie on your side of the bed to warm it up before you joined him beneath the covers.

Sasha does his best to fill the void. "What am I, chopped liver?" he asks as you refuse his tenth attempt to get you to go out to a club with him after a show.

"I'm just tired," you tell him.

"You are pining," he retorts. "It's really kind of pathetic." Then he smiles. "You are really into this guy, aren't you?"

You look at him and shrug. "I guess I am."

"Well, I have to admit it. He's the best one yet."

"Really?"

"Don't you think so?"

"Of course I do, I'm just happy to hear you say it."

"I'll deny it if you repeat," Sasha says with a smirk. "But I am glad you are happy."

* * *

On the tour bus to Louisiana, you call Serge at almost midnight. The time difference means that the only time you can really talk is very early morning or very late at night. So far, the trip is going brilliantly.

"It's been a whirlwind," Serge tells you. "We are being driven place to place, never knowing what our next appearance is. We just say yes to everything."

"And how are your mom and Nikolas?"

"They are very, very happy. They want us never to leave. They ask why can't we make a career in Kiev. Nikolas is trying to bribe us with a private recording studio. He promises to build it in the basement of the apartment building. He is very persuasive."

"Sounds tempting," you say, wondering whether Serge and Niko might actually be considering it.

"It is tempting," Serge admits, "but not as tempting as what awaits me when I step off of the plane and have you back in my arms, *Sladkaya.* I miss you very much."

"I miss you too."

Serge lowers his voice, speaking quietly into the phone. "Just wait until I am back, *Sladkaya.* I have many plans, for when I have you all to myself."

"Oh really?"

"Oh yes, really."

"What kind of plans?"

Serge speaks slowly, his voice low. "First, I am going to undress you very, very slowly, then I am going to kiss every inch of your body, and when I finish, I am going to slide under the covers and pay special attention to your—"

"Sergei!" a familiar voice yells in the background. "Come, the car is waiting!"

"*Chyort!*" Serge exclaims. "Okay, I am coming!"

You laugh. Though you don't know what the expression means, you get the gist. "Tell Niko I say hi," you tell Serge.

"I am sorry." He sighs into the phone.

"It's fine. Believe me, I understand. To be continued?"

"Oh yes," Serge says, "definitely to be continued."

You laugh again, and smile into the phone. "Have fun," you tell him before you end the call.

Sasha breezes by you on his way to bed. He lays the back of his hand against your forehead. "That must have been Serge," he says.

"It might have been," you answer, a smile playing on your lips.

"Sweet dreams, Henrietta," he tells you, switching off the overhead light.

Your dreams that night are very sweet, indeed.

Everything about Louisiana is oppressive. Since there's no hotel close to the venue, you stay on the bus. Wispy tendrils of steam rise from the gravel backlot into the broiling August air after a brief summer storm as you make your way into the venue.

Freddie waits for you in the dressing room, looking like he's seen a ghost.

A sense of dread overwhelms you as you take in the pallor of his skin, the look in his eyes.

"What is it?" you ask, bracing for the worst.

"I think you need to see this." Freddie thrusts his phone into your hand. The screen glows, a stark white backdrop against the rows of black text which take a moment to focus. A single photo of Crispin, smiling at some red carpet event, sits below the headline: CRISPIN HERSHEY HOSPITALIZED AFTER WILD NIGHT OF PARTYING. WHAT WE KNOW SO FAR.

You look up at Sasha, who exchanges a quick glance with Freddie, then you scroll slowly down to read the full article.

Crispin Hershey was hospitalized today after being found unconscious in a Los Angeles hotel room. The star reportedly spent the last two days partying in Hershey's VIP suite with long-time friend and recent rehab co-attendee, Trixie Taylor. Taylor, who made the 911 call, reporting that Hershey was having a seizure, was arrested at the scene for drug possession. According to sources, Hershey was unresponsive upon arrival at Cedars Sinai Hospital and remains in critical condition. Hershey's off-again-off-again love, Honey Noble, has not yet been contacted, according to a source close to the star.

An ugly sob escapes your throat as you look desperately up at Sasha and Freddie.

"I need to go to him," you say.

"Henrietta, think this through," Sasha beseeches.

"No!" you tell him. "There's nothing to think about."

You do your best to stay calm and focused during the show, but the heat and the events of the day do nothing to help. You know it's not your best performance, but the audience doesn't seem to care.

Freddie arranges a private plane and alerts the venue that tomorrow night's show is uncertain. You fly through the night, arriving in LA at almost two in the morning, local time. A car takes you to the VIP hospital entrance. Even the halls of the ICU are hushed at this hour, lights dim, the only activity is the bustle of the nurses, who never stop darting in and out of patient rooms and back to the nurses' station.

Tears immediately spring to your eyes as they adjust to the dim light of Crispin's room. His body looks frail in the hospital bed. Tangles of wires are draped across the metal bed rails, disappearing under the thin sheet covering Crispin's frame. Tubes seem to spring from every orifice and machines beep incessantly from every corner. A nurse walks into the room, wheeling a cart.

"How is he?" you ask her.

"He's stable," she tells you. "But he's not out of the woods. The doctor will be here in the morning. He can tell you more."

You keep vigil by Crispin's side throughout the night, willing him to open his eyes. You sing softly to him, hoping your voice gets through whatever fog he is under. The room begins to brighten as dawn breaks. At last, the doctor, who remains determinedly unflustered by your presence, gives you what information he has. A battery of tests is to be run today, but initial bloodwork revealed a mix of drugs and alcohol which should have been fatal.

"He is very lucky to be alive," the doctor tells you. "But we won't know what damage has been done until the test results are back."

"When will that be?" you ask.

"Some will come in today, some will take a day or two. And the brain activity tests will be ongoing."

"Brain activity?"

"There's no way to tell how much, if any, damage has been done to his brain, until he regains consciousness. There's a chance he was without oxygen for some time. And the person who made the initial call reported a seizure."

"I see," you tell him—although you don't understand completely.

A hefty nurse comes into the room, arms laden with sheets and blankets.

"Sorry to interrupt your visit," she announces, "but it's time for his bath and linen change."

"Oh, I can help," you offer.

"No, no, miss," she says. "Visiting hours are over for today. Go home and get some rest. You're going to need it."

Summarily dismissed, you take a car back to your house. The clean, black-and-white tile suddenly seems jarring. You realize you are beyond exhausted. You retreat to your bedroom and fall onto your still-made bed into a dreamless sleep.

You wake with a start hours later, uncertain where you are and what time of day it is. You grab your phone and see a stream of texts filling the screen. It's two p.m., almost twelve hours since you arrived in LA. You quickly brush your teeth and splash water on your face in an attempt to wake up, then quickly scroll through the texts.

Several are from Sasha—those you'll answer later. One thread is from Crispin's mother, Marjorie, telling you she's about to board a flight and will arrive in LA this evening. Interesting that she assumes you are there with her son. The last texts are from Serge:

Sladkaya?

Then a few hours later:

Do you have time for a call?

An hour after that:

I guess you are sleeping. Sweet dreams.

Then this morning:

I am getting worried. But I am thinking maybe your phone has died?

Hello? Can you please text or call me back. I will keep my phone on all night

Serge's final text knocks the breath from your lungs:

Please call me. Something has happened.

You quickly calculate the time difference—it's just after midnight in Kiev—and call Serge.

The call goes directly to voicemail. "Serge," you say, "it's Honey. I'm so sorry I'm just seeing your texts. Please call me back."

You turn the ringer volume as high as it will go then slide your phone into your bag. You add a change of clothes, a hairbrush, and your toothbrush and call a car to take you back to the hospital. On the way, you text Freddie instructing him to cancel the rest of the Louisiana shows.

The day quickly becomes evening as you sit by Crispin's bedside. Strangely, no one returns your texts and your phone doesn't ring once. The cycle of nurse visits is almost hypnotic. The doctor reappears at the end of his shift with an update.

"We've downgraded him from critical to stable," he tells you. "We've managed to push most of the toxins through his system, and his liver and kidneys appear to be unharmed, but we still need to run more tests to be certain. We need to keep him on IV meds for a least the next few days, just to be safe. He'll stay here in the ICU for that time period."

"Why hasn't he woken up?" you ask him.

"There could be a number of reasons," the doctor tells you. "It could be the body's way of protecting the brain. We see that sometimes with traumas. Or it could be something else. Right now it's too early to speculate."

You don't want to ask what the "something else" might be, so you thank the doctor and let him leave.

A few hours later, Marjorie bursts into the room with Crispin's sister, Maxine, in tow. Maxine takes one look at Crispin and bursts into tears.

"Do stop it, Maxine," Marjorie admonishes. Ever the stoic and elegant Brit, Marjorie considers such emotional outbursts beneath her. No doubt she's done everything she can to keep Crispin's latest scandal as quiet as possible.

"But look at him, Mummy!" Maxine cups her hand over her mouth. You offer her the box of tissues. "Thank you, Honey!" Maxine pulls you into a sloppy embrace, wetting your shoulder as her body trembles, wracked with sobs.

"Really, Maxine, that is quite enough!" Marjorie pulls her away and frowns at her daughter's tear-stained face, mascara smudged and running underneath each eye.

"It's okay," you tell her.

Marjorie looks at you, and sympathy washes over her face. You must look worse than you imagined. "Thank you for being here, Henrietta." Marjorie is one of the only other people outside of your immediate family and Sasha who calls you by your given name. Somehow it sounds lovely, in her clipped British accent.

"What have they told you?"

You fill Marjorie and Maxine in on the little you know. Marjorie glares at Maxine each time a new detail elicits a gasping sob.

"Well, I suppose we can only wait," Marjorie sighs when you finish. Then, "I think I'd like a cup of tea," she announces brightly, getting to her feet.

"We can't just leave him here," Maxine sniffles.

"He can't come with us, can he?" Marjorie asks, a little too tartly. "Why don't you stay with him, Max. Henrietta and I will bring you something."

"I'm not hungry," Maxine dabs at her cheeks, never taking her eyes from her brother.

"How about you, Henrietta? You must be famished."

You cannot remember the last time you ate. "I actually am starving," you tell her, and accompany her down the hall to the bank of elevators leading to the lobby. The second you walk through the elevator doors, your phone begins to buzz. More texts than you've ever seen fill your screen and the voicemail icon shows twelve missed calls and five new voicemails. "What on earth?" you mutter as you scroll through the phone.

"Is everything quite all right?" Marjorie asks.

"Um, I'm not sure. Looks like I missed a bunch of phone calls. Do you mind if I meet you in the cafeteria in a few minutes?"

"Not at all."

You make a quick escape through the glass lobby doors and immediately call Serge. He picks up on the first ring.

"*Sladkaya,*" he says, his voice strained and anxious. "I have been trying to call you."

"I know," you tell him, pacing the hospital sidewalk as you talk. "There must be no reception upstairs. I'm at the hospital—I'm fine, though."

"Yes," Serge interrupts you. "I know. Sasha told me. I called him when I couldn't find you. I was very worried."

"I'm sorry," you tell him.

"No, no, it is fine," he assures you, his voice more even. "I am just glad you are safe. How is Crispin?" His question sounds genuine and devoid of any hint of jealousy.

"He's in bad shape," you answer. "He really did a number on himself this time. His mother just arrived—and his sister—so hopefully that will help, though his sister's a bit of a mess. The doctors don't seem to know the extent of it yet. And he hasn't opened his eyes since they brought him in. No one seems to know what that means."

"I am sorry, *Sladkaya,*" Serge tells you. "It is good of you to be there."

"I guess," you tell him. "I'm not sure I'm really helping."

Serge is silent for a moment. "What will you do? Will you stay there?"

That gives you pause. Since you arrived at the hospital, up until this moment you hadn't thought past the present. Driven by adrenaline, you just went. You think for a long moment. "I don't know," you answer honestly.

Serge breathes in a long breath. "Well, you will do the right thing, *Sladkaya,*" he tells you. "I may not know you that well, not yet, but I do know you have a very good heart."

"Thank you." Your chest tightens and suddenly you feel completely torn. "Serge, can I ask you something?"

"Ah, I am being summoned, once again," Serge says. "Will you call me tomorrow?"

"Okay," you tell him. "I'll call you."

"Goodbye, *Sladkaya,*" Serge says, and you hear the line go still.

You gaze down at the black phone screen, wondering what Serge meant when he said you would do the right thing. It takes you a moment to realize that at just past midnight in Kiev it is highly unlikely that Serge was being called away. And that you didn't even ask him how things were going there. Or what his text meant. *Tomorrow*, you think, and walk back into the chilly hospital lobby to go find Marjorie.

After a cup of coffee and a semi-hot meal, actually not bad for hospital cafeteria fare, you check back in on Crispin. Maxine has found a magazine and she reads it aloud to Crispin.

"It's meant to be a good thing to read aloud to them," she explains, in answer to Marjorie's puzzled expression.

"I think that's said about people in a coma," Marjorie corrects.

You smile at Maxine. "Anyway, it can't hurt."

You excuse yourself to return the rest of your voicemails. Three were from Serge, two from Sasha, and one from Freddie, which you'll deal with later.

Sasha answers after a few rings. "How's the patient?" he asks without preamble.

"Not great," you answer, without elaborating.

You know Sasha is using great restraint to keep his opinions to himself, which you appreciate. "So, what's your plan?" he asks you.

"Why, is Freddie breathing down your neck?"

"No, not yet. I want to know for my own information. And in light of the phone call I got from Serge yesterday, of course."

"What do you mean?" you ask. "I just talked to him a little while ago."

"Oh, so you know then."

The familiar sense of dread washes over you. "Know what?"

"He didn't say anything?"

"Seriously, Sasha, just tell me."

"He didn't say anything about Niko's father?"

"No."

"Oh. That's odd." Sasha pauses for a second. "I guess there's no reason not to tell you. Apparently Niko's father suffered a massive heart attack yesterday morning—evening their time. He didn't make it."

"What do you mean he didn't make it?"

"I mean, he died, Henrietta. Do I have to spell it out for you?"

"Oh, God," you gasp, as the realization hits you. "Serge didn't say a word."

"He probably figured you were dealing with enough."

You can't even imagine what Niko and Serge must be going through, having just reunited with their father after all this time. "God, I'm an idiot," you say.

"You couldn't have known."

"I could have. I didn't even ask.'' Your mind is racing as you try to figure out what to do. "Listen, Sasha, can you do me a favor? I owe Freddie a call back but I can't do it right now. Can you buy me some time with him please?"

"I can try," Sasha says. "But you know Freddie."

"I know, I know. Let me just figure a couple of things out. I'll call you before I do anything, I promise."

On the long drive back to your house, your mind reels. You feel pulled in two completely different directions. In one, there's Crispin, lying in a hospital bed fighting for his life. The two of you have a long history, and part of you can't help but think that if you hadn't abandoned him when he needed you most you might have saved him from this terrible turn. In fact, the two of you might be back together now and he might be clean and sober had you not hung up the phone that day. Still, another part of you knows that Crispin has brought this fate upon himself, and that no amount of support from you can get him to want to turn his life around. Besides, now that his mother and sister are here, there's no real reason for you to stay—aside from your own sense of guilt and the hope that somehow your presence can help him recover.

In the other direction is Serge, hundreds of miles away in Kiev, mourning the loss of his father. Though your relationship is still new, there's something you feel when you look into Serge's eyes that you've never felt before. He makes you feel safe and cherished, something no one has ever made you feel. The future could hold anything for the two of you, or your romance could fade, unable to stand the grueling tests of distance and fame. The fact that Serge didn't even tell you about Nikolas when you called, that his only concern was your well-being, speaks volumes. He's selfless, which is something new to you, too.

You tumble into bed with conflicting thoughts spinning through your mind. Your last thought before sleep overtakes you is a desperate hope that you will awaken with some clarity.

To go to Serge in Kiev, turn to page 219.
To stay in LA with Crispin, keep reading.

You awaken with a clarity you haven't felt in months. You know you have no choice but to stay with Crispin, at least until he is on a solid road to recovery. You pack a fresh change of clothes and head back to the hospital, calling Freddie on the way to let him know that at least the next leg of the tour needs to be canceled. He is less than pleased, but you promise you'll be back as soon as Crispin is well enough to be on his own. Fifteen minutes later, your phone begins to ring. Sasha calls incessantly when you refuse to pick up, so you turn the phone off completely the minute you walk through the hospital doors, knowing it won't get reception once you step off of the elevator into the ICU anyway.

Marjorie is snoring loudly in the corner chair when you enter the room. Maxine continues her bedside vigil, reading to Crispin in a raspy voice. She looks up and cuts her eyes toward her mother, acknowledging the noises coming from her usually elegant nose.

"She would be mortified to learn she snores like a lumberjack," she snickers.

"We'd better not tell her," you agree.

"How is he?" you walk toward the bed where Crispin lies. He appears not to have moved a millimeter since you last saw him.

"The same," Maxine answers miserably. Cavernous black bags underline Maxine's eyes.

"You look exhausted," you tell her. "You two should go get some rest. You're welcome to stay at my place."

Maxine looks perplexed. "But don't you have to fly back? Mother says you're in the middle of a tour."

"I am. But I'm taking a little hiatus, just until Crispin is out of the woods."

Just then, Marjorie lets out a loud snort, startling you both into laughter. She opens her eyes in a state of confusion.

"Is something funny?" she asks sleepily, sitting up and straightening her crumpled clothes.

Maxine shares a conspiratorial look. "No, Mum. Honey just gave me the good news that she's made plans to stay on until Crispin is feeling better. Isn't that right, Honey?"

"Yes, I just told my tour manager. I want to be here for him, when he wakes up."

"Henrietta, that's—" Marjorie pauses, looking past you, her eyes wide. You and Maxine follow her gaze and turn to see what has rendered her speechless.

Crispin has turned his head and is gazing at you in a dead stare. Your heart leaps into your throat and then you see him blink, and you can breathe again. The sheet moves, and Crispin manages to edge his hand out and reaches toward you.

You close the gap between you in two steps, Maxine at your side.

Marjorie races out of the room calling, "I'll get a nurse."

You gently take Crispin's hand, careful not to interfere with the IV lines running to it. He locks eyes with yours and, trying to tell you something, but unable to speak around the tubes that pump oxygen into his lungs.

A nurse bustles into the room, all business. "Well, good morning," she says, beginning to take his vitals.

Marjorie stays out of the way, but reaches to take your hand. Her eyes brim with tears. "Thank you, Henrietta," she manages and gives your hand a little squeeze.

You turn back to Crispin, wondering whether this is a sign you've made the right decision after all.

Four days later, Crispin is free of almost all of the wires and tubes that have tethered him to the hospital bed. His voice is still raspy and dry, vocal cords likely scratched in the process of intubation.

"Do you think I'll ever sing again?" he asks, only half-joking.

"I think that's the least of your worries." You smile, spooning a wobbly mass of red Jell-O into his mouth.

Crispin's communication and verbal processing appear to be unaffected by the trauma, but the doctors are concerned about his fine motor skills and possible attention issues. So far, he's been unable to guide a utensil to his mouth or to write a word.

"He has months of physical therapy ahead of him," the doctor tells you when he visits one morning. "But I predict a full recovery."

Thrilled, Marjorie and Maxine decide to take you up on your offer to stay at your house. Crispin is discharged two weeks later and joins them. The main level bedroom and on-site gym offer Crispin the perfect place to rehabilitate. The arrangement enables you to return to your tour, although you fly home between stops to help as much as you can.

At first, Serge texts and calls you daily, just to check in. You tell him how sorry you are about his father and try to engage him in conversation, but you can feel that something has changed between you. Soon, your conversations become only text exchanges, and those become briefer and farther apart. Sometimes Serge takes days to return a single text.

Serge and Niko resume their performance as the warm-up to your opening act the second week you are back on tour. It's awkward when you first reunite, but only a little. Seeing Serge in person confirms what you already knew, that the distance between you is now too vast to bridge. "I'm so sorry for your loss," you tell them both, encircling Serge in an embrace. He is stiff and hesitant, and you look at Niko, trying to read his eyes for any clue about how Serge feels. Niko's eyes telegraph nothing but sadness.

That night in the wings, you cross paths with Serge at the moment he comes off the stage and you prepare to climb the steep staircase to the catwalk. For one crazy moment, you have the urge to run to him and to jump into his strong arms, just to see whether he will catch you. But of course you can't. You put one hand on his strong bicep, and feel the familiar chemical zing. You have no choice but to deny it. Every spare moment and ounce of energy you have has to be focused on Crispin's recovery. "Thank you for understanding," you tell Serge.

"Of course, Honey." Your name sounds artificial and cold on his lips. A shiver runs through you as you walk past him, and you wonder whether there was ever anything more between you, whether you only imagined him calling you by another, sweeter name.

Sasha proves surprisingly understanding as well. For all of his vitriol toward Crispin, he seems genuinely concerned for his recovery. "You are nothing if not loyal, Henrietta," he tells you as he hangs your costumes and drives you to the airport for yet another flight back to LA after a set of shows.

Crispin recovers in fits and starts. Some days he seems like himself again, and others he regresses, needing help with almost every task. But little by little, he becomes independent. At last, he feels ready to reemerge into the public eye. He chooses one of your shows to make his first appearance. To their credit, Sasha and Freddie throw him a pre-show party and even Serge and Niko attend and are polite and congratulatory.

Crispin is featured in all the tabloids, the classic comeback story. He begins to spend hours in the studio, releases a single, and breaks a record with presales of his upcoming album, "Phoenix."

"Better watch out," Freddie says after a swarm of usually loyal Honey Bees migrate in Crispin's direction after a show. "He's stealing some of your thunder."

You are more than happy to let him. After all he has been through, he deserves it. You are incredibly proud of the work he has done to get to this point and you are grateful for his recovery. In many ways, Crispin is like a new person, and you feel as though you're beginning your relationship all over again. The day "Phoenix" drops, you come home to find the house filled with thousands of roses, the lights low, and Crispin waiting at a candlelit table set for two. Soft music plays in the background.

"What's all this?" you ask, smiling.

"This," Crispin says, rising from the table and taking your hand, "is my way of saying thank you. It's not nearly enough, of course, but it's just a start."

"You don't have to thank me," you tell him. "You've done the hard work."

"That's what I love about you, Honey." He pulls you to him and kisses you tenderly. "You continue to give me the credit. But you do know I couldn't have done any of it without you, don't you?"

"I don't know about that." You look up into his warm, clear eyes, and smile. "But I'm glad we could do this together."

"I'm back," Crispin says, "and now we are going to celebrate." He sweeps you off of your feet and carries you to the bedroom.

"What about dinner?" you laugh.

Crispin kisses your neck and kicks the bedroom door shut behind him. "Dinner," he says, "can most definitely wait."

One month later the Maxamillion invites Crispin to headline the opening of a new outdoor club. You both know Vegas poses a threat to Crispin's sobriety, and so you accompany him to Vegas. Sasha decides to tag along, too. The three of you check into a suite at the Max, and it feels almost like old times, only this time Crispin is the center of attention. For once, Sasha and Crispin actually seem to enjoy each other's company.

"You're much more tolerable when you're not wasted out of your mind," Sasha tells him as you prepare to leave for the evening.

"Why Mr. Fortier," Crispin responds. "That may very well be the nicest thing you've ever said to me."

"Don't get used to it," Sasha teases.

Crispin manages the appearance spectacularly, sipping seltzer water and putting in exactly the time required. When he finishes, he twirls you in a little victory dance.

"That went splendidly," he grins. "Let's go celebrate."

A knot of dread drops into your stomach. The old Crispin's celebration would entail an alcohol-fueled night of clubbing. He reads the look of apprehension on your face.

"Dinner," he tells you. "Somewhere quiet and private. I want you all to myself, just for tonight."

The knot of dread loosens and is replaced by a little thrill. You like this new Crispin, and you eagerly agree.

Crispin takes you to an intimate French restaurant and follows you into the cushioned seat of a high banquette. The booth gives you total privacy and a chance to focus fully on each other.

You giggle as Crispin toasts with sparkling water. "To you, Honey Noble." He lifts his glass, the tiny bubbles rising to the surface as his speaks. "Where would I be without you?"

"God only knows." You laugh, sipping the bubbly water.

"I'm serious." Crispin takes your hand. "I might very well still be lying in that hospital bed, or worse."

"You would have been fine," you run your fingers along his hand, the skin still scarred from the IV needles.

"No, Honey, it was you who pulled me through. Every grueling step of the way. Quite literally."

"You need to give yourself some credit. You did the hard work," you tell him.

"It was you deciding to stay with me; that's what really did the trick. Opened my eyes, in more ways than one." Crispin sets his drink down and gazes at you lovingly. "You know my Mum and Maxine think you are a miracle worker."

"That's sweet." You've never seen Crispin's eyes so focused, his gaze so clear. You feel a warm tingle of energy spread from your core, zip through your arm, and join you to Crispin. *This is what love feels like*, you think.

As if feeling it too, Crispin's hand jumps just slightly. His eyes widen and he seems to realize something, all at once. A flush rises to his face, and he takes a sip of his water. "I could never have done this"—He sets the glass gently back down on the table with a slow, controlled motion—"or this," he says, leaning across to give you a soft kiss. He rises to his feet, steady and sure. "And I'm fairly certain I couldn't have managed this." He drops to one knee, reaching to take your hands in his.

Suddenly your breath and heartbeat quicken as you realize what Crispin is about to do.

His clear, whiskey gaze is locked to yours, making your head swim. "Life can be very uncertain. But there are three things I know with absolute conviction: I would not be alive without you. I do not want to spend one more day of my life without you. And I am absolutely, one hundred percent, completely in love with you."

Dizzy, you do your best to focus on his words as he asks, "Honey Noble, would you do me the great honor of becoming my wife?"

Turn to page 91.

From page 213 . . .

The flight to Ukraine seems endless. You distract yourself by scribbling lyrics and watching old movies on the little airplane screen. The plane lands at daybreak and you quickly deposit your bags in the hotel Sasha arranged for you. You pull on a long, black dress and twist your hair into a subdued up-do.

The funeral mass is just beginning when you arrive at the church. The huge cathedral is packed with mourners, with standing room only left by the rear doors. You squeeze in as close to the aisle as you can manage. The organ begins to play a somber dirge, and the doors open, revealing pallbearers hoisting the shining casket on their shoulders. First in the line, closest to you, is Serge, his jaw set in a hard line. He sees you immediately, and locks eyes with you for a long moment. His eyes soften, and the look of relief and love there tells you everything you need to know. Once the casket is in place, Serge walks back up the aisle, every eye following him as he takes your hand and guides you to the pew in front, making a place for you to kneel beside him. He stares straight ahead as the priest recites the mass and swings the incense over the casket. Serge sheds not a tear but he grips your hand tightly, never letting go. You are glad that for once, you can be the strength he needs, the strength he's given you from the moment you met him.

Serge remains in Kiev with his mother for the three weeks following the funeral. Together, he and Niko help her to go through Nikolas's belongings, deciding which pieces to donate and which to store. Serge and Niko take a few sentimental belongings for themselves: their father's billfold, a fountain pen, each son takes one cufflink from their father's favorite pair. At last, the brothers return to the tour. Embraced by the Nobility family, they resume their performances, pouring a new intensity into their act.

Slowly, Serge begins to recover from his loss. You spend long nights together, Serge holding you close in the narrow tour bus bed. You cover him with kisses, never tiring of the warmth of his muscular body, the gentle strength of his touch, the love in his eyes.

Sasha allows you your space, and is equally present when you need him. One day backstage, as he zips you into a costume, he whispers, "I have some news."

You turn to look at him, concern in your eyes. "It's good news, Henrietta! Don't stress."

"Good, I've had enough surprises lately," you say, relieved. "Tell me."

"After the show," he promises, giving you a little nudge toward the stage.

Serge is waiting to wrap you into a hug when you step off of the stage. He takes your hand and leads you into the dressing room, where the cast and crew await with flutes of champagne. They raise their glasses as Serge walks in, joining Niko and Sasha in the center of the room. Last to join the circle is Freddie. He hoists his glass into the air and the room quiets.

"A toast!" he announces. "To the newest member of Powers Records, *Burya*." He rolls the R impressively, eliciting a whoop of approval from Niko. "To our very own Serge," he puts an arm around his shoulder, "and Niko." He puts his other arm as far as it will reach around Niko's shoulder. The two huge men make even Freddie appear diminutive. "And, last but certainly not least," he reaches out for Sasha and pulls him into their circle, "to their new tour manager, Sasha!"

"What?" You catch Sasha's eye, thrilled but utterly confused.

"That's my news, Henrietta," Sasha tells you. "Go ahead, take a drink."

You take Sasha's advice and down half of your glass. "Is someone going to explain?" you ask, trying to sounds lighthearted.

"Looks like you're losing your opening-opening act," Freddie says pragmatically.

"But you're not losing your costume designer," Sasha assures you. "I can do almost everything I need to do for the boys in my downtime, now that Nobility is running like a well-oiled machine. I've already started their performance schedule. And we'll coordinate it so that they perform where we are, whenever we can. So far it's all working out."

"That's amazing!" you tell them, and you mean it. It's one of those rare perfect moments, where everything comes together. The dressing room bursts at the seams with cast and crew as you celebrate well into the wee hours of the night.

No one promotes a new act better than Powers, and *Burya's* album release is an immediate success. The act is booked at every tour stop, Serge and Niko often appearing on both morning and late-night talk shows, even fitting print and radio interviews in around their performances. Powers capitalizes on Serge and Niko's compelling back-story, and the long-lost brothers who spent their childhoods under each other's noses become instant media sensations.

"It is exhausting," Serge tells you one night, wearily rolling into bed after a long day of appearances and performances. "I do not know how you do this."

"Red Bull," you remind him.

"Ah, right."

"Get in here," you tell him. "You need some rest."

"Yes, some rest." He laughs, nuzzling your neck. "And maybe a little something more." He tucks his hand under the sheets, finding you bare and ready. *"Sladkaya,"* he groans, sliding his hand between your legs. He gives you a long, slow kiss and joins himself to you completely.

"There is nothing like springtime in Washington," Serge says, leading you down a now very familiar path. "Isn't this beautiful?"

"It's snowing!" Nikki yells, running just enough ahead to make her father uncomfortable.

"You must stay with us, *Malyshka*," Serge yells. "There are too many people."

"Okay, Papa," Nikki obediently skips back, braids flying out behind her as she bridges the few feet between you. She fits one small hand into yours, and takes Serge's hand with the other. "Swing me!" she cries, and lifts her feet off of the ground.

You lift her as high as you can, trying to even out the height difference between you and your husband. Nikki tilts her face to the sky as she swings, giggling as the soft petals fall across her cheeks.

"Do you remember the story?" Serge asks, setting Nikki gently back onto the path.

"The one about you and Mommy?" She squints up at her father, towering over her as he walks. "And all the trees?"

"Oh, so you do remember!" Serge pats the top of her head, pleased.

"I think I remember," she says, smiling. "Can you tell me again?"

"Maybe Mommy wants to tell it this time," Serge suggests.

"No, no," you protest. "Papa does a much better job."

"Okay, I will tell it." Serge begins, smiling to himself, "Papa and Mommy used to work together."

"In Mommy's concert," Nikki says.

"That's right, in Mommy's concert. One day, Mommy heard Papa playing his cello. The music was so beautiful that she fell immediately in love."

"That's not exactly how it happened," you correct him.

"Yes, that is exactly how it happened," Serge continues, unde-terred, making Nikki giggle. "But before Papa could ask Mommy to marry him, Papa had to go on a long journey."

"To Kiev!" Nikki interrupts excitedly.

"Right again. And an evil wizard tried to put a spell on Mommy to make her forget about Papa, but Mommy was too smart for that wizard so she escaped and flew to Papa's side."

Nikki jumps in front of Serge, her little sneakers causing a pile of pale-pink petals to fly into the air. "To the castle in the sky!" she cries.

You roll your eyes at the romanticized version of events, but you can't help but smile at how much Nikki loves the tale, tall as it is.

"Yes! And so they flew back together with *Baba,* who was very sad and lonely, and they brought her back to live with them."

"And Uncle Niko," Nikki reminds him.

"Yes, Uncle Niko, too." Serge smiles. "Now, pay attention. This is the best part."

Nikki beams up at him in anticipation.

"Papa was very grateful to Mommy for rescuing him, and decided he never wanted to be away from her ever again. So, he bought her a beautiful ring."

Reflexively, you glance down at the gorgeous ring, still glittering brilliantly almost five years later.

"Yes?" Nikki prompts him to go on.

"And he brought Mommy here, to this very spot."

"This one?" Nikki glances around her. "Was it this tree?"

"Yes!" Serge says. "How did you know?" Then he walks a few steps and stops in front of another tree, laden with pale-pink blossoms. "Wait, maybe it was this tree."

"No," Nikki giggles, moving onto the next tree. "It was this one!"

"Hmm," Serge says. "I think it was this one."

"No, this one!" It's become a familiar game, and one Nikki has been dying to play ever since you arrived in DC for your annual Cherry Blossom Festival pilgrimage. The fact that you and Serge were asked to headline this year's Festival made this time even sweeter.

"No, no," Serge laughs. "It was definitely this one!"

They continue down the path, laughing and stopping at random trees, proclaiming each to be the spot of your storied engagement. You follow along, laughing with them, and smiling to yourself.

At last, you come to the familiar fork in the path, and the tree that is the most special of all.

"Here it is," you announce.

"That's not it!" Nikki wrinkles her nose at the denuded tree, its gnarled branches twisted, some bluntly cut. "That's an ugly old tree."

"This is an old tree, you are right about that," Serge tells her, laying his hand against the tree's thick trunk. "But it is a beautiful tree, and it has a magical ability. This is the indicator tree."

"The what?" Nikki looks up at the tree with curiosity, warming to the idea that maybe it holds a hidden secret.

"This is the tree that tells us when all of the other trees are going to blossom. This tree can tell the future."

"No it can't!" Nikki giggles, sure that Serge is teasing her.

"Really, it can," he assures her. "And it is never wrong. Next time we come I will show you. But for now, you will have to believe me."

You lean down to Nikki, looking into her eyes, the same dove grey as Serge's. "I knew this tree was special as soon as I saw it," you tell her. "And when your Papa told me all about it, I knew he was special, too."

Serge smiles at you and sweeps Nikki up into his arms. "Let's go. *Baba,* Uncle Niko, and Uncle Sasha are waiting for us."

"Hold on," you lean into the tree, pretending to listen. "I think the tree is trying to tell us something right now."

"What, Mommy?" Nikki whispers, her eyes wide.

"That's funny," you say, placing your hand lightly on your still-flat stomach. "It says that there's something else getting ready to blossom."

Serge tracks your hand with his eyes and breaks into a wide smile. "Really?" he asks, a sheen of tears in his eyes.

"Really," you answer. "It's early yet, but the tree is never wrong."

"That is wonderful, *Sladkaya,* wonderful!" He spins Nikki around in the air and leans in to give you a long kiss.

"What is'?" Nikki begs. "What?"

"Our family is going to get a little bigger, *Mulyshka.*"

"Are we getting a dog?"

"Oh boy," you sigh. "Are you two ready to go to dinner? We have a lot to celebrate."

"Wait!" Nikki says. "Papa didn't finish the story!"

Serge locks his eyes with yours, his cool, grey gaze piercing your heart as he takes your hand and finishes the tale.

"And they lived happily ever after."

THE END

POP STAR and STAR STRUCK are Meredith Michelle's first two novels and combine her lifelong fascination with celebrity culture and her childhood love of trying to figure out different endings for her favorite books. Meredith has been an avid writer since her youth, penning plays, poetry, and short stories. She is a native and current resident of the Washington, DC area, where she resides with her husband and her three children.